PHANTOM LIMB

A Gripping Psychological Thriller

Lucinda Berry

Copyright © 2016 Lucinda Berry

All rights reserved.

Published in the United States by Rise Press

ISBN-10: 1541034953
ISBN-13: 978-1541034952

This book is a work of fiction. Names, characters, places, events, and businesses are used fictitiously. Any resemblance to actual persons, places, or events is purely coincidental.

DEDICATION

To my mom who read every draft.

1

It was always the same phone call. Always the same desperate pleas.

"Don't say a word," she'd beg.

Who would I tell? Had I ever told? I'd been keeping her secrets for years.

I pulled my car into my parking spot and looked up at the third story of our apartment building at the last window on the left. The shades were sealed shut. They'd been that way for days. I stepped out and walked into the entryway, passing Mrs. Jasberson by the mailboxes. She checked her mail at least five times a day so she could interact with someone other than the characters on her TV.

"Hello, Elizabeth," she called when she spotted me. "How was work today?"

"Great," I replied without turning around. No need to tell her that, once again, I'd left three hours before the end of my shift.

"You tell that sister of yours she needs to get out in the sun more often."

I turned around and smiled at her as I waited for the elevator. "I will."

I waved to her over my shoulder and stepped inside the box as soon as the doors opened. They closed in front of me, and I stared at the numbers as they lit up, anxiously tapping my feet back and forth against each other. The familiar *ding* sounded and then the doors opened to the long hallway.

Stale cigarette smoke greeted me when I opened our door. I took a deep breath before walking down the hallway and into our bedroom. A small lump hid underneath the yellow comforter. I stepped over the scattered piles of clothes as I walked to the window and pulled on the blinds' string, flooding the room with light and making it more cheerful. I opened the window, letting the fresh air sweep into the room, and took another deep breath to fortify myself for what I had to do next. I sat on a spot on the edge of the bed and peeled back the comforter, revealing Emily's small body tucked into the fetal position, her arms cradling her head. She was wearing her purple pajamas. Not a good sign. The last time she'd worn them, we'd almost ended up in the emergency room. I'd grown to hate the color purple.

I stroked her brown hair away from her face. "Hi, sweetie. I'm home."

Her arms reached out for me like a small child reaching for her mother. I lay down beside her and wrapped my arms around her. We'd been through this routine many times. She nestled her head on my chest and began to cry.

"Shh." I stroked her hair. "It's going be all right. We always make it through."

"I couldn't even get dressed." Her tears wet my shirt. "I tried, Bethy. I really tried. I did."

"I know you did, honey," I said.

"Don't you get tired of me?"

She looked up at me and I looked down at my twin's face—our features the same, even down to the small mole on each of our foreheads, right below the hairline. I shook my head. I always shook my head.

Even though she was the one to come out first, I looked after her. I'd devoted myself to protecting her through the tragedy we'd faced together as kids, through her depressed teenage years, and I was still doing it. She'd spent the first three minutes of her life without me, but that was it.

"Let's get you showered, all right?"

I didn't wait for her answer. I stood and pulled her up with me, her stick-thin arms and body leaning against me for support. Her hair was matted against the side of her head.

"Then maybe we can go out and get dinner. Someone at school told me there's this really great Chinese buffet that opened up downtown a few weeks ago. The teriyaki chicken is supposed to be amazing."

Her eyes widened and her mouth dropped open in fear of going out in public as if I'd suggested she cut off her arm.

"Or we can just order a pizza and watch a movie. I've been in the mood to watch a romantic comedy."

Her face instantly relaxed.

I chattered away about my day and laughed about Mrs. Jasberson's gossipy interest in our lives as I moved us into the bathroom. I flicked on the fluorescent lights and ran the bathwater. Emily walked in to join me, hanging her head, her arms wrapped tightly around her stomach. I stopped filling the silence and let out a deep sigh.

"What'd you do?" I asked.

She shrugged and began undressing, her head still hanging low as if she were a puppy who'd been caught peeing on the floor or getting into the garbage. She slid off her pajama pants. Dried blood was smeared all over her legs like crusted trails of rust. There was a lot of it, which meant she'd been cutting herself all day. She undressed slowly, wary of her raw skin. I stared at the jagged edges of her wounds, new and old, as they spliced their way over her pale skin in a tangled web. Three deep gashes scarred the left side of her stomach. We'd ended up in the emergency room that time. It'd taken over thirty staples to stop the bleeding, but they'd done an impressive job with her skin. If you didn't know otherwise, you might think it was an abdominal surgery scar. Her name was crudely etched on her upper right thigh. She'd methodically carved the letters into her skin with a razor on our fourteenth birthday. When I saw it, I threatened to cut myself too if she didn't stop hurting herself, but it didn't do any good. She kept cutting, and I could never follow through on my threat. I would hold the razor blade to my flesh but could never slice myself. I didn't have it in me. I didn't say anything about her cutting anymore. There was no need. I understood why she crucified herself.

I held her hand as she stepped into the tub and sank into the warm water. I picked up the washcloth and began washing her back.

"Tell me about your day," she said as her body relaxed.

I filled the bathroom with more stories from my day as I washed her fresh wounds. I told her about the test I'd taken in my Introduction to Psychology class that morning and how surprised I'd been at how easy it was since the reading material had been so dense and difficult to get through. I sprinkled in stories about the nice weather and how good the breeze felt while I walked to my car, hoping it'd motivate her to start leaving the house again. By the time she was ready to get out of the tub, I'd moved on to my telemarketing stories.

"How many times today?" she asked.

I smiled. "Twelve." I kept track of how many times I got hung up on every day. We kept a running tally. So far, my record was thirty-two.

I couldn't convince her to watch a romantic comedy. She insisted on another episode of *Law & Order: SVU*. I didn't understand her obsession with the darkest and most depraved parts of humanity. I couldn't stand the stories of kids kept in cages or sold into prostitution, but she loved them. If I had my choice, we'd never watch the stuff again.

As she cuddled up next to me on our beat-up couch and got

ready to solve the latest sex crime with Olivia and the SVU team, I tried to shake the images of her mangled body. It never got easier for me to see the pain she inflicted on herself.

"Haven't we already seen this one?" I asked as a vaguely familiar story about a kidnapped girl found in a trunk unfolded in front of me.

"Yes, but only once and it's one of my favorites." She didn't break her gaze from the TV.

I made it to the second commercial break before I couldn't take any more. "I'm going to make dinner."

I walked into the kitchen and started rummaging through the refrigerator. I didn't like cooking but was willing to do it so I didn't have to watch the show. I didn't know what I did wrong when I cooked. I followed the same recipes as Emily, but my dishes never tasted like hers. She was a great cook, and back when she used to leave the house, she'd make exotic meals for us like Chicken Makhani or Modenese Pork Chops. She still loved to experiment in the kitchen on her good days, but her options were limited when I did all of the grocery shopping.

I settled on pasta, something easy that I couldn't screw up, and hoped by the time we finished eating, I could convince her to watch something happy. I daydreamed about my boyfriend, Thomas, while I waited for the water to boil. He'd brought me flowers at work again. He loved to give me flowers when it wasn't a special occasion and never brought roses because he knew I hated them. He'd tucked in another cheesy poem and I'd teased him about it for the rest of our shift. By the time the water came to a boil, I was smiling and humming to myself. He always had that effect on me.

"What are you smiling about?" Emily came up behind me and leaned over the stove to peek into the pot.

"Oh, nothing," I said. It'd been over a year and I still hadn't told her about Thomas. "Just something one of the jocks said in class today. It wasn't remotely related to what the professor was talking about, and he sounded like a complete idiot."

"Why do you always have to be so hard on the jocks?"

I rolled my eyes. In high school, she'd loved their chiseled bodies and hadn't minded their stupidity, but they were only interested in how many points they could score on the field and how many girls they could score with. During our junior year, the football team had a competition where they awarded point values to each girl and then proceeded to see who could earn the most points by sleeping with them. They got extra points if they didn't wear a condom. Emily ended up on their list, but I didn't. I wasn't sure if college jocks were the same as the jocks in high school, but I had no interest in finding out.

"There are plenty of openings in my health class, and it's filled with half of the hockey team if you want to come and meet him yourself."

"Subtle, Bethy. Real subtle." She grabbed the spoon from my hand and moved to stir the sauce simmering next to the pasta. "Let me help you with this so that it's actually edible." She flashed me a wide smile.

We moved through our small kitchen in a perfectly choreographed dance, sliding around each other smoothly and effortlessly like we'd done so many times in the past. I was continually amazed at how quickly her moods changed. She'd already forgotten that less than an hour ago we'd been in the bathroom washing blood off her body.

We skipped setting the table and balanced our dishes on our laps in front of the TV instead. *SVU* was over and Emily switched to *Dateline*. They were doing a documentary on teenage depression and the increased rates of girls cutting themselves.

"No way, Em. I'm not watching this." I reached for the remote, but she pulled her arm away, keeping it out of my reach.

"C'mon, just for a minute. Please?" She batted her long lashes at me.

I gave in to her like I always did. "Ten minutes. That's it. Then we're watching reruns of *Friends*."

The news anchor launched into a detailed discussion about a mother who discovered her twelve-year-old daughter cutting herself and how her daughter lied to cover it up. He interviewed the girl and her friends, trying to understand why she did it.

"Do you remember when I started?" Emily asked when the focus of the show turned back to the mother's horror at finding out her daughter was injuring herself.

"Of course I remember."

I'd never forget the day she'd started to carve herself. It was the day designed to mark our liberation from Mother. We were eight, and our adoption was finally complete. It'd been a long process. We'd been living with the Rooths for nine months, but everything was finally legal. We were officially theirs and they were officially ours. The papers had been signed in black ink and Mother could never get us back. There was nothing left to do except throw a party.

It was supposed to be a happy day, and it might have been if Mother hadn't shown up. We'd only seen her three times since Child Protective Services had taken us away from her, and each visit had resulted in some form of emotional meltdown, especially for Emily. Living with Mother was harder on her than it was on me. I'd given up trying to get Mother to love me, but Emily never gave up hope that she could get Mother to love her. I understood why Emily held on, because she'd always been Mother's favorite. She was the one who got the sparse hugs and affection when Mother needed to pretend as if she cared.

Our adoption party had been thoughtfully and lovingly designed to look like a birthday party, a valiant effort by our new family to symbolize our birth into a new world. Our therapist, Lisa, who we saw twice a week, had suggested the party. The Rooths had loved the idea and had spared no expense. There were pink balloons floating everywhere and purple streamers hanging from the tall oak trees in the backyard. The Rooths had rented a big bounce house that had a huge princess with her arms wide open as if she were trying to give you a hug before you went inside. We each had a beautifully decorated cake with our names scrawled across the center, and Dalila had let us each pick a flavor. Mine was vanilla and Emily's was chocolate. We'd spent the morning arguing over whose was going to taste better. There was a table stacked with brightly wrapped presents, and we couldn't wait for the party to be over so we could tear into them since we'd never had presents before.

Emily and I stood off to the side, holding hands and watching the activities go on around us, even though we were supposed to be the center of attention. Our new family was still so foreign to us. They flitted about and laughed with each other, effortlessly doling out big hugs. Every few moments, one of them would point in our direction, wave, and flash us a huge smile.

The party had barely gotten started when we heard her impossible-to-miss voice, a high-pitched, Valley Girl squeal, even though she'd never spent a day of her life living in Southern California.

"Hi, Bob! Hi, Dalila. It's so good to see you," she gushed, flashing one of the smiles I'd seen her practice in the mirror. "I can't tell you how glad I am that you're taking such good care of my girls."

We watched as Mother, Bob, and Dalila made their way toward us. Lisa trailed behind the trio, ready to step in if we needed her. Mother squeezed her way into the middle of our new parents and linked her arms through each of theirs.

"Did I tell you I'm going into the military? I'm taking the test on Monday. It's gonna be good for me. Real good. It's not as hard as I thought it'd be. Boot camp is gonna suck, but ya know, I'm kinda tough. I work out. Haven't been working out much lately. I'll get back—"

Bob interrupted her. "Girls, your mom is here to see you."

She wasn't there to see us. I didn't know why she was there, but it had nothing to do with us. Mother grabbed Emily and threw her arms around her in a showy hug. Emily stood with her arms at her sides, looking around Mother at me, apologizing with her eyes.

"How's my precious Emily? My sweet baby girl. You've gotten so big, darling. So big." She raised Emily's arms up in the air dramatically. "Remember when we used to do that when you were little? You're so tall. Must've grown at least a couple inches. Let me look at you."

She stepped back, hands on Emily's shoulders, and sized her up. "Absolutely. Two inches. For sure." She turned to look at Bob, fluttering her dark eyelashes, and said, "She looks so cute. Just like her mama." She tossed her hair back over her shoulder and giggled.

Bob flushed and instinctively put his arm around Dalila. "They're both beautiful."

"When do I get to see them again? You'll probably have to come pick me up since I don't have a car. Jeremy gave me a ride here today. He's waiting outside. Too scared to come in. You know men." She poked Dalila in the side. Dalila laughed nervously. Mother turned back to Emily and squeezed her cheeks in her hands. "I just had to come see my baby."

Emily stepped back and reached out, grabbing my hand and pulling me close to her again.

"Hi, Elizabeth," Mother said without glancing in my direction.

I stared at her, saying nothing, hoping she could read the hate in my eyes. Mother coughed and flipped her hair over her shoulders again. Too much time with us made her uncomfortable, and she'd reached her limit.

"I can't wait for us to go on vacation, girls. I think we're gonna go to Disneyland. I'm getting it all planned now."

She might as well have been promising to take us to the moon. She put her arms around both of us, kissing the top of Emily's head.

"Now, your mama loves you. Don't you forget. I love you."

She skipped off, turning around when she reached the garage to dramatically blow us a kiss good-bye. We never saw her again.

Later on that night, while we were supposed to be sleeping in our separate bedrooms, Emily crept into my bed like she did every night. We had our own rooms as part of the differentiation process that Lisa talked about all the time. It had something to do with separating us and treating us as individuals instead of grouping us together like one person. Lisa had suggested ways for Bob and Dalila to do it, and sleeping apart was one of them. We hated it. It didn't matter, though, because nothing could separate us. Every night after they tucked each of us into our own beds, Emily would tiptoe through the "Jack and Jill" bathroom connecting our rooms and crawl into bed with me. Each morning the Rooths would find us wrapped up together.

"I hate Mother," Emily whispered as she curled up next to me.

I sat up, shocked. It was the first time she'd said it. I said it all the time, but not her. She didn't hate Mother like I did. She sat up next to me with an odd smile on her face. It was one I'd never seen before and I thought I'd seen them all. She pulled up her pajama leg.

"Lookit." She pointed in the dark.

I leaned closer to her leg, squinting. There were scratches on the side like a cat might've clawed her.

"What'd you do that on? Where'd you fall?"

She giggled. "I did it myself. Tonight, before I brushed my teeth. I was in my room and a tack fell off my bulletin board. I just picked it up and did it." She giggled again.

I stared back at her. "Did it hurt?"

She shook her head. "It felt good." She smiled as if she'd just won an award.

"Why'd you do it?"

She shrugged. "I wanted to see if I'd bleed. I tasted it. It tastes funny." A huge smile spread across her face, but her smile quickly turned to a look of concern. "Bethy, don't tell anyone. They'll think

I'm a weirdo. Promise you won't tell anyone. Promise, Bethy?"

"Course not," I replied.

And I didn't. And I hadn't. And I wouldn't.

2

"When? Just tell me when." The frustration in Thomas's voice bordered on begging. You could only have the same argument so many times before running out of patience, and we'd reached that limit a long time ago.

I sighed. I was as tired of the argument as he was. "You don't understand. You don't get it."

"Yes, I do. I get it. I mean, as much as I can. You don't even have to tell her I'm your boyfriend. You can just introduce me as your friend."

"She'll know."

I shot him down like I always did. He thought he understood, but he didn't. Nobody understood our relationship or why it functioned like it did. Even Bob and Dalila didn't, and if they couldn't get it, I was sure he wouldn't either.

We sat in silence as I played with the string hanging off the bottom of my shirt. I could feel him staring at me with hot intensity and even though I didn't look up, I felt the heat boring into the side of my face. I didn't know how he could be so patient with me. Tears welled in my eyes and I pulled them back before they had a chance to slide down my cheeks.

"Honey."

I loved when he called me honey.

His voice softened and he wrapped his arms around me,

pulling me close. The frustration in his voice was gone. "Everything's going to be all right."

I breathed in his scent. He smelled like a forest even though he spent all of his time inside, locked behind a cubicle at work or the library on campus with his head buried in a book. I liked being in his arms and wanted to kiss him, but still hadn't kissed him first. I couldn't initiate. I waited for him to kiss me and then kissed him back.

I looked up at him, trying to understand how he cared about me so deeply when there was still so much I couldn't tell him. I'd shared who I was more than I'd shared with anybody else, but there were lots of things I hadn't told him yet. He saw me as a strong, focused, and independent woman who was determined to make a better life for herself. I was afraid his image would change if he got closer to me, but I longed to be more intimate despite my fears because I wanted to be with him. I was beginning to need him, and I was going to have to take risks if I wanted our relationship to work.

I spat the words out as fast as I could before I changed my mind or lost my courage. "Okay. I'm going to tell her about us."

He pushed me back to arm's length with a huge smile on his face and looked me in the eyes. "You sure? I don't want to pressure you, but it's been a long time. We've been together for almost a year, and I still haven't been able to meet the most important person in your life. I care about you. Whoever is important to you is important to me too."

I'd never met anyone like Thomas. He was kind and patient. Unlike most people, who only professed not to care about what other people thought of them, he really didn't. I didn't either, outside of Emily. Emily's opinion was important to me, but I didn't spend much time worrying about other people's opinion of me. Thomas told me this was what attracted him to me, too.

He was his own person and I found myself drawn to him in a way I'd never been drawn to a man before because I had Emily—

my other half. She was the only person I needed or wanted to be close to, but as she was getting sicker, a small part of me had begun to wonder what it would be like to be attached to someone other than her. I'd started to question if it was possible to be close to someone who didn't already know everything about me or if I could develop a bond with someone if I hadn't gone through traumatic events with them.

I'd pushed away the longings to get close to someone else. Until Thomas. Thomas was different. I couldn't push away my feelings. There was nothing striking or exceptional about his appearance. He looked like an average college kid, with skinny jeans and red Converse that were so worn you could see his socks through the holes in the fabric. If you passed him in the mall, you wouldn't look twice. His confidence and strong sense of self attracted me. He was sure of himself without being arrogant. I didn't know how someone could be so sure of themselves without someone else defining them. I didn't know what it was like to just be "me" and not an "us."

We worked together doing telemarketing for a catalog company selling cheap towels that fell apart after the second wash and candles advertised to smell like flowers but really smelled like cheap soap. It was boring and a four-hour shift felt like twelve. The callers on the other end of the line were as annoyed by the call as you were at making it, and they usually took it as an opportunity to unleash all their pent-up anger and call you names they'd never say to your face. Thomas was never bothered by the rude comments like the rest of us were. He didn't get upset about them, and unlike most of us, who'd give back equally rude responses, he'd smile, say "thank you," and go on to his next caller.

Telemarketing wasn't anybody's first career choice. Everyone had a reason for being there and it wasn't to become rich or successful. Most of us did it to get by or because we couldn't get a job anywhere else. Our shift was mostly college students because of the flexible schedule and short shifts. Thomas started a few months before me and was there to put himself through seminary school. Unlike me, who still couldn't decide which career I wanted, Thomas had known since he was eight that he wanted to be a youth pastor.

He was a born-again Christian and his religion was a badge he wore proudly. His parents were Christians and he'd made the decision to follow Christ when he was three. He talked about God like God was his friend, and even though Bob and Dalila brought us to church for a while when we were young, I'd never felt God in the way he described. I didn't believe in God, but it didn't bother him. I often wondered if there would come a day when it became an issue and he tried to convert me to Christianity, but it hadn't happened yet. It used to worry me in the beginning, but I was becoming more and more willing to try his religion if he wanted me to.

Our coworkers teased and made fun of him constantly about his religious convictions. It was partly his fault because he didn't make any secret about being a Christian. He wasn't the least bit embarrassed about saving himself for marriage, which only made the other college guys on our shift work that much harder to get a reaction out of him. They accused him of being gay or taunted him by taping naked pictures of women all over his cubicle. But no matter what they tried, he stayed strong and never gave them the reaction they wanted. It was after one of their teasing sessions that we spoke for the first time.

"What a bunch of jerks," I said, putting my call on hold and turning to look at him in his cubicle—two down from mine.

He punched his hold button and shifted his mouthpiece. "Ah, who cares? They don't know any better. They're just being guys."

I refrained from stating the obvious fact that he was a guy too.

"I'm Elizabeth."

He smiled at me. His smile was warm and inviting, immediately putting me at ease. "I'm Thomas. Please, whatever you do, don't call me Tom."

I laughed. "As long as you promise not to call me Liz or Beth."

"Deal."

It was easy for us to talk in between taking calls because he was only two cubicles down from me. You weren't allowed to put your calls on hold for longer than two minutes without permission from your supervisor, so our initial conversations were short and clipped. He made me laugh with his funny descriptions about our customers.

"She definitely isn't going to remember making that order. I'm pretty sure she was talking in her sleep," he'd say. "I could've sold her every towel we have."

He'd mute the call in the middle of it, make faces and exclaim things like, "Oh my God, I don't want to hear about his hemorrhoids." Unlike our other customers, our elderly customers welcomed our calls and took them as opportunities to describe in detail all of their medical issues.

I was surprised at how normal he seemed despite his strong religious convictions. His smile and laugh started creeping into my thoughts, and I started imagining what it would be like to kiss him and feeling excited before work, knowing I'd see him. I'd never worried about what I looked like at work, but I began making sure I wore makeup and did my hair.

He started taking his lunch break at the same time I took mine. He took his break later in the day and I liked to eat early. I was always starving by noon because even though I knew I was supposed to, I never ate a good breakfast. The first time he took his break with me, I thought it might be because he had to leave work early, but I secretly hoped it was to spend time with me. The second time it happened and he took a seat next to me at the table in the break room, it was everything I could do to contain my excitement and act nonchalant.

"What are you reading?" he asked, noticing my open textbook. I always did homework on my lunch break.

"Kant. My English teacher is obsessed with him."

"Ugh, yuck, I remember those days."

"You read Kant? Like in college?"

He laughed. "Yes, we do more than just read the Bible all day."

Heat rushed to my cheeks. "I'm sorry."

He put his hand on my shoulder. It was the first time he'd touched me. "Don't worry about it. I was only teasing you. Everybody always assumes all we ever do is sit and talk about God, but you'd be surprised. It's exactly like regular college. We take all of the same classes and prerequisites as you. We just take other classes that have to do with whatever field we've chosen in the ministry."

"What field of ministry did you choose?"

"I want be a youth pastor. What's your major?"

"I haven't decided yet. I go back and forth between going into law or medicine. One day I think I want to be a doctor and I'm totally convinced it's the right choice for me, and then a few days later I'm convinced it's the worst decision ever and that I want to be a lawyer. It's so much pressure and I don't want to make the wrong decision."

"You'll figure it out." I waited for him to say more, but instead, he started digging into his reheated pasta. It looked Italian, and I loved Italian but hadn't been to a good Italian restaurant in a long time.

We developed our routine quickly. We had three shifts together each week and took our lunch break together at noon. I started bringing him things I'd baked. I couldn't cook like Emily, but I was a better baker than her. I'd bring in different cookies, cakes, and brownies for us to share. After a while, I started bringing a few extra for him to take home with him. I'd just given him a slice of carrot cake to take home when he asked me out on an official date.

"We should start eating more than lunch together. Want to see if we get along as good at dinner as we do lunch?"

I froze. I loved our lunches and enjoyed spending time with

him, but it couldn't be anything more than that. I'd stopped dating when Emily had gotten sick. She got jealous when I spent time with anyone other than her, and I avoided upsetting her.

I shook my head. "I can't."

He shrugged his shoulders. "No worries."

I was afraid he'd give up on our lunches since I said no to dinner, but he didn't. He carried on as if it had never happened and it didn't stop him from asking me out again. Every Friday he worked in a way to subtly or not so subtly ask me out for dinner and each time I found a reason to decline. Finally, after two months, I agreed to go out with him because I enjoyed spending time with him and was starting to like him. I told Emily I'd picked up an extra shift and would be home late. I didn't like lying to her, but I didn't have a choice.

We went to a small Italian restaurant after our shift. I was so nervous the only thing I dared eat was plain spaghetti. I didn't know if it was more of me being nervous or if it simply felt good to be out with somebody else, but I couldn't stop talking. I chatted and chatted about my classes, the books I was reading, and my favorite movies. Most of the time on dates I let the guy control the conversation while I listened, but I felt comfortable with Thomas. It felt so nice to talk to someone who wasn't depressed. He was a great conversationalist, and I liked that he was smart because I didn't have to pretend like I wasn't intelligent. Most guys were intimidated by my intellect, but he enjoyed it. We talked until it was time for the restaurant to close.

It'd been almost a year since our first dinner. I pulled his hand next to mine and intertwined my fingers with his, squeezing. "I care about you, too." I felt the red filling my face and looked away. "I want you to meet Emily. I know if she gives you a chance, she'll feel the same way I do about you."

The alarm on his watch sounded, signaling the end of our break. We didn't take our lunch in the break room anymore. We brought our own and retreated to his white Honda to eat in private. We started doing it as a way to spend time together shortly after our first date and we'd been doing it ever since. We were both busy balancing school and work and cherished our alone time during lunch. We put our stuff away and headed back inside.

I took my seat and slipped my headset over my head shifting into automatic mode. If I told Emily about Thomas, everything would change about my relationships with both of them. As much as I blamed Emily for my reluctance and hesitation to disclose our relationship to her, there was a part of me that was scared to do it. Telling Emily about Thomas would be the first step of separation between us. Even if it was a small one, once I took it there wouldn't be any going back. Things would never be the same between Emily and me.

It wasn't like we hadn't dated. Emily used to do more dating than me. Guys loved her. In high school, she had a new one attached to her every other week, but she quickly tossed them aside for the next one waiting in line as if she were just trying them on, shopping for a new pair of jeans. But neither of us had ever been serious about a guy or seen a future with one. Deep down, I knew there'd come a day when one of us would meet a man and start to build our own life without the other, but I'd assumed she'd be the one to do it first. It was clear now that it wasn't going to happen that way. She hadn't been on a date in years and I couldn't remember the last time she'd left the apartment.

The thought of building a life with someone other than Emily made my stomach flip with excitement and fear. It had always been the two of us because our survival depended on it. We were a team and couldn't have endured our childhood without the other.

When we lived with Mother, she'd disappeared and left us locked in our bedroom for days. Emily was the one who'd figured out how to get rid of the itchy and painful red rash all over our legs and inner thighs. The rash was a result of wearing the same urine-and-feces-soaked diapers for days, but we didn't dare take them off. The one time we had, Mother had been furious. She'd grabbed the wire hanger that she used to beat us and added painful welts on top of our open wounds. There was a big red plastic bucket in our room that Mother had left behind once. Emily started taking her diaper off and squatting over it to go the bathroom. I did too, and we both used the bucket as a toilet. While one of us peed, the other listened for the sound of Mother's keys in the front door. For some reason, Mother didn't mind when she found out we were using the bucket and she let us dump our bucket in the toilet once a week. We no longer sat in pounds of our waste, and the rashes on our legs finally went away. We still had to smell it, but at least we no longer had to sit in it.

The hours of hunger and isolation were endless, but we filled them up with each other. We told each other stories about imaginary families and made each other laugh. But our favorite game was to take turns pretending to be the mother. When I was Emily's mother, I knew how she liked to have her hair stroked, so she would lay on my lap and I'd stroke her hair over and over again while I hummed. When Emily was my mother, she knew I liked to have my back stroked in circles, so she would draw pictures on my back before she fell asleep. We spoke in a secret language so when Mother was around she wouldn't know what we were saying to each other. We sang and played pretend in our crib, performing for each other. When there was nothing left to eat and we were starving, we slept cuddled close to each other like puppies trying to stay warm.

Sleep during starvation was fitful. It was like being halfway between asleep and awake. I would slip in and out of lucid dreams. Sometimes we shared the same dream. We moved in and out of consciousness together.

We were five when Mother started letting us out of our bedroom and into the rest of the apartment. We knew nothing of a world outside of the four walls of the bedroom and to us, the small apartment was an expansive universe. At the time, we didn't know it would eventually imprison us in the same way our bedroom had; we were completely enraptured with it. On the other side of the living room, Mother had her own bedroom that she kept locked. She gave us strict orders for being out of our bedroom.

"You do not go into my bedroom. Ever," she said. "Do you understand me? If you do, I'll put you back in your room and never let you out again."

We nodded our heads.

"When you're out here, you're quiet. If anyone hears the two of you, I'll use the belt again. I mean it. Do you understand me?" She smacked me on the side of my head.

"Yes, I get it, Mother. I do. Be quiet," I said.

She grabbed Emily's face in her hands and peered into her eyes, "How about you, little miss thing? You gonna be quiet if I let you out?"

Emily nodded her head and looked at me. She grabbed my hand. Mother jerked her away from me.

"Speak up, look at me. I'm your mother. What are you looking at her for? You can talk too, or are you the dumb one? They always say there's a smart twin and a dumb twin. I guess you're the dumb one."

Emily started to cry.

"Shut up! Stop crying. God, you always cry. That's one thing you could learn from your sister. She never cries. She knows how to be strong. You're just pathetic. You know what? Get back in your room. Both of you."

We scurried back to our room as quickly as we could. I held Emily while she sobbed without making a sound because loud crying angered Mother more. We thought our chance to be let out was over, but it wasn't long until Mother brought us out again and gave us the same instructions a second time. That time we passed her test and she started to let us out of our bedroom occasionally when she left. She introduced us to the TV and it was the same routine every time.

"Don't turn this off. You leave it on while I'm gone. If anyone comes to the door to knock, you don't answer it. No matter what. I don't care what they say or who they say it is. You shut up and stay where you are. You do not lift the shades of the windows." She walked over to the window in the living room and pointed at the blinds. "These stay closed at all times. Period. If I find out either of you have broken my rules, I'll beat the shit out of both of you."

And then she'd leave. Sometimes for hours. Other times for days. We never knew how long she'd stay gone. We were fascinated with the TV because there were new voices and faces, so many things we'd never seen and didn't know existed. There were people who had skin that wasn't peach like ours. They'd been painted with a different color. We sat on the floor in front of it, mesmerized and enthralled. We never knew when Mother was going to set us free from the bedroom, but knowing another world existed made the time we were locked up more bearable and gave us new things to play with each other.

It wasn't long before we met our first person from the outside world. When he came through the door with Mother, Emily and I stared at him as if he'd walked out of our TV set. He wore blue jeans and a black T-shirt with words we didn't know how to read sprawled across the center. He had short blond hair and big glasses framing his squinty eyes. His stomach protruded over his waist and it shook while he laughed with Mother, rolling up and down as if there was something inside it. He smelled like Mother—the same putrid smell of rotten cheese.

"Girls, stand up and come meet the special friend I was telling you about this morning." She'd never told us about anyone, but we did as we were told and stood up. "Come here. Come closer. Don't be shy." We took a few steps in their direction. "I told you they were adorable." She looked up at him, but he wasn't looking at her. He was looking at us, licking his lips with a half sneer tugging at the corner of his mouth.

He stuck out his hand. We stood with our hands by our sides.

"Girls, don't be impolite. Shake his hand." Mother's syrupy sweet voice was one I'd never heard before but would grow to know well over time. I stuck out my hand, and the special friend took hold of it and shook. Emily followed suit. He reached into his back pocket and took out two sticks that held round circles on the top covered in colorful paper and twisted at the bottom.

"I brought you a treat. I thought you might like it," he said. His voice was low. He sounded like he had a mouthful of marbles that he had to speak around.

"Go ahead, girls. Take it. Don't be rude."

We took the object from his hand. We didn't have a clue what to do with it, but we dared not move or ask any questions.

"They're nice and clean. I gave them a bath this morning. I even used my special lotion." He nodded his head in approval, still smiling his strange smile. Mother pointed to her bedroom. "You can take them in there. Just like we discussed." She walked to her bedroom door and turned the knob, revealing a bedroom like the ones we'd seen on TV. There was a beautiful bed in the center of the room shrouded in white wisps of material that looked like clouds. Unlike the rest of the apartment, which was covered in dingy white walls, her bedroom was a soft pink bordered with vibrant flowers and a plush pink-and-white rug on the floor. He hungrily took in the bedroom in the same manner we were.

"They're all yours," she said.

He walked through the door. We stayed glued to our spots. Mother turned to look at us with a look we knew well.

"Go on, girls." Her eyes carried the threat of punishment if we didn't. "There's nothing to be afraid of."

Robotically, we followed him into the bedroom and she shut the door behind us. I heard her ice cubes clink in the glass that she used to drink her dark liquid. The sound of the TV went from its normal volume to blasting, and rock music filled my ears. The special friend took Emily's hand and led her to the bed. I rushed to the bed and sat down next to her, gripping her hand in mine.

"We're going to play a special game," he said, taking off his black T-shirt.

The first time we played the game was the hardest because we didn't know how to play any special games. We'd never played games with anyone else besides each other, so we didn't know how other people played. I went first. I didn't like his game. It didn't make any sense. It wasn't fun and it hurt, but he didn't care that it hurt. He had a special toy he used in the game. It was attached to his body and I couldn't breathe when he put it in my mouth. It choked me and made tears stream down my cheeks.

I had super powers and used them to float into the ceiling tiles to watch myself. I waited to come down from the tiles until the game was over. When it was Emily's turn, I helped her through it because I didn't know if she had the same powers I did and wanted to help her get to the end of the game. She looked at me while she played the game and I was glad we knew how to talk to each other without words so I could keep telling her it was going to be okay.

We met many special friends over the years and played the game more times than I could count. Emily liked the ones who brought us candy. She always took it, but I never did. The candy meant we were going to have to play the game and I hated playing the game. There were times when the special friend left, and Mother hugged us and told us she was proud of us. Those times she'd let us stay out of the bedroom for a few days as a reward. Then, there were the other times when she became furious after the special friend left and beat us with the wire hanger or the belt before throwing us into the bedroom.

Our rescue quickly became a media sensation. Our story was in every magazine and on every news station at the time. Shortly after we turned seven, we'd started a fire in the apartment while Mother was gone.

I'd finally gotten up the courage to start exploring the kitchen. Mother might have beaten us to death if she came home and found us in the kitchen, but Emily listened carefully at the door while I rummaged through the cupboards and drawers. We lived in the upper back unit of an apartment complex. There were creaky wooden stairs leading up to our door, and Mother couldn't walk up without making noise. Once she got to the top, she had to jiggle the key around in the lock and put her shoulder into the door to get it open. It was thirty seconds from the time we heard her footsteps on the stairs until she opened the door, which gave us plenty of time to scurry to our usual spots in front of the TV.

I discovered a package of noodles in the cupboard.

"Em, look," I said, showing her the package.

"What is it?" She jumped on the counter next to me, taking the package from my hand and turning it around.

"It's noodles. Just like Mother made." I recognized the red package and small sticks inside. I'd seen Mother make them before. She didn't cook very often and when she did, she never shared. She'd scarf it down in front of us, never offering a bite. She only cooked when she had that funny, sweet smell and sometimes she forgot she was doing it. "She'll think she cooked them. She won't even know."

I was convinced I could make the pasta even though Emily wasn't so sure. We figured out how to turn the burner on, but I didn't know anything about stoves and tossed a towel onto the burner after it was lit. It ignited quickly and the smoke alarm started wailing.

"Ohmigod! Ohmigod! Bethy! Bethy!" Emily screamed as loud as the alarm. "She's gonna kill us! Make it stop!"

The kitchen was filthy because Mother never cleaned. There were leftover pizza boxes next to the stove, and as quickly as the towel started to burn, the pizza boxes were next. I stood there watching the fire as if I was in a trance. Smoke began to fill the kitchen. The cupboards above the pizza boxes caught the flames next. Emily was pulling on my arm.

"Do something! Ohmigod! Do something!"

I grabbed her arm and ran back into our room as fast as I

could, slamming and locking the door behind us. We huddled in our crib, clutching each other. Emily buried her head against me and sobbed. It wasn't long until we heard the sounds of sirens from a distance and listened as they grew closer and closer to us.

"Fire department," we heard a male voice yell.

And then the crashing started. The sounds of wood breaking. Male voices called out to each other. We jumped out of our crib and hid in the closet. Both of us were shaking. It seemed like we were in the closet for hours. We heard the sound of heavy footsteps moving throughout the apartment. We braced ourselves as a giant man dressed all in blue opened the closet door.

"Oh my God." The giant let out his breath slowly, peering down at us as we looked up at him in terror. "Get back here, John. There are kids in here."

I couldn't remember much of what happened next. The only thing I recalled was panic at the flurry of activity and the strangers' faces flashing in front of us. Emily and I held on to each other, refusing to let go and unable to answer any of their questions. We didn't speak, not even to utter our names. We let ourselves be poked and prodded by the doctors and stared blankly at all the characters who pressed in on us, wanting to know who we were, but most importantly, where our mother was.

They couldn't locate Mother and we didn't have any information to help them. She didn't come back to the apartment for three days and there was yellow tape on the front door when she did. We stayed in the hospital for a week. She never visited or called. Child Protective Services wasn't about to let us go. We went directly from the hospital into foster care with the Rooths.

Every media headline included a picture from our bedroom and Mother's bedroom followed by some version of the question: How did they survive? The truth was simple—we had each other. I didn't know how we'd done it, but we had. We were still doing it and I didn't know how to bring someone else into our world. Even though we'd lived with the Rooths until we graduated from high school, they'd never been able to make their way into our inner world. I wanted Thomas to be different.

It wasn't the first time I'd considered telling Emily about our relationship. I'd worked up enough courage before, but then she'd plunged into one of her dark episodes. It wasn't fair to tell her in her destroyed state. Not when brushing her teeth brought her to tears. So I waited for any sign that she was getting better.

There'd been brief glimpses of the old Emily that kept my hope alive, like the nights when I came home and found the apartment cleaned spotless or got off work late to find she'd cooked an elaborate dinner for us, complete with the table set for two. She was thoughtful during her flashes of normalcy; the dinner she made was always the meal I'd mentioned craving the day before, or the housecleaning would happen on a particularly stressful day at work. However, my hope was always short-lived. The next day or the day after she would retreat to the sanctity of our bed, draw the shades, and pull the covers around her. She didn't move or shower. She barely spoke.

I searched my memory trying to pinpoint the exact moment when she gave up trying to live a normal life and gave in to the suffering. I was obsessed with trying to figure out when she gave up because if I could find the moment where she quit trying, I might be able to fix it and get her to fight again. I'd been through the routine many times before and each time my search had come up empty.

I tried to talk her into meeting with our old therapist, Lisa. We'd liked therapy with Lisa because she was the only person who treated us like we weren't fragile. She talked to us in a normal voice. Everyone else, including Bob and Dalila, talked to us in soft, quiet voices as if they thought we might break if they spoke too loud. I needed someone strong to help Emily because I couldn't do it by myself anymore. My suggestions to meet with Lisa were always met with rejection.

"No. I won't do it. I hated talking to her when we were kids and I would hate it even more now," she'd huff, crossing her arms across her chest.

"But, Em, it wasn't that bad. She helped us. Really, she did. You just don't remember. All you can see and remember is the negative stuff right now. Your brain is clouded with it."

She didn't remember the fun games Lisa played with us as kids or how she helped us talk to Bob and Dalila about what we were feeling. She'd also forgotten how much she helped her depression when she was a teenager.

I'd put my hand on her shoulder, trying to get her to soften to the idea. "Please. I don't know what to do. I really don't."

"I'm sorry. God, I'm so sorry. I'm such a mess. You'd be so much better off without having to worry about me. You really would."

"Don't talk like that. You know I hate it when you talk like that. It's just stupid."

"Seriously. I'm never going to be anything except a huge burden on you. I'm worthless. My life is pointless."

Her self-pity would drone on until I was suffocating in it. Eventually, I'd drop the conversation because I wasn't going to be able to convince her to see Lisa. I'd considered going to see Lisa by myself but never did.

As I dialed my next unsuspecting potential customer, I decided to make an appointment to see her as soon as I could. Maybe I could convince her to come to the apartment to work with Emily. She used to come to Bob and Dalila's to visit, and I didn't see why she couldn't come to our place too. Emily would have to talk to her if I brought her to the apartment, but even if Lisa couldn't come to the apartment, she'd help me figure out a way to help Emily. She'd always been able to point out ways I could be there for Emily without losing myself, and I needed her guidance now in the same way.

I Googled Lisa as soon as my call ended. She was at the same office. I put my customer line on hold, looked around to make sure nobody was watching, and punched in the number on my cell phone.

Her receptionist answered on the third ring. "Hello?"

"I'd like to make an appointment for Lisa as soon as I can get in," I said, looking around to make sure none of my supervisors were walking by.

"You're in luck," she said. "She has a cancelation for tomorrow at nine thirty. Any chance you could make it in then?"

"Absolutely."

"Great. Have you been here before? Who do I say it's for?"

"Yes, but it was a long time ago. I was a kid."

"What's your name?"

"Elizabeth. Elizabeth Rooth." I tapped my fingers on my desk as I waited.

"I don't see your name ... I wonder if—"

"Look, can you just put me in as a new patient, then?"

"Okay." I listened as she tapped on her computer. I was afraid I was going to get caught. I'd never been in trouble at work before. I hated getting into trouble anywhere. "Do you know if your insurance will cover it?"

"I'll pay cash. I don't care."

"All right, Elizabeth. We'll see you tomorrow at nine thirty. Be sure to bring your insurance card with you since we don't have you on file."

"Okay. Thanks. Bye." I quickly hung up before I got caught.

I didn't tell Thomas about my appointment when I said goodbye to him at the end of our shift and didn't tell Emily about it when I got home. She didn't stir when I walked in the door. She stared at the TV as if she was looking through it. It reinforced what I was about to do. I couldn't live this way anymore. I needed help.

3

I was surprised Lisa didn't look different. I half-expected her to have a pile of white hair and round old-lady glasses perched on her nose because it seemed like a lifetime ago since I'd sat in her office. Instead, she looked exactly how I remembered her. She had the same straight black hair, except it used to be long and now it was in a cute bob framing her narrow face. She still had kind blue eyes and perfectly straight teeth, the kind that were only possible from years of braces. We'd spent countless hours in her office and for a while, I thought she'd adopted us along with the Rooths because of the amount of time we spent together.

Bob and Dalila were devastated again and again as they tried to conceive. Bob wanted a child as much as Dalila and after many heartbreaking tries with IVF, they'd turned to adoption. For Bob, adopting a child simply meant being given the opportunity to be a parent, but for Dalila, it was something more. She took all the pain she'd experienced from not being able to conceive and channeled it into finding a child she could save. She didn't want just to adopt a baby—she wanted to rescue one.

After our examinations at the hospital, we were taken to the Rooths in a police squad car. Dalila loved to describe how her heart melted when she saw us, watching the police officer let us out of the backseat as if we were the world's youngest felons. We were too afraid to move forward, so the officer had to keep reminding us to walk up the sidewalk. Dalila opened the door before he knocked. Emily and I clung to each other on the front steps. We still hadn't spoken to anyone since the firemen rescued us from our apartment.

"Come inside, sweethearts," she said. The sound of her voice was kind, and we followed it into our new world.

We didn't function like normal kids, and nothing could've prepared Bob and Dalila for our list of problems. Eating was a huge one. I didn't eat and Emily ate everything she could get her hands on. Both extremes made us sick. Emily threw up after her binges while I got skinnier than I'd been before they took us in.

The only solid food we'd ever eaten was cheese pizza and bread. There was a small all-night pizza place two blocks down from the strip club where Mother worked, and occasionally when she didn't have a man, she'd grab one on the way home. The grease always gave us diarrhea, but we didn't care. It was worth it. Other than that, we survived on water, formula, and bread. The cupboards in the kitchen in our apartment were stocked with formula and bread. Nothing else. We used the water from the sink to mix up the formula we drank. The social workers told Dalila that although drinking formula from bottles had rotted out many of our front teeth, it kept us from starving to death or developing mental retardation from the lack of important nutrients over the years. We were still drinking formula from bottles when we were brought to the Rooths.

Eating was foreign and the food felt weird in my mouth. I didn't like to chew, or the texture and squish of it between my teeth. I spat out mouthfuls, because if I tried to swallow, I couldn't breathe, which sent me into a frenzied panic attack. Emily, on the other hand, couldn't get enough food. She was in Heaven. She'd eat everything on her plate and mine. She hid food all over her room. She'd sneak down to the kitchen in the middle of the night and eat half the contents of the refrigerator. Sometimes I'd go with her and watch her eat pickles straight out of the jar, followed by whipped cream and the leftovers from dinner.

"Yuck. How do you eat that?" I'd ask, completely repulsed and disgusted.

She'd giggle at me with food smeared all over her mouth. "Because it's so delicious."

We'd learned how to eat, but it wasn't easy and took a long time. The process involved forced feedings, coupled with small rewards for me and locks on the kitchen cabinets and refrigerator for Emily.

We didn't like to be separated, which was a problem since everyone was determined to sever our dependence on each other. If someone separated us, we went into horrible rages that escalated into biting and head banging. I bit and Emily banged.

There were other adjustments too. Neither of us had any semblance of a regular sleep/wake routine. We'd never been on a schedule, so we didn't know the difference between day and night. Neither of us could sleep through the night. It was as if the Rooths had two newborns, except we were seven. It made it even harder on them because we'd never been properly toilet trained and traded off on nightly accidents, but since we slept together there was only one set of sheets to wash. It took a year before we were able to sleep through the night without accidents.

Bob and Dalila were patient through all of our struggles, but our refusal to make physical contact hurt them the most. We were physical and affectionate with each other, but recoiled from anyone else's touch. Dalila liked to hold and cuddle us before we went to bed. She put a rocking chair in each of our rooms. She'd pull me on her lap and wrap her arms around me, but I didn't like to sit on her lap or anyone else's. Some of Mother's special friends made me sit on their laps and it was all I could think about when she plopped me on hers. I'd wiggle and squirm, trying to get comfortable, but was never able to find a spot that felt right. I loved when Emily stroked my back, but her rubbing made my skin itch like bugs were underneath it. I pushed her hands away.

I had an easier time connecting with Bob than Dalila. I was mesmerized by the safety in his eyes. They twinkled when he smiled and laughed. Every man I'd met had had eyes clouded with demons that came to life as soon as Mother's bedroom door closed, but Bob's eyes bore no sign of demons. He didn't expect as much of us as Dalila. He accepted much sooner than her that Emily and I had some wounds no amount of love would erase. He was content to focus on what he could give us and didn't try to change us into something we weren't.

He developed his own routines with us. He'd sit and draw for hours with Emily, and he loved to watch *Friends* with me. It didn't matter that he could quote almost every line Joey said or knew each twist during the scene. His belly jiggled up and down with laughter each time as if it was the first time he'd seen the episode. I spent many nights on the couch with him watching *Friends*. He had his side of the couch and I had mine. There was an invisible line between us, and unlike Dalila, he never tried to cross it.

Lisa played a central role in helping the Rooths navigate our issues. Changing our behavior involved charts and stickers that the Rooths brought home and taped on the refrigerator. There was a chart on the refrigerator right up until the day we started high school.

Lisa referred to things like "insecure attachment" and "reactive attachment disorder" when she talked to the Rooths about us. I hadn't understood the words then and still didn't. Sometimes they forced me to sit in Dalila's lap in Lisa's office with her arms wrapped tightly around me while I kicked and screamed. Emily hated it too, but unlike me, who fought, she'd just go limp in Dalila's arms when it was her turn. It might have helped them work with us if we'd told them what Mother's special friends made us do to them, but we never told. Never. Mother had warned us that if we ever told, she'd kill us, and her threats were still very real to us even though her physical presence was gone from our lives.

We spoke to no one about it, not even each other.

Despite their efforts, neither Emily nor I responded to Bob and Dalila as they'd hoped, but we grew to love them in our own way and became familiar with the routine and stability they provided. It was just never the way they'd imagined it'd be.

"Elizabeth," Lisa exclaimed when she saw me and threw her arms around me. She laid her hand on my back and ushered me into her office. It was still the same too. Games and toys were stacked on the shelves. Blocks and puzzles littered the floor. The huge bin of stuffed animals that I used to love to jump into headfirst was still there. Her small desk was buried in the corner, with her degrees hanging on the wall behind her, peeking out from crayoned artwork and finger paintings. I stood eyeing the blue beanbag chair I used to sit in. It seemed too weird to sit in it now. She pointed to a straight-backed chair in front of her desk as she took a seat behind it.

"Have a seat. I'm so happy to see you."

I plopped down on the wooden seat, feeling like a giant. Everything was so much smaller than I remembered. Even Lisa looked like she'd shrunk a few inches.

"You look great," she said.

I smiled at her. Being in love had a way of making everything look brighter and more vibrant. I'd been noticing it myself.

"I can't wait to hear what's going on with you. Dalila sent me an email that you got a full scholarship for college. It made me so proud. Where are you at now?" she asked.

"I'm in the first semester of my second year."

"At Galston?"

I nodded. "Yep. After this year, I'm hoping to transfer to a four-year university on my scholarship. I'm just starting to look at schools. I still haven't decided if I want to go into law or medicine."

"I can see you being a lawyer. You've always been so logical and analytical. It seems like it'd be a good fit."

I crossed my legs and looked to the side, avoiding her eyes. I'd forgotten about her eyes. She had a way of looking right into you as if she could see into your insides.

"Do you have a job?"

"In telemarketing. It's a mindless job, but I get paid well enough and they work around my school schedule, so that's good."

"Wonderful."

There was an awkward pause.

"Do you live on campus?" she asked.

"No, I live in an apartment off campus. It's only a few blocks away. It works out to live so close to school."

I hated small talk.

"So, what brings you here to see me today?" she asked.

Apparently, she hated small talk too.

I cleared my throat. Cleared it again. I wasn't any better at this kind of talk either. "Well, um, I have a boyfriend."

"It's about time." She laughed. "He's a lucky guy. Tell me about him." She leaned back in her chair, resting it against the wall.

"His name's Thomas and we work together. We've been dating for almost a year. I think I'm in love." I blushed.

She smiled. "That's great. I'm so happy for you. Love is a good thing and I think it's a wonderful problem to have."

I smiled shyly. If only it were that simple.

"Then there's Emily ..."

The sentence hung in the air.

She got up from her desk and walked over to sit in the chair next to me. She smelled different. She used to smell like flowers. Now all I smelled was vanilla, like she'd just finished baking cookies. She placed her hand on my knee.

"Elizabeth, it's okay." She paused, letting her words take effect. "It's okay to love someone other than Emily. You know that, don't you? It's okay to let go."

I took her words in, digesting them slowly. Dalila used to say the same thing back when we were talking regularly and not just checking in every few weeks.

"Sweetie, I know I've said this to you before, but I think it would help you so much if you allowed yourself to let go of Emily. She's holding you back from moving on with your life and being happy," she'd said after I complained about Emily refusing to get out of bed again.

She'd never understand us. Emily and I were like two bodies who shared one soul and I didn't know how you were supposed to give up your soul. I'd hung up on Dalila after she said it and didn't talk to her for another month. I started talking to her again after a while but kept our discussions focused on school and trivial things.

I heard the words in a new way when they came from Lisa. Her words always had a different effect on me. Maybe it was because she knew our early history so well or had years of training on how to say the right thing at the perfect time, but something about them made me stop feeling guilty about loving Thomas. I had enough love for both of them. I'd just have to prove to Emily that I'd still take care of her even with Thomas in my life.

"Thank you."

She smiled again. "Anything else you want to talk about? Do you need anything from me? Anything at all?"

"I don't know if you know this or if Dalila told you, but Emily's been really depressed again. Worse than before. I've been keeping Thomas a secret from her because I'm afraid of hurting her, but I want to tell her. I just don't know how."

Lisa cocked her head to the side, studying my face. She was silent as she gathered her words. She always chose her words carefully. "I think Emily will understand."

"Do you?" My heart swelled. Lisa knew Emily as well as anyone besides me. I felt excited again.

"I'm always here to help you. You know that. What do you think about us having a few sessions to talk about your relationship with Thomas and the effect it's going to have on your relationship with Emily?"

I didn't even have to think about my answer.

"I'd really love that," I said.

I wished I'd come to see her months ago when I first thought about it. She'd been there for every important milestone in our lives and could help us navigate this next transition.

"Tell you what, why don't you schedule a session next week? We can really start digging into what's going on and come up with a plan."

"Absolutely." I liked plans. I stood up. "How much do I owe you for today?"

She rolled her eyes at me. "It was just really great to see you. Don't worry about today. We'll take care of all of the financial stuff next week when we start working together. I'm excited to be working with you again."

She smiled at me and then stood up and walked me to the door.

"How are the Rooths?"

"Good, I guess," I said. "We don't talk much since Emily got sick."

She opened her mouth and then closed it quickly.

"I think it's hard on them, too. I don't think they want to deal with her depression again," I explained. When we were in high school, Dalila became almost as depressed as Emily when she found out she was cutting herself. They didn't like to talk about Emily anymore and had quit asking me about her. I played along because Emily didn't want me to share how bad it'd gotten with them anyway, so it made it easier for everyone if we didn't talk about her.

"It was so good to see you. And I'm always here if you need me. Always." Lisa put her arms around me and squeezed. "Take care of yourself and I'll see you next week."

"I will," I promised.

4

I didn't get a chance to spend any alone time with Thomas until two days after I met with Lisa. It was important for me to tell him about it in person, so I waited until we were alone in his dorm room with a shoe propping the door open. It was seminary policy whenever a girl was in a guy's room and vice versa, but it still made me giggle because it was so old-fashioned. It was as if I'd stepped into a weird time machine every time I was on his campus.

"I've decided I'm ready for you to meet Emily," I announced from my position on his bed with my homework laid out in front of me.

He swirled around in his office chair scooting away from his desk and towards me. "Really?"

I nodded.

My announcement elevated our relationship to a different level. It was like asking your partner to meet your parents and I was sure he was beginning to doubt it'd ever happen. "But before you do, I'm going to need a few days to get her ready. I've got to prepare her and I also need to tell you a few things about her ... about us."

The details of my and Emily's life had trickled out in small chunks over the last year. He knew we were neglected by Mother because her main priorities were to get drunk and sleep with wealthy men. She searched for her Prince Charming in bars downtown, hoping one of her conquests would result in riches, but all she'd ever ended up with was us. I'd never known why she didn't get rid of us or give us up when we were born. I'd spent years asking why she'd decided to keep us, but I'd given up on finding an answer a long time ago. None of her decisions made sense, and I couldn't expect her decision to keep us to be any different.

I'd shared with Thomas how she kept us locked in our bedroom for days while she was gone, but purposefully left out the parts about what happened when she let us out or how she usually kept us locked up even when she was there. This small window into her actions was already so incomprehensible to him and I didn't want to shatter his innocence about humanity any more than I already had. His innocence was one of the things I found so attractive about him, and I didn't want to defile it. He was naïve, even though he thought he was well traveled, given all of the mission trips he'd taken. Lots of women might've been turned off by his childlike faith in the world, but it was one of the things I liked the most about him.

The only other part of our story I'd shared with him was how we'd been taken away from Mother—about the fire and going to live with the Rooths. I didn't tell him how many healed fractures the doctors found when they x-rayed our bodies, the lice they found in our hair, or that we had to have a feeding tube because we were so malnourished. The pain I saw in his eyes when I'd told him my edited version of the rescue made me want to cry, and just remembering that look still had the power to move me to tears. Sometimes I thought my past hurt him more than it hurt me. What he didn't understand was that back then, I didn't know anything else existed. I had no idea what the world was like outside of our apartment besides my fleeting experiences with the things I saw on TV, so I didn't know I was missing out on anything. I had no idea there were other people who didn't live like we did. And besides, I always had Emily.

I also hadn't told him about how bad things were now. He had no clue Emily was depressed and what a hard time she'd been having since we'd graduated high school and moved out on our own. If he was going to meet her, he had to be prepared for what he was getting himself into.

"Emily has had a hard time since we moved out. I don't know why. I think it might be because we left all the routines we had at the Rooths or something."

"But I thought you told me she was the one that wanted to move out?" he asked.

"She was. She couldn't wait, but I don't think she knew how it would affect her until it actually happened. I know I told you she doesn't work and that she doesn't leave the house without me, but it's more than that."

How could I explain what she was like now and who she'd become? I had to try.

"She's really depressed. She'll sleep for days and then not sleep at all. Sometimes she doesn't even shower or eat anything. I've never seen her so moody. She's always been emotional, but it's more than that. Like, one minute she'll be bawling her eyes out and the next minute she'll be angry for no reason. She gets really worked up and it can be impossible to get her to calm down. Sometimes she doesn't talk at all. Other times, when she does talk, it's completely incoherent. You just never know which Emily you're going to get."

As soon as the words were out, I wanted to take them back. I never talked about Emily with anyone and I'd just told someone her secret. In our twenty years, I'd never betrayed her. Even when Dalila discovered her cutting and questioned me about it, I'd refused to say anything. I wanted to cry but held the tears back. I still hadn't let Thomas see me cry.

He got up and sat next to me on the bed, putting his arm

around my shoulders. "My freshman year was awful. It took me over a year to get used to not living with my parents. It makes sense that it's even harder for her. I get it. There's no judgment here."

He was the most nonjudgmental person I knew. He was going to make a great pastor, even if I didn't understand his religion.

"You don't have to feel guilty that you aren't miserable and she is."

"But I do. It eats away at me. I pay all my bills by myself and I'm getting straight As, which should make me happy, but I feel bad about it. Like I'm a horrible person for leaving the house every day. I even feel bad that I love you."

His head snapped up. "I've been waiting a long time for you to say that."

I kissed him tenderly and pulled back. "I love you."

It still sounded right the second time.

"Now if you could just work on the whole God thing," he laughed.

I punched him in his arm and he reached over, pulling me into his arms. "I love you, too."

I floated through the rest of the week. I was in love for the first time and it felt wonderful. It was like every romantic movie I'd seen where the girl walks like she's dancing on clouds with a huge grin on her face. I didn't change the station on the radio when the sappy love songs came on. Instead, I turned them up and tried to sing along. I'd been freed from a prison I didn't know I was in. I'd always been cynical about falling in love, because I was afraid I wasn't capable of it, and it was exhilarating to discover I was.

I picked Saturday to tell Emily about Thomas because she did better on the weekends, when I was there. It didn't matter if I was sitting in front of the computer or buried in one of my textbooks. She just liked having me around. When Saturday morning rolled around, I was happy when she got up before noon and joined me for coffee at the table because it meant it was one of her good days.

"You slept good last night," I said.

She'd only kicked me once and hadn't talked at all in her sleep.

She smiled at me and lit a cigarette. "Do you have lots of homework to do this weekend?"

"Not really," I said, shaking my head and pointing to my pile of textbooks lying open on the table. "Just a lot of reading."

She picked up my economics book and began thumbing through it. "Yuck. God, I hate anything that has to do with math. I don't know how you do it."

I shrugged my shoulders. "It's not so bad."

She picked up another book. *Theories of Mind.* I was taking Introduction to Psychology this semester. "Now this is more like it. I think I could do this stuff," she laughed. "Maybe I'd figure out what the hell is wrong with me. Is there a section in here on blood tasting?"

She laughed again, but I didn't think it was funny. Her compulsion to cut was terrible, yet understandable, but the things she did with her blood were disgusting. Over the years, she'd tasted it, written with it, and lately her new thing was to save it in empty water bottles. It was the one part of her sickness I chose to ignore completely. I didn't like to see it or talk about it. Not even with her. I shot her a knowing look that she'd stepped over my line.

"That's not funny," I said.

I stared into my coffee cup, searching for the words to begin the conversation, trying to figure out what her response would be and how I'd respond to it. This was unfamiliar territory for us. I had lots of secrets but never one I'd kept from her.

"What's up?" she interrupted my thoughts.

She knew me too well.

"I …" I cleared my throat. "This is really weird for me. I don't even know how to start."

Her eyes froze in fear. She sat back in her chair.

"It's nothing bad. Don't worry. It's actually a good thing." I reached out and squeezed her hand. She clung tightly to mine. I took a deep breath. "Em, I met a really great guy at work."

"You should go out with him, then."

Guilt washed over me.

"I already have. We've been going out for a while," I said, surprised at her response.

"Why didn't you tell me?"

"I don't know. I guess I never thought it'd go anywhere and I felt bad because of you being so, uh, not well. I guess I felt bad being ... being ..."

"Happy?"

"I feel like I shouldn't be. Like somehow I'm betraying you."

She cocked her head back and laughed. "By not being miserable? It's not your fault I'm crazy."

"You're not crazy." I hated when she talked that way. "You're just depressed and going through a hard time. Things are going to get better again."

All emotion left her eyes and she stared at me vacantly. "No. They're not."

Her emptiness scared me. I could handle her emotional intensity, but her nothingness was frightening. I got up, refilling both of our coffee mugs.

"So, do you want to meet him?"

She shrugged. "I guess I probably should. Where?"

"I don't know. I could call him. He could come over and—"

"No!" She leaped up from her chair. "This is our place, ours!"

She ran through the narrow kitchen, down the hallway, and into the bedroom, where she slammed the door. I took a few deep breaths before following. I walked in and found her face down on the bed, beating her fists onto the pillows as if she was a three-year-old child having a temper tantrum. I sat at the end of the bed.

"Get away from me," she cried. I moved closer. "I mean it."

I slid up next to her, touching her lightly on the back.

"Don't touch me!"

I began to rub circles on her back slowly. Round and round while I hummed "You are my Sunshine" softly.

I sang through it three times before she spoke, "You must really like him."

"I do," I whispered.

She rolled over and pulled herself up to sit next to me, looking me in the eyes. She looked like little Emmie. Lately, it felt like each day she grew backwards.

"I'm sorry I'm being such a whiner about it, but this is our place. It's my safety. My sanity. To bring someone else here feels like they'd be contaminating the only space I have to feel safe in."

I nodded. "I understand. I don't know why I suggested he come here. It was a bad idea. I just got excited about you guys meeting each other. It was the first thing I thought of. You could meet him anywhere. We could all go out for coffee or dinner or—"

"What's his name?" she interrupted.

"Thomas."

"Your eyes lit up when you said his name." The emptiness was back in hers.

"He's a great guy. He wants to be a youth pastor and works so hard at it. You'd think he'd be this huge dork or something because of the whole preacher deal, but he's not. He's amazing. Just this really well-rounded guy. I don't know what he sees in me." I laughed.

"I do. He sees the you that I see. Beautiful."

The words made me blush even coming from her. "So, when do I get to meet him?"

"When do you want to?"

5

"I met your sister," he announced as soon as we shut the doors in his Honda on our lunch break on Tuesday.

"What? When? Where?"

"Yesterday."

Yesterday was Monday and I never worked on Mondays because I had classes all day. I usually didn't get home until after seven and last night was no different. Emily was home when I got there, watching her trashy reality TV shows. She didn't mention meeting Thomas. Nothing. Not even a word about leaving the house. She hadn't left the house by herself in over six months. How could she not have at least mentioned that?

"How'd it go?" I asked.

He rubbed his nose like he did every time he got nervous and cleared his throat. "I've got to admit, it was pretty weird to see someone who looks exactly like you. I knew you were twins, but I guess I never expected not to be able to tell you guys apart. In the beginning, I had to keep telling myself that she wasn't you. But once I got over the weirdness, it was easy to see she wasn't you. You guys are very different."

My heart was thudding. My ears rang.

"She met me at my car. Asked me if I was Thomas—"

"Wait, how'd she know who you were?"

"I don't know. A twin thing, maybe? She just walked right up to me in the parking lot. I guess she could've seen my name tag or something. She didn't seem depressed ..."

He wouldn't look at me.

"What do you mean? What'd she say? How'd she act?"

A million questions and scenarios whirled through my mind so fast that one started before the other ended. He was visibly shaken and I'd never seen him unnerved. Not even when they'd plastered *Playboy* on his cubicle walls.

"She was pretty pissed off even though she tried to hide it at first. She said she knew who I was because you'd told her about me and that she knew all about our relationship. She kept trying to make me promise not to tell you that she'd come to see me. I kept telling her I couldn't do that, which just made her even angrier. And then she was just like—'stay away from her.'"

"She did? She said that?" I couldn't believe it. What was wrong with her? Why would she do that?

"Yeah. Look, I'm sorry—"

I cut him off. "What were her exact words?"

"I don't think it really matters. She just made it clear she didn't want us to be together."

"Tell me her exact words."

"Are you sure?"

"Tell. Me. Her. Exact. Words."

He let out a deep sigh. "Her exact words were to stay the fuck away from you. I felt like I was dealing with a jealous ex-boyfriend or something. I told her I couldn't do that either because I loved you. I stayed pretty calm, but honestly, I think being calm just pissed her off even more. She said some pretty mean things about you, so I told her I was done talking to her and didn't want to hear anything else she had to say. Then she left."

She must've walked because the buses didn't come down this far, and even if they did, I couldn't imagine her riding the bus alone. She hated taking the bus alone. Always had. Even when she was acting normal.

"What'd she say about me?"

"It's really not important."

"Yes, it is. Tell me. You have to tell me."

The tips of my ears were on fire. My entire face felt hot.

He looked away from me. "I think she's just scared and doesn't know what to do. I'm the first real threat to your relationship, so it makes sense that she's totally freaking out about it."

"Tell me what she said." The anger in my voice surprised me, but I couldn't help it. I was baffled by her behavior and had to know the whole story. It was infuriating that he wouldn't give me all the details.

"I told you it doesn't matter. Everything was said in fear. Fear is a very strong and powerful emotion."

"All right, Dr. Phil."

"Okay," he said, "if you really want to know, I'll tell you. But just for the record, I don't think it helps anything or serves a purpose." He coughed. Coughed again. He was staring at some imaginary spot on the dashboard, rubbing it anxiously. "She said you were crazy and that I just didn't know it yet. She told me you were really great at pretending to be fine and I had to be a fool if I believed you were normal. She went on and on about how damaged you are. Oh, and she kept saying she felt like it was her duty to warn me about you because she knew you'd hurt me. That's pretty much all of it."

I felt like someone had taken a baseball bat and slammed the end of it into the middle of my gut. For a moment, I felt like I might throw up and rolled the window down in case I did. The breeze didn't reach my face. I couldn't believe Emily had said those things about me.

The silence between us was deafening. The timer on his watch went off, signaling the end of our break. He looked at me.

"I'm not going back to work," I said. "Tell Josh I threw up in the parking lot or that I got hit by a car. I don't care what you tell him. Just tell him I'm gone for the day."

He nodded. "I understand." He reached for my hand, but I pulled it away. I felt like being touched about as much as I felt like going back to work. "I need you to know I don't believe any of the things she said about you. None of it. I don't think any differently about you now than I did in the seconds before she came to the car. I know your past and I respect your past. But I don't believe for a second that it ruined you. Just look at you. You're amazing."

I faked a smile purely for his benefit, not because his words touched me. I was reeling from Emily's betrayal. I'd never been so furious.

Thomas leaned over and gave me a hug. I halfheartedly patted him on the back, keeping one of my arms at my side. "Promise to call later?"

"Sure."

We got out of his car and I watched him walk in the other direction towards the building. He looked back and waved right before reaching the entrance. I was sure he would pray to his God on the elevator ride and for a split second, I envied his faith. I wished I believed in a God or at least believed in the divine purpose of things like he did. Maybe then I could make sense of what was happening. But I didn't believe in his God or any other person's God and nothing about Emily's words or actions made sense.

The most upsetting part wasn't that she'd tried to keep Thomas away from me. I'd expected her to feel threatened by our relationship. It was her words—the terrible things she'd said about me. I'd never uttered an unkind word about her. I didn't even allow myself to think an unkind word about her.

My hands shook on the wheel and were covered in a clammy sweat. My heart was pounding so hard it made my chest hurt and it was difficult to breathe. I forced my legs to quit trembling and turned the car on. Somehow I drove to our apartment without running a stop light or causing an accident. I was shocked to find her in the kitchen, busy making a pot of coffee and humming as if everything was fine. Something inside me snapped.

"How could you?" I screamed, lunging at her. I grabbed her by the shoulders and shook her. "How could you?"

It was all I could say over and over again as I shook her. And I couldn't stop. She just let me fling her back and forth. When I finally stopped, I looked into my own face, searching for answers. I felt as if I was looking into the reflection of a stranger.

"Calm down," she said and moved to put her arm around me as if she might be about to give me a hug. I slapped her arm away. "Come here."

I walked away from her and into the living room. I traced a pattern back and forth across the floor, wringing my hands together. I was on the verge of hyperventilating. She followed me into the living room, taking a seat on the couch, and waited for me to calm down. She'd never seen me this angry.

"I just didn't want you to get hurt. You're going to get hurt by him. I know you will. I don't think it's a good idea for you to be involved with anybody," she said, not waiting for me to speak.

I wanted to choke her. I hadn't even said anything about Thomas and she knew exactly what I was talking about. She'd done it. She'd gone there and said those horrible things. There'd been a small part of me hoping it was all a misunderstanding.

"I'm sorry. I just don't like the idea. He'll come between us. I know he will. He already has. I mean, you've already been lying to me. You've never lied to me before. Ever."

"Don't you get it?" I screamed at her. "It's not about that. I understand you're afraid of a man taking me away from you. But how could you say those horrible things about me? Calling me crazy? And damaged? I'm crazy? I'm fucking *crazy*? All this time, I've protected you. I've never even thought of calling you crazy. Never. I don't breathe one word about you that's bad. Not one. Ever." I shook my head ferociously. "I can't believe you did that to me. Said those things. How could you do that? How *could* you?"

She was sobbing now, curling herself into a ball on the couch which only infuriated me more.

"Stop crying! Stop! All you do is cry. This is about me—damn it. It's not about you. It never gets to be about me. Just once, I want it to be about me. Two years. Two years it has been nothing but you. All I've done is walk around your fragile fucking emotions. Then you slap me in the face. No, not even slap. You spit in my face. That's worse."

"Stop, Bethy, please, just stop." She was pulling on my arm, trying to get me to sit on the couch next to her.

But I couldn't stop. Something inside of me had been unleashed and it was beyond my control. "No, I won't. I've had the exact same life. We've been the same damn person. For the first time ever, I was doing something for myself. Just me. I had to have somebody because you disappeared on me. You fucking disappeared. What did you think I would do? Live in this crazy isolation forever? I've waited and hoped that you'd get better, that you'd come back to me. But you've ruined everything. You're more fucked up than I thought you were!"

"Stop!" she screamed like a wild animal. "Just stop! I'm sorry. I'm so sorry! For everything!"

She jumped up, ran down the hallway, and slammed the bedroom door like she did every time she got upset. The same routine. This time, I didn't follow her and assume my position at the end of the bed to comfort her. I stayed where I was—I'd never done that before.

I heard the sounds of her sobbing through the wall separating us. It was a loud constant wailing that would go on for a long time. I stood out of instinct, beginning to take my customary steps down the hallway to the bedroom. I stopped in my tracks and turned around mechanically, heading back to the couch. I made myself sit back down again.

I curled up at the end of the couch, hugging my legs against my chest as I listened to her. It took every bit of willpower and strength I had to keep my body from moving towards her. In spite of myself, I desperately wanted to comfort her. I wanted to ease her pain at the expense of my own, but I didn't allow myself to do it this time. I was the one who needed to be comforted. I was exhausted and just wanted to rest. I fell asleep to the sounds of her wails.

When I opened my eyes, it was dark and eerily quiet, all sounds and signals of the previous hours gone. It was still as if nothing had happened. Out of habit, I listened for sounds of her but heard none. I was calmer, and some of the pain had subsided. Things had changed in our world, but I was ready to meet the changes and make something good come out of our horrible fight. I had no idea I'd been that upset. All of my emotions from the last two years had come out during my tirade and even though I'd hurt her and felt bad about it, I felt better to have finally said all the things I'd been holding inside. She would understand once I explained it to her. I eased up slowly from my spot on the couch and tiptoed down the hallway in case she was asleep. I didn't want to wake her. Right then all I wanted was to cuddle up next to her and fall back to sleep. We could talk through our fight tomorrow.

I saw light in the crack underneath the bathroom door. She shouldn't have been in the bathroom in the middle of the night. There was only one reason she'd be in the bathroom this late and it wasn't to use it the right way. For a second, I wanted to get angry again, but quickly pushed the feelings back down. I had to be there for her now.

I walked slowly down the hallway, preparing myself for the emotional mess I'd find Emily in. I reached the bathroom, took a deep breath to brace myself like I'd done so many times in the past, and opened the door. The scene flashed in front of me and burned into my brain like a Polaroid. I stood frozen in the doorway, unable to move.

Emily's body lay crumpled up next to the toilet. Her carving kit lay splayed out on top of the toilet seat. Her legs were contorted like a deer that'd been hit by a car and left on the side of the road. Her arms encircled her head, her fingers digging into her hair. Brown puke was splattered everywhere. Tiny pink pills sprinkled her insides and lay spilled on the tiled floor. Her pale skin was blackened, covered in blues and purples as if she'd been beaten.

She wasn't wearing pants. Just her yellow panties. And there was blood—the blood I'd expected to be there, but there'd never been so much. Her body lay in a pool of red.

I willed myself to move forward, the blood making my bare feet wet. I knelt down beside her, the vomit squishing against my knees. Her chest wasn't moving. The air left my lungs. I grabbed her arm and pulled it away from her face, then let go. It slumped to the floor. Her arm was so cold. She'd never been cold before. Not like this.

I forced myself to look at her face. Her unblinking eyes were wide open, staring back at me. The green was gone and replaced with black marbles covered in a milky film, staring through me. Her mouth was slightly open, brown vomit caked in the corners.

I felt her wrist, trying to grasp everything I was seeing but couldn't comprehend. I felt for her pulse, but knew what I'd find before I touched her. Her lifeless skin revealed what my mind had already absorbed. She was dead and I had killed her. I threw myself on top of her body.

"No!" My scream rang out into the night.

6

Beeping. Machines whirring. Footsteps. Faraway voices. Whispers. Coughs.

I wanted to open my eyes but couldn't. It was as if they'd been taped shut. Held down with something. My body felt heavy. Weighted as if I might be paralyzed. It felt like something heavier than me was lying on top of me, making it hard to breathe. I wiggled my toes. They moved and I was pleased they did. I tried to move my legs and couldn't. They were being held down too. I tried to move my arms and then my body, but something was preventing the movements. I wanted to scream, but no words came out.

What's going on? Where am I?

I was terrified. I had to break free. I struggled against whatever was holding me so tightly. Panic overtook me. I thrashed my body violently back and forth. My head was free. I shook it back and forth, side to side. It hurt.

Oh my God. It hurts.

And then it all ended.

Awake again. The only thing that separated wake from sleep was the sound of the machines and footsteps coming from outside myself. I struggled to open my eyes whenever I woke, but my efforts were useless each time.

I want to see. I want to know.
I tried to concentrate. Focus. Failed. I had to sleep.
Emily.
My first thought when I returned to the world.
Emily.
I wanted to call for her. I wanted to scream for her in this world of darkness. I tried to scream, but her name locked in my throat. There was something in my throat blocking her name from coming out.
I can't stay here. I won't. Emily.
Sleep was easy.
Images blurred in front of my eyes. Everything melted together, moving in one image. I squinted.
Concentrate. Focus.
There was a doorway. A frame. Hazy white in a halo of yellow. I looked down at my body and saw a white blanket and the metal rails of a hospital bed. There was a sink across the room in front of me. A closet next to it. The beeps were coming from machines with wires leading into my body. I couldn't see where they were planted, but they were neat and organized as they wound their way into me, performing unknown functions.
I'm in a hospital and Emily is dead.
All my mind would let me see when I opened my eyes was her small lifeless body on our bathroom floor. I didn't want to see it anymore. I wanted to return to the world of sleep and didn't care if I woke again.
But I did. Too quickly. This time when I opened my eyes and performed a search of my surroundings there was a hand covering mine. The fingernails chewed down to nubs. I followed it up to Thomas's brown curly hair lying on his arm, resting on the side of the bed. I moved my head and he snapped his head up.
"Elizabeth? Oh my God! Elizabeth!" He bent down and started kissing me all over my forehead and my cheeks. "I'm calling the nurse." He pushed a button on my bed.

I tried to speak but couldn't. My tongue felt like sandpaper. I tried again. My voice cracked as I spoke. "What's going on?" It came out in a croaky whisper.

Thomas's eyes darted back and forth across the room, lingering on the doorway. He rubbed his nose. Then rubbed it again. "I um ... I um ... it's ... that, well ... I think we should wait for your doctor."

"Just tell me. Why am I in the hospital?" My throat was on fire.

"You ... you ... I—"

Before he could get the words unstuck, a nurse entered the room.

"She's awake." He jumped up from his chair next to the bed.

The nurse had a plump round face that rolled easily into a smile. She began checking all of the machines next to me methodically.

"She's asking me questions," Thomas spoke softly, directing his statement to the nurse as if I wasn't there.

"I'll page the doctor immediately. He can answer all of her questions," she said, nodding at him.

I couldn't stand the way they were talking about me as if I wasn't in the same room, lying on the bed in front of them. I wanted to scream that I didn't want the doctor. All I wanted was Emily and she was gone. A cry slipped past my lips. It came out sounding like a moan. The nurse put her hand on my forehead.

"How are you feeling?"

I turned away from her. Cries were coming from my lips, but the tears to accompany them were frozen. Thomas rushed back to my side, his face lined with concern and heavy dark circles underneath his eyes. He looked worse than he did during finals week.

"Emily," I croaked.

He nodded, swallowing hard. He stroked my hair.

"Emily," I said again.

"I know. I know," he whispered. "I understand."

His tears splashed on my arm. I shook my head and closed my eyes. No, he didn't understand. He had no idea.

"Elizabeth. Elizabeth." A deep unfamiliar voice startled me awake again.

This time when I opened my eyes, both Thomas and the nurse were gone. I was in the same room. Same bed. Next to my bed stood a short, overweight man with thick, curly black hair and matching facial hair. It looked like it'd been several days since he last shaved. He wore a gray collared shirt with a matching tie.

"I'm Dr. Larson," he said, stretching out his hand to shake mine, which I could barely lift to meet his. His hands engulfed mine. I'd never met a doctor who wore a suit.

"This has all got to be very confusing for you, so we're going to take it really slow. Do you know where you are?"

Of course I knew I was in a hospital, but I didn't respond. Nothing mattered. I hoped he was going to tell me I was dying.

"You're at Kennedy Memorial Hospital. Here in Galston. It's Tuesday afternoon at three thirty. What is the last thing you remember?"

The last thing I remembered was killing her. She was so cold.

"Emily."

Maybe if I kept saying her name, calling out for her, I would open my eyes in our bedroom and she'd be lying next to me, shaking me awake from a bad dream.

"What's the last thing you remember about Emily?" he asked, peering down at me with inquisitive eyes.

"Her body. The bathroom. I found her. She was ... she was ..." My voice stopped. I couldn't bring myself to say the words. They didn't fit in my mouth.

He grabbed a small notebook along with a pen from his pocket and wrote something down.

"That day was a week ago. You've been in the hospital for seven days, and we've been treating you here. You were in intensive care for the first three days. The last four days you've spent in this room." He paused, giving his words a chance to sink in.

Intensive care? I was in intensive care?

"You made a very serious attempt to end your life."

End my life? He meant suicide. I didn't remember doing, it but of course I had. She was dead because of me and there was no way I could live without her. I knew it a week ago and I knew it now.

"Do you want to talk about it?"

I shook my head. I wanted him to leave my room. To go away so I could return to sleep. Nothing mattered now. I wanted to die with her. My sister was gone and I was still here.

"Okay. I understand you feel that way right now. I'm sure you've got lots of confusing emotions going on and we'll take the talking real slow. There's no rush."

He was still looking at me intently, searching for some kind of answer in my face. I wanted him to stop.

"We're going to have you transferred to the fifth floor tomorrow morning. You'll have your own room, but you'll be surrounded by other people with similar problems. We need to give you a safe place where you can process this situation."

A situation? That's what he was calling losing the only person in my life who ever meant anything to me—not to mention that I was responsible for it?

"We'll talk more tomorrow. I think you've had all you can handle for the day," he said. "I'll meet with you once you're checked into the fifth floor tomorrow, but the nurse will page me if you need anything from me before then."

He left the room quietly and I was glad, but my relief was short-lived because as soon as he left, Dalila and Thomas appeared in the doorway. She looked worse than she had when she'd found Emily in the bathtub with blood pouring down her legs, and I didn't think she could ever look worse than that. I hadn't forgotten the look of pain in her eyes when she discovered her, as if Emily had stabbed Dalila instead of herself. Dalila had cried for three days and barely spoken. She'd broken out in a rash then, and the same rash covered her now—red, scaly patches of a stress-induced psoriasis breakout. Her eyes were puffy and swollen. She was unsteady on her feet and Thomas guided her towards me. It was as if she'd aged ten years since I'd seen her last. Seeing her pain made losing Emily more real and I had to look away.

"Hey, sweetie," she said with a forced smile on her face, trying to be strong for me despite her own loss. Big tears were in her eyes. She leaned over and kissed my forehead. "We've been praying night and day for you. I think I've even been praying in my sleep." The tears rolled down her cheeks. "I couldn't stand the thought of losing both of you."

She sobbed, her shoulders trembling. I looked away. It was too hard to see her so raw, in so much agony. Thomas came around to the other side of my bed and grabbed my hand. I pulled it away. I didn't want to be touched. These two people loved me and a week ago I'd loved them too, but it felt like a lifetime ago. They could've been strangers to me if I didn't recognize their faces.

My twin was dead, which meant I was only half-alive, and the intensity of the loss screamed at me, shattering every wall I'd built over the years to keep myself strong. The space she occupied within me was immense and limitless, and the loss of her left an empty, aching void inside of me that could never be replaced with anyone else's love. Not Thomas's or Dalila's. No one's.

Her death surrounded me, punishing me for not being there or doing enough to keep her alive. The weight of it was unbearable and never going to go away. Never going to get better. It didn't matter how much they loved me or how much they prayed. Without Emily, the cord that connected me to the world was severed. I couldn't live without her.

"What do you remember?" Dalila asked after she regained her composure.

I told her the same thing I'd told the doctor. "Emily."

She sighed, "What do you remember about that night, honey?"

"I remember that I'm the one who killed her," I said.

"But, Elizabeth, you know that's not—"

Thomas cut in, "Remember what Dr. Larson said?"

The two of them stared at each other for a long time, engaged in a silent war of words.

"You were not responsible for Emily's death, Elizabeth," Dalila said.

She leaned forward to kiss my forehead again, but I turned away because I couldn't bear it. I didn't deserve her expressions of love when I'd failed Emily and let her die. I'd failed her too by not being able to save Emily even though she'd never admit it. For a moment, she looked stricken, but her shock faded to the same dejected look I'd come to know so well. For a moment, I wanted to say something to comfort her, do something to reach out to her, but I couldn't bring myself to do it. I was engulfed in my own suffering.

"You know that, honey, don't you?"

I didn't want to answer. Of course it was my fault. She was only saying it to try to make me feel better.

"I've got to work tonight, so Dalila's going to stay with you," Thomas said.

"I don't want anyone to stay with me."

"Are you sure?" Dalila asked. She swallowed hard, desperately trying to keep it together for me.

I nodded. "I'm tired."

"It's just, the thought of you being up here all alone. It just—" She stopped herself. "But certainly. You have to rest. I'll be here tomorrow after they move you."

Thomas piped up, "Me too. I'll come as soon as I finish class." He looked into my eyes, searching for some kind of clue as to how he was supposed to act. I looked away and he leaned down to give me an awkward sideways hug, careful not to tug on any of the wires attached to me. I patted his back stiffly. I stared at him as he left, surprised he could smile. I was never going to smile again.

"I'll wait for you outside," he said to Dalila.

"I love you, darling. And so does Bob. He couldn't get away from the factory today, but he's been up here as much as me and Thomas. By the way, he absolutely adores Thomas. He's been so helpful throughout all of this. I'm sorry we have to meet him under these circumstances, but I'm so glad we did. I can't believe you never mentioned him before. Maybe when you're feeling better, you can tell me the story of how you guys met. You know how much I adore love stories." She waited to see if I would respond.

I had to give her something. "Sure."

She smiled and the lines in her face eased for a second. "Great." She fluffed the pillows behind me. "Bob is going to be so happy to know you're awake. I could've told him if I could reach him while he's at work, but you know how he is about carrying a cell phone. Maybe someday I can get him to move into the twenty-first century. He's going to be so disappointed that he didn't get to be here today."

"It's fine," I assured her.

Bob was one less person trying to touch me and reach out to me in this place.

"I'm going to call Lisa when I leave and let her know you're awake. She's been visiting, too. She's been a huge help for us through all of this. I don't know how we would ever manage without her." Dalila brushed my hair back from my face. "It's going to be okay. It really is. You'll get through this. You will." Her big blue eyes were wet again. "You're so strong. You've always been so strong."

I was never going to be okay. There was no getting through this.

I closed my eyes and pretended to sleep, hoping she'd leave. She watched me for several minutes, and when she was convinced

I was sleeping, she tiptoed out the door. I opened my eyes into the stark white bleakness that comprises every hospital room, the stale air, tainted only with the smell of alcohol to mask the smell of sickness. I pushed the button for the nurse. She appeared quickly, a different nurse from the one who came before when Thomas pushed the button.

"Can you give me something to sleep?"

"Sure." She left and returned with two small pink pills and a glass of water. My throat screamed as I swallowed them. I closed my eyes and was momentarily comforted—sleep was coming.

7

The plump nurse from the previous day woke me at eight in the morning. She turned off the machines next to me and disconnected the wires attached to me. The beeps and whirring stopped. She pulled off the red light device on my pointer finger. She was careful as she took out my IV and managed to do it without hurting me. She threw the gauze in the garbage and brought a wheelchair from the hallway over to my bed.

She shrugged her shoulders at me when I looked at her skeptically, and said, "Standard hospital procedure. You've been in bed for a week."

I pushed the covers off and stood. My knees wobbled and I felt lightheaded. I took a seat in the wheelchair and felt a flash of gratitude. The nurse attempted small talk as we began winding our way through a series of hallways, but quickly abandoned her efforts because of my nonresponsiveness. It was like a maze as we twisted and turned until finally reaching an elevator. I watched the numbers light up until they arrived at five. With a ding, the door opened, and she pushed me through. As we walked down the hallway, she unlocked each door we came to and I held my breath each time as if something bad was behind it.

"This is it," she said, sliding her key into another door.

The sign next to it read: Adult Psychiatric Unit. I wasn't being moved to some other room in the hospital to finish healing but was being tossed into the nut ward. Every scene from movies I'd watched about psych wards flashed through my mind in snippets and my chest tightened. It was hard to breathe. We moved through another series of locked doors and with each click the sense of impending doom heightened. My panic escalated.

We arrived at a see-through door with a small sign that read: Secure door. Flight risk.

I was rolled through a short, wide hallway to an open area with hallways branching off each side. There was a square nurses' station bustling with activity in the center, where all of the hallways met. Most of the nurses were dressed in ordinary, everyday clothing rather than scrubs as they answered phones, scribbled ferociously on papers, and carried around big, thick black binders. It seemed out of place and character to me, but I'd never been in a nut ward before, so I had nothing to compare it to. My nurse walked up to a petite redheaded woman at the station. They exchanged words, nodded, and looked over in my direction. My nurse returned with the redhead.

"Hi, Elizabeth, I'm Polly. I work here on the unit." She stuck out her hand as if we were acquaintances meeting at a party or something. I declined the gesture. It seemed pointless. "I'm going to show you around and help you get settled."

"I'm going to go now. You're in good hands," my nurse said. It took a moment for me to realize she wasn't waiting for me to say something, but to get up from the wheelchair. I stood up and felt as dizzy as I had getting out of bed.

"This is the nurses' station." Polly pointed to the activity in the center of the room. "There is staff here twenty-four hours a day. If you need anything, you just ask."

She motioned to the hallway directly behind the station.

"Those are the rooms where group sessions are held and where you'll meet with your doctor. Everybody sees their doctor at least once a day. There's a big conference room at the end of the hallway where you'll meet with the team. The team is everyone who is responsible for patient care. Doctors, nurses, social workers, OT people, and such. You'll meet all of them in time. Don't worry about it now. The team is responsible for making the decisions about your care, but they rely heavily on the recommendations from your primary doctor. I think you should have met your primary doctor yesterday, did you? Dr. Larson?"

I nodded. So, he wasn't really a doctor but some kind of a shrink. No wonder he'd looked at me so intensely.

She pointed to the hallway on the left side of the station.

"Down there are the men's rooms. Men and women are at separate sides of the unit. They mingle during the day, but at night we keep you guys separate."

She laughed. I didn't. The idea of crazy people having sex wasn't amusing.

"Everyone is expected to be in their rooms at nine thirty. Lights out is at ten. Come on."

I followed her around the desk and into a huge room that opened up in front of the nurses' station.

"This is the family room," she announced as if it was something to be proud of.

I stood in the doorway.

"Come on inside."

I scanned the room. Magazines thrown around everywhere. Cards spread out on a round table as if someone had left during the middle of a game. There were mismatched padded chairs on wheels strewn about. A big TV stood against the far wall. It was housed in an old-fashioned wooden entertainment center that nobody used anymore. Windows lined an entire wall. Two couches were haphazardly tossed together.

"When you aren't in scheduled activities during the day, this is where you'll spend your time. You won't be allowed in your room outside of sleeping and illness. At least for now. Patients can earn room time once we're assured of safety, but for right now you'll just be one-on-one. That means that you must always have a staff member present. The team will determine when this restriction can be lifted."

The sound of footsteps and laughter broke into her detailed instructions. I watched as bodies filed into the room. The voices hurt my ears, forming a joint throbbing verse in my head.

"It's time for morning check-in. Just have a seat and I'll explain more when it's through," she instructed.

I sat in the nearest chair. The aluminum was cold and made me shiver.

Another woman walked into the room. She was dressed in a sweater and jeans. Her body was completely disproportionate. Her upper body was small and slender, but from her waist she ballooned into a wide bottom and huge hips. As if on cue, the other bodies in the room stepped into action, moving chairs and taking seats as they created a lopsided circle. They made me a part of the circle. I stared at the floor. Dingy gray institutional flooring, like in an elementary school cafeteria. Voices carried on around me, but I didn't let them register. I drowned them out with a humming in my ears and by focusing intently on counting the specs of brown within each tile. I was on my third tile when someone tapped on my knee. I looked up. A woman was peering at me from across the circle. I could feel other eyes on me as well, but I stayed focused on hers.

"Can you tell us your name so we can welcome you?" she asked cheerfully.

She didn't fit on the chair. Her fat folded over the chair like rolls of dough spilling out of the pan. What were they welcoming me to and who cared what my name was? I said nothing. Just returned her stare.

She waited for a few moments and then spoke for me. "Everyone, this is Elizabeth."

The focus shifted from me to the person sitting in the chair next to me. I didn't pay any attention to what was happening around me. I wanted to die. I recalled reading somewhere that the body shut down after three days without water. Would my body quit working if I refused to eat or drink? It would be a relief to waste away in my chair, but there was no way it was going to happen. There were too many nurses around to allow it. I was sure they'd stick an IV in my arm and pump me with fluids to keep me alive. I glanced at the windows lining the wall on the other side of the room and considered jumping, but I was sure they were locked since we were on the fifth floor and every crazy person here would jump out the window if given a chance.

It was foreign to be trying to figure out a way to die. I'd never wanted to kill myself before. Giving up had never been an option for me and I'd always tried to prevent Emily from doing it too. When she was a teenager and experienced her first bout of depression, I'd encouraged her by promising her that her hopeless feelings were due to her hormones and eventually, they'd level out and she'd start to feel normal again. But as her depression grew worse and she became more self-destructive, I worked hard at being her cheerleader.

"Come on, Em. You've got to fight this. I know you can do it. We didn't go through everything we went through just to quit." I must've said it to her hundreds of times over the years.

If my cheerleading didn't work, I switched my tactics to pointing out all of the good things about her and what she had to live for.

"Think how much Dalila and Bob love you. It would devastate them to lose you. Everybody loves you. They always have. You've got that special thing that people are naturally drawn to. You can use that. You could use it to do all kinds of other things. Maybe even help other people. You'd probably be good at it because you'd be able to understand exactly what they were going through."

And then, when there weren't any more words left, I held her until the despair passed. I'd always refused to give up and to let her quit. Until now, until I failed to keep her alive.

Emily and I were each other's life support. My purpose in life was to take care of her and keep her safe. It always had been. I went first with the special friends and if Emily was too afraid to play one of their games, I played them for her. When Mother came at us with the wire hanger, I stepped in front of Emily and took the brunt of the beatings whenever I could. The times when I couldn't were torturous. I kept Emily going when she didn't have the strength to keep going on her own, but she kept me going too because she gave me a purpose for living. She defined me, gave me the role I had to play.

Mother's neglect and abuse started it, but by the end, it was more than that. I took care of Emily like we'd pretended to when we were little, trapped in our room and inventing ways to mother each other. But even though she ended up being the sick one, the one who needed help, she gave my life meaning. In high school, she'd kept on cutting herself, and I'd help her clean the wounds. Whenever any of the mean girls in high school would tease her for not getting good grades or making out with a boy she barely knew, I stood up for her. I was a master at pointing out the mean girls' flaws and making them feel bad for things they'd done to shift the attention away from Emily. We were a formidable unit. I didn't know how to exist without her. She'd taken her life and with it, she'd taken away my reason for living.

She'd tried to kill herself so many times I'd lost count, but I'd never considered her suicide attempts as being real death threats. I saw them as a desperate cry for help because she strategically timed her attempts so I would find her before it was too late, or she'd do something crazy in front of me because she knew I'd stop her. I was sure she'd expected me to interrupt her again.

How long had I been asleep? What if I'd woken up five minutes earlier? Would she still be alive? Would it have ended like every other time? What if I'd gone to her instead of staying on the couch? My questions tortured me. All I wanted to do was die, and I wondered if anyone had successfully killed themselves in a nut ward. I almost laughed out loud at the absurdity of it. I had to find a way to get released. There was no way I could stay. Dr. Larson had said yesterday that I needed to be in a safe place until I worked through my situation. If working through my situation meant getting over losing Emily, it was going to be impossible for me to get out.

People around me began moving their chairs out of the circle and putting an end to the strange gathering that had taken place. The bodies scattered throughout the room. The other bodies belonged to actual people. The voices had faces and stories like mine. What brought them into this locked world?

A few sat in chairs by the window, staring intensely out of it as if something really exciting was happening outside that they didn't want to miss. There was a man over in the corner all by himself staring out the window as he sat in an old wooden rocking chair. His eyes were glazed over and he didn't even seem to be blinking. There were three women playing cards in the middle of the room. They all had their hair done and makeup on. One of them was dressed in a low-cut shirt with her cleavage spilling out. They were animated and laughed obnoxiously as they played a card game like they were in someone's living room on a Friday night. They looked like they were having fun.

There was an elderly woman in the opposite corner, rocking back and forth even though she wasn't in a rocking chair. She was pulling hair out of her head, strand by strand, and putting each strand in a neat pile on her pants. She didn't even flinch when she tugged it out.

There were a black man and a white man facing each other on one of the brown couches. At first glance, it looked like they were having a heated conversation with each other as they gestured and pointed wildly. It took me a moment to realize they weren't looking at each other when they talked—they were actually talking to themselves.

"Pretty scary, huh?"

A girl was sitting next to me. She looked ill. Not mentally, like

I'm sure I did, but physically, like she should be in the cancer ward instead of a psychiatric unit. Her cheekbones were protruding through thin, pale skin so translucent I could see the blue veins below. Her hair was thin and there was weird brown fuzz growing on her face. She was dressed in a baggy hooded sweatshirt and jeans, but the clothes lay flat, unfilled, as if her head was simply a clothes hanger.

"Yeah, kinda strange," I said.

"I'm Rose. I hate my name. Doesn't really go well. Roses are supposed to be beautiful. Elegant." She snorted. "And then look at me."

"I'm Elizabeth."

She looked me up and down. "You don't look like an Elizabeth."

I didn't respond, but I didn't think she expected me to.

"Is this your first time here?" she asked.

People came here more than once?

"Yeah."

"My fourth," she replied.

"Oh. Really. So, have you been here long?"

She rolled her eyes. "Four weeks and two days."

"They keep you here that long?"

"If you're me," she laughed. "Gotta gain more weight. Five more pounds. Can you believe it? I have to look like a big fat pig before I can get out of here."

I looked at her body again. She couldn't have weighed more than ninety pounds. She had the body of a little girl with the face of a very old woman.

"What are you in for?" she asked.

"I tried to kill myself."

It sounded weird coming out of my mouth, but I'd better get used to saying it. It was true.

"Oh." She smiled and waved her hand as if it was nothing. "Then they can only keep you for seventy-two hours. It's an automatic seventy-two-hour hold when you try to kill yourself."

I could last seventy-two hours.

"Who's the team?" I asked.

"A whole bunch of doctors and stuff. You, like, sit at the head of this great big table and they all ask you questions. And stare at you. I hate it. Everyone does. It's so uncomfortable. It's one thing you never get used to no matter how many times you've been here."

I trusted her because she had to know what she was talking about if she'd been here four times. Polly was sitting in one of the aluminum chairs behind us but appeared to be engrossed in a book.

"I really want to get out of here. How do I get them to let me out?" I whispered, just in case Polly had good hearing.

"It's easy for you," she explained. "All you have to do is tell them you aren't going to kill yourself. You just have to be like— hey, I felt really bad at the time and I did something stupid. I won't do it again."

I listened to her stories about all her other hospitalizations and the forced feedings she had to endure. I knew how hard it was to eat, but I didn't tell her that.

"You've got it easy. The suicidals usually make it in and out of here pretty quickly. It will probably be the longest three days of your life, but there's stuff you can do to pass the time."

"Like what?" I asked.

"Like reading all the trashy magazines you want." She tossed an *Us Weekly* onto my lap and giggled. "And believe me, there will be plenty of drama to keep you entertained. Some of the people here really are crazy. See that dude over there?" She motioned to the guy staring into nothingness by the window. I nodded. "He doesn't talk. Like at all. Ever. You could go up behind him and yell in his ear. He wouldn't even flinch."

Rose and I were interrupted by Dr. Larson, who motioned for me to follow him down the hallway and into one of the offices. It was small and cramped. Completely bare. Not even a picture on any of the muted blue walls. There was only a single table with a chair on each side. I sat on one while he took the one across from me. It reminded me of the interrogation rooms I'd seen on TV, and it wasn't anything like Lisa's therapy room. He wasted no time.

"How are you feeling today?"

I took a deep breath. I could do this.

"I feel much better than I did yesterday. Yesterday was tough, trying to figure out what was going on."

He nodded attentively. "Do you remember more about what happened the night before you came to the hospital?"

"I felt like everything was my fault, maybe I was too overwhelmed? You have to understand how close me and Emily are—were—I didn't want to live without her. So, I just did it. I didn't think about it. I wanted to die with her."

"I understand how you could feel that way," he said.

He still hadn't taken his eyes off me and I still hadn't looked at him. I kept my gaze focused on the desk in front of me. We sat in silence that seemed to go on for hours. I wanted him to ask me questions. Something. Anything to give me a clue as to what to say. I didn't want to start talking without some sort of idea about what I was supposed to say, because what if I said something wrong and he kept me longer? Finally, he broke the silence.

"What's the last thing you remember about Emily?"

"Her body. Like I told you yesterday. I found her in the bathroom. I can't get the picture of it out of my head. I keep seeing it."

"What happened before that? Do you remember?"

"Yes, we had a fight about my boyfriend."

"Tell me about your boyfriend."

I told Dr. Larson about Thomas and our relationship, how sweet he was to me, and his persistence in the beginning when he first started asking me out. I told him about how we'd started dating and how I'd kept him a secret from Emily. I shared how much I treasured our lunch breaks in his car, and how sometimes I would try to make them even more special—baking him cookies, packing a thermos of homemade soup, surprising him by decorating the inside of his car with flowers so we could pretend to have a picnic. I didn't tell him what Emily had said to Thomas or the fight we'd had afterward. He didn't need to know how badly she'd hurt me with the mean things she said. It wasn't important and I didn't want him to think badly of her.

"It sounds like you really care about him," he said.

"Yeah, I do. He's a great guy. I think he's going to be very supportive in helping me to get through this."

I congratulated myself for sounding like I was ready for some kind of recovery. I even used the words he used yesterday.

"It's good to have people in your life that can provide you with a support network. It's going to be really important for you in your treatment to have people that are there for you."

He pulled out the small notebook he'd used yesterday from the front pocket of his suit. "What's going on in your life right now?"

I didn't know how to answer that one. What was the response Rose had said would get me out of here? I chose my words carefully.

"I think I've gone through a really big loss. The biggest one in my life. I think it was too much for me to handle. Especially because my life has been so hard. For that minute, I just didn't want to live anymore. I was so sad and wasn't thinking about any of the good things I have in my life. Only the bad." I added as an afterthought, "I don't really want to die."

I hoped I sounded believable.

He was still looking at me as if he expected me to say more, but I'd run out of words.

"I'll be your psychologist while you're here. I realize it's really hard to talk to a complete stranger. My hope is that you'll take a small risk and begin to trust me enough to share your pain with me."

I wasn't going to trust him. Not in seventy-two hours or any other amount of hours for that matter, but I nodded my head in agreement.

"I'm going to meet with the team early this afternoon. We'll discuss how to proceed with your treatment. It's important for you to know that you'll be able to voice your thoughts about your treatment with the team. You'll be included in all decisions. And I want you to know we're all here to help you."

"Thank you."

It seemed like the polite thing to say.

"Do you have any questions for me?"

I shook my head.

Just like that and it was over.

8

Nothing could've prepared me for how intimidated I felt when I met with the team, even though Rose had warned me about it. The room was filled with a long conference table, and black high-backed office chairs, all occupied, circled it and made me feel like I was at an important executive business meeting. Nine people whom I'd never spoken to before or even met, except for Dr. Larson, filled the chairs and were responsible for knowing how to take care of me.

I was expected to sit at the head of the table. Dr. Larson was on my right. I was crawling out of my skin as I took my seat. There was a possibility I could fool Dr. Larson into believing I was okay, but an entire room? I sat there waiting for whatever horrible meeting was about to take place.

"Elizabeth, we're having this meeting so you can have an opportunity to meet the team. We're going to go around the room and have everyone introduce themselves," Dr. Larson said.

One by one they went around the table, stating their names and job titles. There was one psychiatrist. Three therapists: two males and one female. A slender woman with her hair drawn back in a tight ponytail identified herself as my social worker. Another woman who looked like she was my age identified herself as my occupational therapist and a female doctor announced she was the one responsible for my medical care. An overweight bald man said he was the family therapist. And last, an elderly man announced he was the supervising counseling associate. I had no idea what any of their titles meant or what kind of care they provided. By the time we went around the table, I couldn't remember any of their names.

"Elizabeth, why don't you tell us a little bit about yourself?" one of the women on the left asked.

"I'm twenty years old. I'm a full-time college student at Galston Community College. I plan on transferring to a four-year university at the end of the school year. I work as a telemarketer. It's for a catalog company. Kinda boring, but my shifts work around my class schedule. I have a boyfriend, Thomas, who works with me and I like to watch movies and drink coffee."

My throat was dry. Had I said too much? Too little? They were all just staring at me.

"Elizabeth, I noticed you didn't say anything about your childhood," the woman with the ponytail said.

Why did they keep saying my name every time they talked to me? What was the reason for it? The room was silent. All eyes bored holes into me.

"I ... um ... didn't say anything about my childhood because I didn't think it was important."

"Why is that?" the bald man asked.

"I don't know. Of course childhoods are important."

They were unnerving me. They were all scribbling into notebooks exactly like Dr. Larson did. What were they writing? Did I get to see it?

"What are you guys writing?" The question popped out before I could stop it.

"Does it bother you?" Dr. Larson asked.

"Yes." I quickly changed my response. "Not too much. Just wondering."

They kept scribbling. Heads down and then back up.

"Can you tell us about Emily?"

I didn't know who was asking the questions anymore. They were coming from everywhere.

"Emily and I are identical twins. She was born three minutes before me. Our mother hated us and kept us locked up in our apartment. She didn't feed us. Sometimes we got pizza, though, but mostly just bread. Oh, and we drank a lot of formula. She liked to beat us with a hanger whenever she was mad or we got in trouble. It was really bad, but Emily and I had each other so we managed to survive. But then I started a fire." I immediately realized saying I started a fire was not a good idea and I needed to explain myself so I kept blabbering on. "Not on purpose—I didn't start the fire on purpose. It was an accident. People from the county took us away and brought us to the Rooths, Bob and Dalila, and they adopted us."

I paused. Nobody said anything. I assumed they wanted more so I kept going. "The Rooths were really good to us. We went to therapy with Lisa. A lot of it. She was super helpful. I even went to see her the other day. I had to go by myself because Emily refused. We managed to grow up all right even though we had such a bad beginning. We moved into an apartment together after we graduated high school. It was on Eighty-Sixth Street. A nice place. We did all right. Even though Emily struggled."

"Why do you think Emily struggled?"

I'd asked myself the same question many times in the last two years. I'd never been able to come up with a good answer, but I had to try now.

"Our lives were hard and I think she was severely depressed."

I looked around the table into all their faces, searching for some sort of a clue or sign as to how I was doing, but there was nothing. Only expressionless faces staring back at me, completely ambiguous.

"Elizabeth, we've asked you a lot of questions, do you have any questions for us?" a woman at the end of the table broke in.

"Do you guys know when I'll get to go home?"

"That will depend," Dr. Larson said.

Depend. On what? What did that mean? What kind of an answer was that? But I nodded my head as if he'd given me a logical response.

"You can go back and—"

"Wait one second," the woman at the other end of the table interrupted. "I noticed you didn't ask about Emily's funeral. Is there a reason for that?"

"I guess I assumed I'd be able to go."

My words hung in the air. Finally, Dr. Larson motioned to the door. I jumped up and nearly sprinted out. Polly was waiting for me and led me back to the family room, taking a seat next to me. I was sweating and my hands shook. I hoped I wasn't going to have to do the team meeting every day. The idea of a repeat performance made my stomach churn. I kept telling myself to breathe.

It was odd that the woman at the end of the meeting had brought up Emily's funeral. I had to be able to go, didn't I? Bob and Dalila couldn't bury Emily without me being there. There was no way. It would be too cruel. Where'd people keep dead bodies? They could wait as long as they needed to for a funeral, couldn't they? I was on the verge of panicking and couldn't panic because if I did, I might start screaming and never stop. I calmed down as I remembered Dalila was going to visit today because I was sure she'd have all the details about Emily's funeral.

"When can our family come see us?" I asked Polly.

"After dinner. Six to seven are visiting hours each night," she said. "Are you all right? You look a little pale."

"I'm fine. Just tired."

"Do you want to talk about anything? Sometimes the patients find us easier to talk to than the doctors. I think we're less intimidating. A little more of a normal conversation if you know what I mean."

I looked around the room for Rose. She was sitting across the room on one of the couches, reading *Star* magazine.

"Can I go talk to her?" I pointed. Asking permission seemed strange but somehow appropriate.

"Sure. You don't have to ask me permission. You can pretend I'm not here if you want."

I got up and went over to the couch and sat down.

"The team meeting is just as bad as you said it was going to be," I said.

She laughed. "Told you it was. It always makes me want to freak out just because they're all staring at me or say something crazy to get a reaction out of them."

"Totally." I smiled and instantly felt guilty for smiling.

"Look at her," Rose said, showing me her magazine and pointing to Jennifer Aniston. "She's so beautiful and skinny. How does she stay so skinny?"

I looked at her and not at the picture. "You know you're really skinny, right?"

"Thanks, but you don't have to say that. I know I've gotten fat here." She looked like she was going to cry. "But you should see how I looked before they brought me to the hospital. I was really skinny then."

She motioned for me to come closer. I scooted near her, and she whispered in my ear, "I can show you what I used to look like when I was skinny. I have a picture. You can't tell anyone I have it, though. I'm not supposed to."

I pulled away and looked at her, nodding my head, communicating with my eyes that her secret was safe with me.

"Here, you can read this. I've got another one."

She handed me *Star* and picked up an issue of *People*. I aimlessly thumbed through the magazine. I couldn't help thinking they shouldn't let her read them. Looking at stick-thin models probably didn't help her feel better about herself. I was quickly bored with the magazine. I had no interest in Hollywood. I loved movies, but didn't care about what the actors did in their real lives.

I'd never been able to understand people's obsessions with celebrities. Emily and I used to make fun of the amount of time people spent focusing on everything they did like they weird gods to be worshiped instead of human beings like the rest of us.

"So, we just sit here all day?"

She looked up at the clock. "Yes and no. We go to group in ten minutes. Then dinner."

I watched the clock until it reached 3:30. At 3:30, one of the men, who looked like one of the men on my team, appeared in the doorway. Without any instruction, everyone got up and followed him. We walked after him like a herd of cattle, down the back hallway and into the room across from the one I'd been in earlier with Dr. Larson, except it was bigger. It was painted in the same muted blue and there were plastic folding chairs in a prearranged circle. I grabbed a seat next to Rose.

"Okay." He clasped his hands in front of his chest. "Who wants to start first?"

I squinted at his name tag. Mark Underwood. The title underneath read "Clinical Psychologist." He looked too young to be a psychologist, with his clean-shaven face and sparkling blue eyes. It was hard to imagine he'd experienced a serious problem and I couldn't help but wonder how he was going to help a room full of psychiatric patients. I had a hard time with people who'd had easy lives trying to pretend they could help people who hadn't. It was one of the things I liked about Lisa. She'd spent the first five years of her childhood living on the streets with her drug-addicted parents, so she knew what it was like to have to overcome hard stuff.

"I will," the elderly woman who'd been pulling out her hair volunteered.

"Okay, Arlene. Go ahead," he instructed.

"My name is Arlene. I'm bipolar. Mostly depressed, though. I've been here for fourteen days and today I'm feeling sad."

"Great, Arlene. Next." He motioned to the man sitting next to her. The white man from the couch.

"Rick. Schizophrenic. Twenty-one days. Fine."

Next in line was the young man who was staring into space at the window. He was skipped over without any prompting. He didn't appear to notice.

"I'm Shelly, but y'all know that already, don't ya?" Shelly giggled.

She was one of the women who had been playing cards earlier.

"Let's see, I've been here almost a week this time. I've got major depression, an anxiety disorder, and I'm a recovering alcoholic. Seventeen days sober. Yay!"

The woman who sat next to her was one of the other card players and she patted her on the back.

"I've got PTSD. I'm a cutter. And yeah, borderline." She rocked her head back and forth while she announced this and the woman next to her laughed loudly as if what she said was hysterical. "And today, I feel really happy and hopeful."

The woman next to her took her turn and her list was just as long as Shelly's. Her name was Tobi and she sang out "borderline" at the end of her list, too, which caused the two of them to collapse in laughter again. I didn't get the joke. I was glad I wasn't them because their lists were too long.

The last card player was Denise and she was not nearly as loud or dramatic as the other two. Her list was much shorter. She said she was depressed and she'd only been there for four days.

Good. Four days. That was encouraging.

The black man from the couch went next.

"Sunday. Sometimes I buy a purple sweater on Sunday, but what about Diana Ross? I have to tell you about Italy. That's okay. Never really minded. My mama did. Smells funny, though. Always—"

Mark broke in, "Thank you, Darin. Let's hear from Sally."

Darin snapped his mouth shut. I watched him as Sally, the woman next to him, began her announcement in this bizarre ritual. As soon as she began talking, he opened his mouth. I watched his eyes nervously skirt around the room. He wasn't making a sound, but his lips were moving animatedly.

Rose went next.

"I'm Rose. I'm anorexic." She said the word *anorexic* as if she was cussing. "I've been here four weeks and two days. I feel really sad today because I'm fat."

It was my turn now. Every part of me wanted to be skipped like the other guy.

"My name's Elizabeth. I've been here for one day. Today I feel ... I feel ... overwhelmed?"

"And why are you here?" Mark asked.

"I'm here because I tried to commit suicide."

Mark nodded at me and moved on. I'd just announced that I tried to commit suicide and everyone responded as if I'd announced I used Crest to brush my teeth. The woman who followed me introduced herself as Doris. She didn't talk about why she was here and didn't say how she was feeling. She spoke with an accent I couldn't place.

Mark started talking once everyone in the circle had made their proclamation. "I did notice one thing while we were going around the room. Some of you said 'I'm bipolar' or 'I'm borderline.' I would like you all to try and remember that you are not your mental illness. Your mental illness is only a part of you. I want to encourage you all to say your name and then say 'with a disorder.' For example, if I had depression I could say, 'I'm Mark and I have depression.' Or if I had anxiety I could say, 'I'm Mark and I have anxiety.' It's important to keep who you are separate from your diagnosis. Now, are there any issues on the unit that anyone feels need to be addressed in group?"

It was quiet for a minute as everyone looked around the room.

Rick blurted out, "I heard them talking about me. Saying nasty things about me."

Mark leaned forward. "Who did, Rick?"

He pointed to the three women who were playing cards earlier.

"Did you ladies talk about Rick in a negative way today?" Mark asked.

They all shook their heads in unison.

Shelly spoke up and her eyes looked angry, "Absolutely not. We didn't say anything about him. He's so fuckin' paranoid."

Tobi and Denise nodded their heads in agreement.

"I heard it. They said I should kill myself. Hang myself in my room. I'm a worthless piece of shit. Die." Rick's voice rose more with each word.

"Rick," Mark began in a calm voice, "I don't think they were saying those things. What you heard was horrible and mean. I don't think anyone here thinks those horrible things about you. Is it possible what you heard was part of your mental illness?"

"Maybe it was Archeus," Rick said.

I looked around the room. Weren't we all here? Were we missing somebody?

Mark nodded.

"I think you're right, Rick. It probably wasn't the ladies. Doesn't Archeus usually say bad things about you and tell you to hurt yourself?"

Rick bobbed his head up and down. He sat back in his seat.

"Shut up. Done."

"All right, then. I'd like to go around the room again, and this time, I'd like everyone to talk a little bit about their treatment goals and the progress they're making towards them," Mark directed. "This time we'll start with Doris. Doris?"

Doris looked around the room, eying the door, and returning to Mark's face.

"I kill me mudda," she mumbled under her breath.

I couldn't make out her words, but it sounded like she said she killed her mother. I didn't think it was what Mark had in mind when he said we were supposed to talk about our treatment goals.

"Can you speak up so we can all hear you?"

"I kill me mudder!" she yelled. This time, there was no mistaking her words.

Mark remained calm and spoke in an even tone. "Doris, do you know it's not okay to kill your mother?"

Doris was wearing a pink floral-print muumuu and you could almost feel the sting as she pounded her fist against her leg. It made a sharp slapping sound against her skin.

I looked around the room. Everyone was calm. Some of them weren't even paying attention. Shelly was busy whispering to Tobi while Rick and Darin had gone back to talking to people only they could see. They were uninterested in this woman freaking out because she wanted to kill her mother, or maybe she already had. Now she was rocking back and forth in her chair, still punching her leg and chanting "kill my mother" in her weird, thick accent.

"Doris, I need to ask you to calm down. I need to ask you to take some deep breaths. Practice the breathing exercises we worked on in session."

His words had no effect on her. It was as if she hadn't heard them. Suddenly, she jumped up, picked up her chair, and launched it in Mark's direction. It landed at his feet. She lunged towards him. He reacted quickly, jumping up and pushing a round metal button on the wall. She reached him and flailed her arms at him wildly, trying to grab his face. He tried to grab her arms and restrain her, but she was too quick.

Now everyone was paying attention. Everyone moved their chairs back. Shelly was sobbing, holding her face in her hands. Tobi and Denise wrapped their arms around her as they watched wide-eyed. Rick and Darin stood up and paced the room, mumbling and swearing softly.

"Christ, here we go again," Rose whispered beside me.

Suddenly, the door burst open. Three huge men rushed in and tackled Doris. She was kicking and screaming. They looked like they spent hours at the gym, but they struggled to contain her, even though she couldn't have weighed much more than a hundred pounds. She kicked, bit, clawed, and scratched at them. They pinned her down to the ground. She spat in their faces, screaming that she would kill them.

Mark was still telling her to breathe, but she was beyond breathing. A nurse ran into the room, rolled up Doris's sleeve, and quickly stabbed her in the forearm with a needle. I expected this to calm her down. It always did in the movies and I felt as if that's what I'd stepped into. A modern-day *One Flew Over the Cuckoo's Nest*. But whatever drug they gave her didn't have any effect on her. She struggled even harder. They stabbed her again with another stick. She continued to fight. It took every staff member in the room to pick her up even though she was rolled up in some weird-looking yoga mat. They carried her kicking and screaming out into the hallway. Her screams echoed down the corridor until fading away.

Other nurses rushed into the room. Two of them began talking to Darin and Rick. They paced back and forth alongside them. One of the others put a soothing arm around Shelly and rubbed her back along with her friends. Arlene went back to pulling her hair out of her head while Sally sat as still as a statue next to the boy who still hadn't even blinked, despite the chaos erupting around him.

I looked at Rose, my eyes filled with questions.

She burst out laughing. "Welcome to another exciting day of group therapy."

9

Dinner was as strange as group. This time, it was Rose who freaked out for no reason. One minute she was sitting next to me at the cafeteria table, pushing her food around her plate and gushing about how much she loved Taylor Swift's new song, and the next minute, without any provocation, she threw her tray of food against the wall.

"I'm not eating this!"

Polly appeared unfazed by her outburst and pushed the intercom button on the side of the door without looking at Rose. "She won't eat."

"All right," a voice cackled back.

Before I had a chance to say anything to Rose to try to calm her down, the door flung open and the same bouncer-looking men who'd pinned down Doris earlier in the day arrived.

"C'mon, Rose. Let's go," the shortest one said. "You know the rules."

Rose sat in her chair, arms folded tightly across her chest, and glared at them.

"Let's not make this any harder than it needs to be."

Rose still didn't move.

They stepped towards her and in one quick movement swooped down at her, grabbing both of her arms. Rose fought like a cat that'd been thrown into a tub of water, scratching and clawing at them as they tried to lift her from her chair. Her chair fell backward and she kicked at it wildly with her stick legs. They carried her out wailing and screaming in the same way they'd carried Doris. I was shocked by her explosive outburst because she seemed like such a meek and timid girl.

"What a freak," Tobi piped up from across the table as soon as the door clicked shut behind Rose.

"Right? I mean, can't we ever eat in peace? Some of us actually like to eat," Shelly said. They burst out laughing along with the other girl, Denise, sitting next to them.

"Maybe she doesn't want to," I said. I wanted to tell them it might do them some good not to eat since none of them could be mistaken as skinny, but it was mean and I didn't like to be mean. Instead, I said, "You don't know what she's going through."

Shelly raised her eyebrows at me and sneered. "And you do?"

I shrugged. She had a point. I'd known Rose less than twenty-four hours.

After dinner, I was surprised to find her back on the couch in the family room, absorbed in her magazines as if nothing had happened. I took a seat next to her.

"Damn, girl. You put up a fight."

I was amazed that it had taken three huge men to restrain such a small girl.

She looked up, her eyes red and puffy. They were still watery. Her pupils were the size of pinpricks. "So much for eating with you guys. Back to forced feedings alone."

"That sucks."

I knew what it was like to be forced to eat. In the first few months at the Rooths, Bob used to hold my mouth open while Dalila shoved food into it as fast as she could. Then, Bob would tilt my head back and grip my mouth closed for me, forcing me to swallow. But whatever food went down came right back up, and they ended up wearing the food they'd worked so hard to get in me.

"How do they force you to eat?"

She sniffled. "It's awful. They give me these huge protein drinks that look and taste like chalk. But that's not even the worse part. The drinks have over a thousand calories. Can you believe that? I have to drink one of those plus whatever else they put on my plate. They're not going to be satisfied until I'm a fat slob."

"What happens if you don't eat it? Do they force the food down your throat?" My throat reflexively closed in response.

"They'd love to. Assholes." Rose snorted. "Nope. If I don't eat, then they put the tube back in."

"A tube? Oh my God, how do they do that?"

"They used to put it in my nose, but I kept pulling it out and making it get infected. So now they do it through my stomach." She pulled up her shirt and pointed to her side. "Look."

I leaned closer. Her right side had three big puncture wounds as if she might've been bitten by a vampire in the last week.

"Whoa." I'd never seen anything like it. "Why don't you just eat? Wouldn't it be easier that way?"

She glared at me like I'd suggested she commit a felony. She pulled her shirt down and folded her arms across her chest. "Do you have visitors coming?"

"Yeah. I do," I said.

She leaned in closer, speaking in a hushed tone. "You should know the team talks to your family, too. They ask them how they think you're doing. So, you might wanna, you know ..."

I nodded knowingly. I turned behind to look at Polly, to see if she heard, but she wasn't there anymore. She'd been replaced with a heavyset hippy-looking guy wearing Birkenstocks. He was too busy staring at Shelly, Tobi, and Denise playing cards in the middle of the family room to notice us. Every few minutes one of them would laugh loudly and turn to flash a smile in his direction. He returned their smiles, welcoming their attention with a goofy grin.

I didn't want to see Bob, Dalila, and Thomas. It was going to be weird and uncomfortable seeing them together, but I didn't have a choice because I needed to talk to Dalila about the funeral. I wanted to know where it was going to be held and what Emily was going to wear in the casket. I wanted to be buried next to her, and if I killed myself as soon as I got released, then they'd be able to do a funeral for us both at the same time. It was the only thing that mattered to me right now. My plan had to be efficient and foolproof.

Shooting myself would be fast and easy, but I didn't know how to get a gun. Even if I did, it would take weeks to get one and I didn't have that much time. Taking pills was another option, but pills were never a sure thing. I'd watched Emily swallow enough to know that most of the time they didn't kill you. You just got really sick, puked them up, and woke up feeling hungover. Waking up wasn't an option. I'd woken up last time. I wasn't doing it again.

Slitting my wrists was a possibility, too. I knew the right way to cut them—vertical, not horizontal like so many people thought. But what if I didn't hit the vein you were supposed to or didn't cut deep enough? The thought of cutting open my flesh made me cringe like it always did. How had Emily done it this last time?

I hadn't allowed myself to think back to the night it happened. It was too painful, but I wanted to know how she'd done it because I might be successful if I copied her. I swallowed my emotions and braced myself to try to remember that night like I was a scientist, replaying the scene as if it were a video I was watching of someone else.

There were pills everywhere and she'd puked, which meant she must've taken a lot of them. Whenever she'd taken a lot of pills in the past, they'd always made her puke. What had she taken this time that made her puke, but was still enough to kill her? There was also blood, but was it because she was cutting herself like she regularly did, or was she trying to cut deep enough to kill herself? Could she have done anything else that I didn't know about? Maybe she did both things together. Maybe that was the key and I could do it the same way.

Suddenly, it dawned on me that I had tried it before. I was in the hospital for trying to kill myself but had no memory of what I'd done that night. I searched my brain for one, but there was nothing. I kept trying to bring something into my consciousness, but it was futile. All I saw were images of Emily. I could trace my memory all the way back to opening up the bathroom door and discovering her crumpled body, but that was it. Her body and then darkness.

Who had found us and how had I gotten to the hospital? Had I called someone? How was I going to make sure I didn't fail again? I couldn't bear the thought of waking up in the hospital another time, finding out I was still alive and she was still dead. My plan had to work this time. It had to be a good one. Much better than last time.

I decided to find someone to buy me liquor on the way home from the hospital even though I hated drinking and shuddered at the thought of the burn it made in my throat. I'd stop at Walgreens and load up on Extra Strength Tylenol. Most people didn't know it, but Tylenol was a good killer. Emily had explained to me once that it shut down everything in your system. Taking handfuls of Tylenol while chugging the booze would make it easier to slit my wrists, but I would have to make sure I didn't drink too much because I couldn't pass out or puke. It'd ruin everything if I did. Drinking might be a risk, but I needed it because I was afraid I wouldn't be able to cut myself without it. I'd lie in the tub just like Emily used to so I didn't get the blood everywhere.

The more I thought about my plan, the less feasible it seemed. If I killed myself in the apartment, how would anyone know I was dead? I couldn't call anyone before I did it because they might stop me before it was over. The only person I saw regularly was Thomas and he was used to not seeing me for days. A week could go by before he started to get worried and by then it would be too late, and Emily's funeral would be over. Killing myself at home wasn't going to work. Not if I wanted to be buried with Emily at the same time and I did, more than anything else. The only thing keeping me moving was knowing if I made it through the seventy-two-hour hold, I could ceremoniously die with her. I had two more days to come up with a good plan.

My name being called over the intercom broke into my thoughts. My visitors were here.

"Good luck," Rose said, without looking up from her magazine.

"Thanks," I replied, hurrying up to the nurses' station.

Dalila, Bob, and Thomas stood at the nurses' station beaming at me. Both Thomas and Dalila looked much better than yesterday. They were showered and scrubbed. Dalila had done her makeup to skillfully hide the worst of her breakouts and her hair was tightly curled in the same way she'd been doing it for the last twenty years. Thomas's dark circles underneath his eyes had lessened, although he still looked a bit ghastly. Bob had his shirt tucked into his jeans, something he reserved for special occasions, and I couldn't help but feel love towards him for the gesture. He carried a handful of dripping-wet flowers.

"They took the vase," he explained apologetically when he saw me eyeing the wet flowers. "The nurses said you can't have glass. One of them is looking for a Styrofoam cup."

Each of them had a smile spread wide across their face. They each took a turn hugging me and today I allowed it.

"You can visit in your room with your guests," one of the nurses instructed. "Let me take those flowers. I'll find a better place to put them."

Bob handed them to her, and a different nurse came out from behind the desk and led us down the women's hallway. She arrived at a door on the right, unlocked it, and pushed it open. "You do have to leave the door open, though. Sorry."

I walked into my room for the first time since being wheeled onto the unit. Everything was bolted to the ground. There was a hospital bed against the wall with a nurse's call button next to it and a small metal dresser across from it with three drawers. A tiny desk was on the other wall with a chair. The chair was the only thing not bolted to the ground. The walls were painted white and it had the same institutional flooring as the rest of the place. We all eyed the room warily.

Dalila was the first to break the silence. "It's a nice room. Needs a little color, though. Maybe I could bring some pictures."

"That's okay. I'm not going to be here long."

We were all standing, which made the space feel even smaller.

"How was your day, honey?" Bob asked.

"Today was a strange day. The people here really do have a lot of problems. Most of them aren't doing very well. It's made me glad for my problems. My own stuff seems pretty mellow in comparison."

"Do you think so?" Bob asked.

He looked over at Dalila with raised eyebrows. She shrugged.

"I really do. I'm pretty sure most of these people hear voices and they freak out all the time. I guess I can be grateful I'm not as sick as they are." My words landed on dead air and hung there expectantly.

"Lisa said some of the best psychologists in the state work here, so you're in good hands. Oh, she also said that wants to visit you once you're settled in," Bob said.

It would be nice to see Lisa, but she had an uncanny ability to get me to talk about things I didn't want to talk about and I couldn't take the chance of accidentally letting on I was planning to kill myself when I got out.

"I don't think I'm going to be here long enough for her to visit. I'm pretty sure I'll be getting out soon," I said.

"It seems like a nice place," Dalila commented for the second time.

It was silent again. I sat in the desk chair. The three of them sat on the edge of bed together. Bob had his arm around Dalila for support. Thomas was to the right of them at the end of the bed.

His posture was more relaxed now that he was on the bed. They sat together as if they were old friends.

Thomas interrupted the silence this time. "I've been praying for you all the time. I put your name on our prayer list. Don't worry. I completely respected your privacy. I didn't give any details about what was going on with you or anything else. I only said you needed help."

He irritated me. It wasn't because being on his church list bothered me, it was that he'd made his way into very private spheres of my life and I wasn't the one who'd invited him there.

"The food's not bad," I said.

"That's good." Bob patted his big belly that protruded over his waist. It was especially pronounced with his tucked-in shirt. They all laughed and I smiled again. Bob could always find a way to make me smile.

The awkwardness in the room surrounded us. We had no idea how to be together in normal circumstances and certainly not in circumstances as weird as these. I hadn't been in a room with Bob and Dalila since last Christmas. Even then, I'd only made a brief appearance. I'd pretended to have a major school project to get done over the holidays and stopped by just long enough to drop off presents. I rarely talked to Bob on the phone because he hated talking on the phone and since the last time Dalila had offended me about Emily, I only talked to her every few weeks.

I stared at Thomas. He was too busy glancing back and forth between Dalila and Bob to notice me looking at him. It was hard to imagine that a little over a week ago I was singing sappy love songs about him in my car. I looked at him now and felt nothing but annoyed, as if he'd duped me into falling in love with him and setting this entire ordeal into motion.

"Dalila, when is Emily's funeral?" I asked.

Her eyes filled with tears. Bob took her hand in his and began stroking it.

"I know this is hard, but we have to talk about it," I said.

"You have no idea how hard this is," Dalila said with tears running in thick streams down her face, creating mascara trails down to her chin.

"Maybe we shouldn't talk about this right now," Thomas said.

"And what would the right time be?" I was surprised by the sharpness in my tone.

"I just think it's a good idea to let your doctors talk about Emily with you." His tone was cautious.

"You do, huh? Well, I'm pretty sure my doctors don't know nearly as much about Emily as her family does." My tone had gone from sharp to angry. I stared at him until he looked away.

"I tend to agree with Thomas," Bob said.

"You don't even know Thomas. You just met him. When did the three of you become best friends?"

"But, honey, I thought he would be the person you'd want to be around. You spend all of your time with him. I mean, we barely talk to you. We don't know what's going on with you. We had no clue you were in such a bad state. It seemed like he would know so much more than us," Dalila said. "He's been—"

Thomas broke in, "It's all right. I understand she's upset. I can step outside." He started to rise.

"No, sweetie, you don't need to leave." Dalila placed her hand on his leg.

I was mad at him, but I didn't want him to leave either.

"Sorry for biting your head off, Thomas." My irritation with him still surprised me.

He shrugged. "Not a problem. I understand."

I was glad he understood because I didn't understand anything happening right now.

"I still want to talk about Emily's funeral," I said.

"God, Elizabeth, can't you just quit? Please? Just stop this craziness," Dalila cried.

"I'm not trying to hurt you. I promise I'm not. I just want to talk about it. I don't know what's going on with the plans. I want to make sure I can go. Am I going to be out in time to go to it?"

I was hurting her, but the conversation had to happen. Talking about Emily's funeral made the loss real to her in the same way that seeing her pain yesterday had made the loss real to me. I wished there was some way to lessen her pain, but there wasn't.

"You j-just, your mom just ... I-I-I ..." Bob always stuttered when he got nervous.

"Stop, Bob! I'm so tired of all this. So sick of it. I can't take it anymore. I can't!" Dalila yelled.

It was the first time I'd heard her yell. She didn't yell no matter how upset or frustrated she was. I'd never heard her even raise her voice. She'd had plenty of reasons to lose it, but she never did. My feelings threatened to break through the surface, but I swallowed them down as quickly as they came up. I had to stay focused.

"I'm sorry I'm upsetting you. I really am." I got up from my chair and moved towards her. I embraced her, rubbing her back—something I wasn't sure I'd ever done, but I felt responsible for upsetting her.

"Maybe if we took her to the grave," Bob muttered from behind us.

I jerked back as if I'd been slapped, staring at Bob.

"What did you say?" I asked.

He stammered. His face was bright red. "N-nothing. I didn't say anything."

"You said something about her grave. I heard you." My head was swirling. "What? What did you say?"

"Bob, honey, maybe—"

"What did you say?"

I let go of Dalila and stood back to face Bob.

"It's nothing. Really it's nothing." He darted his eyes back and forth between Dalila and Thomas. Thomas's eyes were wide open and Dalila gripped the bed as if she might crumple onto the floor if she didn't.

I heard it even though he wouldn't repeat it. He'd said they should take me to Emily's grave. They'd already buried her. They'd put her in the ground without me. How could they do that? How could they not wait for me? I jumped up from my chair.

"Get out!" I screamed at them, pointing at the door. "Leave. All of you. Now! You buried her. You put her in the ground without me even being there! How could you? Why would you do that?"

They were all moving towards me, arms outstretched in my direction, trying to get close to me and touch me. I recoiled from them as if they were zombies, sliding underneath the small desk and curling into a tight ball.

"Get out! Get out! Get out!" I pounded my hands on the linoleum floor over and over again. They kept trying to touch me, grab me. They wouldn't stop. Their words didn't reach me. My screams reverberated through my brain like shards of glass.

"I think this visit is over," a man's voice said from far away, like he was at the end of a long tunnel.

I pulled my knees up to my chest, wrapping my arms around them, and lay my head down on them. They were trying to say good-bye, but I turned away. I couldn't hear their words. I wanted them gone and didn't care if I ever saw them again. When I finally lifted my head, everyone was gone except the hippy-looking man. He was standing with his arms crossed, leaning against my bed.

"Can I please go to bed now?" My voice strained. It hurt to talk. My head throbbed.

"Sure. Just let me call a female CA."

I waited while he pushed the button next to my bed and a large African-American woman appeared in my doorway. She was carrying a black duffel bag. It was mine, but I didn't remember packing it.

"Get outta here, Mr. Man," she ordered with a wide grin on her face.

He shuffled out of the room.

"My name's Felicia. I'm the best thing ya got up here in this place." She handed me my bag, tossing it at my feet. "I guess you've had a long day, huh?"

I didn't feel like talking. I'd run out of lines for the day. There was a huge lump lodged in my throat. Emily's face kept flashing through my mind and I couldn't stop it. Her smile. Her twinkling, green eyes that lit up and sparkled when she was happy. The laughter that used to bubble up out of her, infecting everyone it touched. The pictures hurt.

"You don't talk much, huh? That's okay. Just gives me a reason to run my own mouth. Lord knows I'll never run out of words. You might decide to talk just to get me to shut up." She laughed heartily. "You gonna stay under there or ya gonna come out and put your nightclothes on?"

I crawled out from underneath the desk. I unzipped my bag and found my clothes neatly folded inside. Dalila must've packed my things. I pulled out a white T-shirt and my favorite pajama pants. I stood, holding them in my hands.

"Sorry, for now, I gotta be here while you change." Felicia shrugged. "But I'll turn around. I won't peek. Promise."

I quickly wiggled out of my hospital scrubs and pulled on my pajamas.

"Done."

It felt good to be in my own clothes.

"That was quick." She turned back around. She handed me a small pink pill and a Dixie cup. "Here. This will help."

I took both and swallowed the pill, not caring what I was taking. I handed the cup back to her.

"Now you just crawl into this bed and get some rest. I'm gonna be right outside the door. You need me, ya just holler, okay?" she said.

I crawled underneath the crisp white hospital sheets. The bed crinkled with the pressure of my weight. All of it stiff. But I didn't mind. I fell asleep quickly, long before lights out arrived on the unit.

10

I was awakened in the morning by Polly as she flooded my room with fluorescent light. I wanted to pull my covers over my head, but I put my feet on the floor instead. I grabbed my duffel bag from the chair where Felicia had set it the night before. Dalila had packed well. All of my favorite T-shirts and blue jeans were there. Polly didn't turn around like Felicia had last night while I changed, but I didn't care.

"It's time for breakfast. Your tray has already been brought up. Since you went to bed early last night, you didn't get a chance to fill out your menu for today so you'll get the standard breakfast. Make sure you fill out a menu tonight. Each patient fills out their meal menu for the following day the night before," Polly said as we made our way into the family room.

I didn't care about food. I felt like I was in a trance as I took my seat in the room. Everyone was already seated except Rose. I wondered where she was, but then remembered she'd been sentenced to isolation while she ate because of the tantrum she threw yesterday. I grabbed a seat in the corner by myself. I didn't make eye contact with anyone. I didn't feel like being bothered by having to make conversation this morning. I stared at the tray sitting in front of me. It was filled with cornflakes, pancakes, scrambled eggs, and toast. The thought of swallowing any of it made my stomach flip. I settled on a cup of coffee and sipped it slowly even though it was lukewarm.

Yesterday I'd had a plan, but this morning I had nothing. The only way I'd made it through yesterday was being able to focus on getting out in time to be buried with Emily. There seemed no reason to give a repeat performance if she was already buried and there was no possibility to share a funeral. Now, I was going to be buried alone. I might not even be laid to rest next to her. The only thing I wanted to do was crawl back into bed and sleep. For the first time ever, I understood why Emily spent so much time sleeping. It was the closest you could get to death without physically dying.

I kept telling myself that even though I couldn't be buried with her, I would follow her shortly. I repeated it over and over again as I drank my coffee because I was afraid I'd stop functioning if I didn't, or I'd start crying and never be able to stop. For a brief moment, the pain written on Dalila's face about Emily passed in front of me and I realized how terribly selfish my plan was. I couldn't help but wonder if terminally ill patients felt like I did when they decided to end their lives. I'd read their stories about how they were in so much pain that they made a calculated decision to die rather than continue to fight for a miserable existence. I hadn't understood their stories before, but I understood now.

Emily and I were two parts that made a whole and I was only half of a person without her. I came into the world in an intimate relationship and had never lived my life alone. Not even for a single day. For the first seven years of my life, I'd spent every moment with Emily. She was never further away from me than arm's length. It was as if our brains were sewn together and there was no place where I ended and she began. Even after we were taken away from Mother and everyone tried to separate us, it was impossible. We'd never spent a night away from each other in our twenty years. We finished each other's sentences and could predict what the other was going to do before they did it. There were times when we would start singing the same song at the same moment. We saw through each other's eyes, felt what the other experienced, and shared our thoughts. We could communicate without speaking. We were more like conjoined twins who'd never been separated at birth.

Now it was as if part of my body had been suddenly chopped off. I was an amputee, and like any amputee I was left with the excruciating phantom pain of being tortured by my lost limb. Every person who'd lost a body part still felt the burning, throbbing ache as if it was still there, and the empty void of Emily would never leave me. Unlike some who learned to live with the phantom pain, I never would. I was condemned to live with the unseen ghost of my lost part.

My coffee was finished and I stared at the food in front of me. I gave up on the possibility of eating. My throat was constricted and my stomach was even tighter. I aimlessly pushed the eggs around on my plate. I wondered how long you could refuse food until they started to force-feed you like they did Rose. I hoped they tried easier methods first before jamming a tube up your nose.

"Elizabeth?" Dr. Larson's voice called to me from the corner of the room.

I looked up. He motioned for me to follow him and I stood quickly, moving in his direction. I followed his brown suit as he led me down the hallway and into the same room we'd met in yesterday. I took the same seat I had before as he did the same.

He wasted no time on small talk or surface chat.

"So, your family visit didn't go well, huh?"

I shrugged my shoulders. "Not really."

"Do you want to tell me about it?"

I didn't want to talk about anything. Today I didn't know what my lines were supposed to be and it took too much energy to form words. I felt empty and depleted, but I had to say something or he'd continue to stare at me in silence until I did.

"It was weird. Dalila got upset and then I got upset too. I think she's having a really hard time with Emily's death and it's hard for her to talk to me about it."

"What else happened?"

So far he hadn't taken out his notebook. I didn't know if this was a good sign or a bad one.

"I ended up freaking out pretty badly. Bob let it slip that they already had Emily's funeral," I said.

"Why did that upset you?"

Was he stupid?

"I wanted to go."

He changed the subject, "Elizabeth, why do you think you're here?"

Why did he keep asking me the same question over and over again? Rose's lines were wrong. They weren't working. What was I saying wrong?

"I tried to kill myself. I found Emily dead and I snapped. But I'm starting to think clearer. I'm not going to do anything stupid like that again."

My words couldn't have been more false.

"We are going to begin your treatment."

What was he talking about?

"The team decided yesterday that it's time to start the work."

Work? What kind of work? I was too tired to do anything.

"Have you wondered why everyone keeps asking you the same questions about being here?"

Had he just read my mind?

I nodded.

"How do you feel about that?"

"It's kinda strange. Feels like a test."

"There are no right answers."

Obviously there were or they wouldn't keep asking me the same questions.

He put his hands on the table and folded them, leaning forward. His brown eyes met mine and the stare was so intense I had to turn away. He really was trying to read my mind. "I want to talk about Emily. Are you ready to talk about Emily?"

No. I didn't want to talk about Emily and I wasn't going to have a conversation about her with a stranger who'd never met her and didn't know anything about her.

"I guess," I lied.

"Good." He cleared his throat. He leaned across the desk. He crossed an invisible line on the desk and entered my space. His breath stunk of stale coffee and dirty socks. "I want to begin by telling you this is going to be really hard. However, it's got to happen if you are going to be able to get well ..."

I wasn't sick.

"Can you think of any reason Dalila may have gotten so upset about Emily yesterday?"

I liked therapy better with Lisa when I was a kid. I wanted to draw pictures. Play games. Cards. Anything. Not answer all of his questions.

"She didn't want to talk about the funeral. Probably because she knew how upset I'd get," I said.

"Get about what?"

I wrung my hands underneath the table. He was unsettling me. He wasn't very good at his job. It was irritating the way I had to break everything down into small pieces of information for him.

"I would be upset they didn't wait for me to get out of the hospital before they had her funeral. She knew I'd be angry that I didn't get to go."

There. Was that simple enough for him?

"Elizabeth, I want you to listen to what I'm about to say and to do your best to be present for it."

I was right here. I wasn't going anywhere.

"The reason Dalila was so upset about the conversation yesterday is because Emily's funeral happened a long time ago and you did get to go to it. You were there."

My head swirled around the room as if it was about to roll off my neck and bounce onto the floor. What was he talking about? Maybe he really wasn't my therapist. What if he was really one of the patients? Or maybe this was just a test of my reality. He was seeing if he could confuse me.

"Do you understand what I'm saying?" He spoke slowly, still intensely staring at me.

He was crazy. I looked at the door. It was locked and he had the key. I was trapped in a room with a madman.

He kept talking. "I told you this is going to be really hard and difficult... process ... small steps ..."

Shut up!

I clenched my jaw so I wouldn't scream it at him.

Shut up! He's not going to stop. He's going to keep going. He can't keep talking.

"All of this is really confusing for you. Sometimes when people experience severe trauma, they create a world for themselves that separates them from experiencing what is really going on ..."

He didn't know what was going on. He didn't understand anything.

"The brain is powerful. I believe the trauma of losing Emily caused a split in reality for you ..."

What was he talking about? Split? Trauma? Why was he using those words? Why was he saying this to me? I wanted to put my hands over my ears to drown out the sound of his voice. It was screaming in my head. His eyes dug into me.

Shut up, you ugly fat man. Just shut up. I don't want to hear what you have to say.

"The reality is that Emily is dead. She's been dead for two years and ..."

My brain was a balloon. My body was a string. The string connected me to the ground. Emily's hand. Her hand, but she'd let go and I was floating. Floating while my body dangled below.

"Derealization ..."

I was still floating.

Can I catch her? Is she there? Is there a way out of this room?

"Dissociation ... extreme ... some cases ..."

The shooting phantom pain.

I'm being stretched. Am I awake? I got out of my bed this morning. Yes, I did. Drank coffee.

I looked across the desk at Dr. Larson. He was still speaking. His lips were moving and his hands were animated. I'd never seen him show any emotion, but his face was alive with it now. I was sure his words had sounds, but they no longer reached my ears. My super powers were taking over. I hadn't used my powers in a long time. I'd started using them with Mother's special friends but over the years, I'd discovered they worked in other situations too.

They took over automatically when Emily and I would go to court. We'd sit in a big empty room lined with rows upon rows of wooden benches that made the courtroom look like a church sanctuary. Our aluminum seats were always freezing as Emily and I sat next to each other at a long table up front, holding hands, with strangers on each side of us. Emily and I never said a word unless someone asked us to. We had lots of practice at being silent and we also knew better than to act up in the presence of adults. Mother's presence at the other table across the aisle was a constant reminder of what would happen if we stepped out of line.

The judge in the courtroom was mean and she towered above the rest of us from her position a top a tall mahogany desk at the front. She said horrible things to our mother, even made her cry. I'd never seen Mother cry. Did she practice her cries in the mirror in the same way I'd seen her practice smiles? I stared at Mother's face, wondering if her tears were real. If I tasted them, would they be salty? Mother always sat on the other side of the room. She'd never even look at us. The man in the chair next to Emily and me carried funny smells with him. Sometimes he smelled like beef stew and Emily and I would giggle about it afterward when we were alone in our bed at the Rooths'.

At some point, the judge would look down from her massive desk and start to ask Emily and me questions. She acted like a nice lady when she talked with us, even smiling at times. It looked real, but we were careful because we'd seen how mean she was to Mother and didn't want to make her angry like Mother made her angry. We also didn't want to say anything that would make Mother upset. The scars on our bodies were a constant reminder of what would happen if we did. Sometimes when the judge was talking, I would stop being able to hear her voice and before long, I didn't just lose her voice—I could no longer hear any of the other voices echoing in the empty vast room.

There was a small window on the right-hand side of the courtroom. It was all the way across the top of Mother's head. I would leave my body and travel out the window. I'd go outside to the tree, to the big one with all the huge green leaves. I'd climb the tree as far as I could go and find myself a good spot. A spot where I could sit without having to worry about falling, where I could simply sit and watch. Stare at the sun. Feel the breeze against my face. Pick leaves and drop them. Watch them flutter down to the ground. I climbed the tree again and began picking the leaves. I dropped a big red one.

The leaf hit the ground and startled me. There was movement around me. Other people. Rose sitting next to me, chattering about something. I looked around.

I'm not in Dr. Larson's office. I've escaped. I'm still breathing. I can hear Rose's voice. It's over. Thank God it's over.

I forced myself to return by listening to Rose's voice. Sometimes when I left my body, it was hard to get back inside.

"And I don't get any more passes. Can you believe that? One screw up. One day and they take it all away. Like I haven't done anything while I've been here," she said. "I hate it here."

I nodded my head in agreement.

I was so glad to be free and that it was over. Dr. Larson was gone and I didn't have to hear his voice, listen to his stupid words, or his ridiculous ideas.

"Did you meet with the team yet? They tell you when you get to leave?" she asked.

"Nope. They haven't told me anything."

They hadn't told me anything but lies. I'd heard that psychologists messed with your head, but the only one I'd ever met was Lisa and she'd never played any mind games like Dr. Larson was playing. He was trying to fool me. But why? Why would he do that? What was the point?

"This place is nuts," I said. Somehow I felt safe confiding in her and I needed to confide in someone. "These doctors really screw with your head."

She threw her head back, laughing. "Uh, yeah. I totally know how you feel. The first time being here is the worst. You have no idea how to play all their stupid games. But you learn. It just takes a while. At least you got to miss group this morning."

"We had group this morning?"

"Yep. You didn't miss anything exciting. Not like yesterday." She laughed again. "Honestly, I kinda like the freak-outs. It keeps me from being bored."

Emily would—

I stopped myself.

Why did Dr. Larson tell me Emily had been dead for two years? There was no way it was true. I wasn't crazy and I'd have to be crazy to believe Emily was alive if she was dead. How did I live with her for two years if she was dead? I'd held her body next to mine every night. I'd listened to her heart beating in her chest when she was in my arms and felt her warm breath on my neck. Dr. Larson couldn't be telling the truth. Other people had seen and talked to her too, like the attendant at the gas station, who would start pulling out her Marlboro Reds when he spotted her walking through the door. Our neighbors knew her too and spoke to her whenever she got the mail, especially Mrs. Jasberson. Even the baristas who worked at the coffee shop down the street from our apartment interacted with her regularly. It was the only place she would go without me, even when she was at her worst. They asked about her when she wasn't with me. They knew her order as well as they knew mine—large vanilla latte with one shot of espresso. Skim milk.

There was no way everyone else would pretend she still existed if she didn't. Bob and Dalila had talked to her numerous times on the phone, even when she was refusing to see them, and they were two of the sanest individuals I knew. The entire story about Emily being dead for two years was impossible. There had to be something else going on, and I was going to find out what it was.

11

I spent the afternoon sitting on the couch in what had quickly become my usual position in the family room, waiting for my meeting with the team. Everyone met with them once a day and so far, I hadn't had my turn.

Everyone had their positions in the family room. Rose was always on my right, usually with her head buried in a magazine. She was obsessed with them. She didn't care if they were new or not. She flipped through them again and again, wearing out the pages. The two wooden rocking chairs stayed occupied by Arlene and the man who still hadn't spoken. His name was Matt but nobody knew anything else about him. Rick and Darin talked to their characters on the other couch opposite me and Rose. I was beginning to not even notice their incessant chatter. Shelly, Tobi, and Denise were glued to their table unless there was a male nurse or doctor at the nurses' station. When that was the case, one of them always sauntered up to the desk as if it were a bar and flirted shamelessly, even though all three of them were married. Doris was the only one who didn't sit. She roamed constantly, walking miles a day without ever going outside.

I stared at the clock hanging above the TV that nobody ever turned on. The minutes inched forward. I was so anxious. By this time yesterday morning, I'd already talked to the team. Rose had told me that there wasn't a set schedule for meeting with the team. You never knew what time it was going to happen or when they were going to come get you. I'd been watching the minute hand go around the black-framed clock ever since.

It wasn't right that the team didn't follow a schedule. They shouldn't do that to us. It was unfair that we had to sit and wonder when they were coming. I was shaking. My heart was pounding and the pressure was back in my chest. My hands were sweaty. My hands were wet but my throat was dry. I didn't drink any water, though, because I'd throw up if I did.

What was going to happen when I met with the team? Was it going to be like my meeting with Dr. Larson? Would they say the same things he did? Was this how the whole thing worked—an entire group of people telling you things about your life that weren't true to see how mentally stable you were? Is that how they were able to tell if you were like Rick or Darin?

I kept glancing at Rick and Darin, alternating between the clock and their antics. Much like yesterday, they were engaged in nonstop conversation. Sometimes they spoke in hushed tones and other times they bordered on yelling, always gesturing wildly and pointing.

Who were they talking to and what were they talking about? Did the voices talk back? What if the doctors were the ones who made them that way? What if the doctors had given birth to the voices and they were normal before? Is that what happened when doctors stuck their hands into the wires of your brain and began to move things around? Is that what was going to happen to me?

Bile rose in my throat.

"I'm going to puke!" I jumped up.

My sudden movements made the bile heave again and it pushed its way into my mouth, filling it with awful-tasting fluid. I clasped my hand over my mouth. My stomach heaved again into my mouth, forcing what was already in it to spray through my fingers.

"Polly! She's puking!" Rose leapt up. "Get her to the bathroom!"

She grabbed my hand as Polly sprang from her chair. Rose pulled me down the hallway and pushed through the bathroom door, and I rushed for the toilet in front of me. I emptied what was left in my mouth into the toilet bowl. Rose knelt beside me, rubbing her hand in small circles on my back. Waves of nausea racked my body over and over again, resulting in water and yellow mucus spraying from my mouth and nose into the toilet. It kept coming until there was nothing left, but my stomach wouldn't stop heaving. It created a pounding in my head unlike any headache before.

"It's okay. You're going to be okay." Rose hadn't left my side. She got a paper towel, wet it in the sink, and pressed it on my forehead. The coolness helped settle my stomach. She got up again and this time brought back a Styrofoam cup filled with water. She handed it to me. "Here. Rinse your mouth out with this. Don't drink it. Just rinse. I don't think you need anything in you right now."

I reached out, taking it from her with my hands still shaking. I rinsed my mouth. I still felt nauseous, but I was done throwing up. I didn't know how long we sat by the toilet together, but my eyelids felt heavy and my eyes burned. My throat was raw.

"Polly, why don't you put her to bed?" Rose asked.

I'd forgotten about Polly, my ever-present shadow.

"No. You know patients aren't allowed in their rooms during the day," she said from somewhere behind us.

"Yeah, except when they're sick. And I'm pretty sure she's sick. C'mon, Polly, don't be a bitch."

Polly laughed. "You ever thought about working here?"

Rose giggled back. "Christ, I should. I certainly spend enough time here."

"You think you can get up?" Polly asked me.

"Here, let me help you." Rose grabbed my hands and pulled

me to my feet.

I felt unsteady. She put her arm around my waist. I was amazed at how small her frame was. I was leaning against bones, but somehow they steadied me. We left the bathroom and walked a few rooms down to mine.

"You have to do something with this room," Rose said, but quickly added, "Only if you end up having to stay. But I'm sure you won't, so we don't need to worry about it. Never mind."

I wanted to smile, but my lips were stuck in a straight line. I crawled into bed and it made the same crinkling sounds as the night before. I didn't care that I was in my jeans. I wanted to close my eyes. Rest.

"I'll be right outside the doorway. I'm going to let you sleep for an hour. Then I'll check and see how you're feeling," I heard Polly's voice from outside my lids.

"And you know where to find me. I'm not going anywhere." Rose giggled.

I focused on the darkness of my lids and nothing else. I didn't allow any thoughts to enter my head. I banished them the instant they tried to intrude. Sleep came with force and with it visions of my last night with Emily. The same scene over and over as if it was a CD stuck on repeat, replaying the moments before I found her in the bathroom.

I walked down the hallway again and again. Each time I put my hand on the doorknob to open the door, I was shoved to the start of the hallway, where I had to begin the journey all over again. I became more and more frantic to get there. To open the door and see her. Each time it ended the same. I never got to open the door or see Emily. I awoke abruptly, feeling wide awake instantly. I saw Polly sitting on a chair outside my door, texting away on her phone.

Polly looked up with my movement and tucked her phone in her pocket. I lay silently in my bed. I was empty and hollow as if my insides had been scraped out like a pumpkin and discarded.

"Do you feel better?"

"Yes," I lied.

I didn't know how I felt. I was a stranger in my own skin.

"I was going to wake you soon." She folded the corner of the book lying on her lap. "I'm sorry you had such a hard morning. This must be very difficult for you. Would a hug help?"

I shook my head.

"Do you want to talk about it?"

I shook my head again.

"Okay, then. Let's join everyone in the family room."

I followed her into the family room. My eyes searched for Rose and I was surprised to find Shelly, Tobi, and Denise had moved their chairs from the table and pulled them up to form a semicircle in front of Rose on the couch. Shelly's sleeve was rolled up and her arm was exposed. All of the women were looking at it. I couldn't help but look as I sat down next to Rose. Her arm reminded me of Emily's body. It was covered in the same scarred madness, as if her arm had been mangled in machinery.

"This is the last one before the hospital," Shelly explained, pointing to a section on her arm, but I couldn't tell the difference between the cuts she was pointing at and the others marking her arm.

"That's nothing," Tobi said as she pulled up her pant leg and exposed holes in her skin. Some were small and others were the size of quarters.

"You burn, huh?" Rose asked. "I've never understood the burning thing. Cutting I get, because you can force yourself to do it and stay still, but how do you stay still while you're burning yourself? Don't you move out of instinct when your skin feels hot?"

"No. It's a total mind thing. That's the beauty of it." Tobi's eyes filled with pride. I'd seen the same look in Emily's eyes. "You go against your body's natural reaction. It's so powerful. It feels wonderful."

Shelly turned to me. "What about you? Are you a cutter?"

I shook my head.

"Oh, what do you do then?" Shelly asked, looking surprised.

I stared at her blankly. "What do you mean?"

"We were talking about the self-injury group. We heard you were going to be in it with us and you have to cut or do something to yourself to get in," Tobi said.

"I'm pretty sure it's not me. I'm not in any special group."

The two of them looked at each other, then me, and smiled back at each other as if they shared a secret. I looked to Rose for some sort of explanation or help. She shrugged her shoulders.

"Tobi, what's the deepest you've ever gone? I—"

Polly interrupted, "Ladies, I think it's time we changed the subject. This conversation is getting unhealthy."

Sometimes I forgot she was there.

Shelly stuck her tongue out at her. "Whatever."

"You guys wanna play Spades?" Denise asked.

"Sure," Rose said. "Elizabeth can be my partner."

"I don't know how to play."

"I'll show you," she said.

We moved to the table. They explained the object of the game and took turns teaching me the rules. I was grateful for the distraction. We played a practice round once they were confident I knew what I was doing. They laughed at my mistakes and joked with each other about their husbands and other times they'd been in the hospital. I stared at them as much as I stared at my cards. Their laughter seemed real and I couldn't understand how they could be happy here. I knew by the number of wounds they carried on their bodies that their insides were filled with tremendous pain. How'd they end up in this strange land and who were they before they came here?

I kept my questions to myself and continued playing cards. We played until it was time for our afternoon snack. Our snack was signaled by a hospital cafeteria worker coming with a cart full of trays and another man who called Rose to go with him.

"Great. My favorite part of the day," she said getting up from the table. "See you after I've gained another five pounds."

"I can't believe how skinny she is and she thinks she's fat," Shelly whispered as if Rose might hear her in whatever room she'd been taken to. "ED girls are so strange."

"ED?" I asked.

"Oh yeah, I forget you're a first-timer." Shelly laughed. "Eating disorder. Everyone I've met with one is completely bizarre. They kinda freak me out."

I disagreed. Rose seemed to be the most normal person here.

"So what's your deal?" Shelly asked.

I was taken by surprise. My face felt hot.

"I'm, uh ... I guess, I'm just ... here."

"You're just here," Tobi repeated rolling her eyes as if I'd insulted her. "You don't just get here. You've got to be really fucked up. Otherwise, they put you on one of the other units." She looked proud.

"I came from the hospital?" It sounded like I was asking permission for something.

Shelly and Tobi exchanged another look.

"We'll find out about your story, little miss secretive," Shelly said. "We know everything that goes on here."

Shelly had to be close to forty, but she reminded me of the mean girls from high school, the ones who liked to pick on Emily for failing math and making out with guys she barely knew or sleeping with their boyfriends. Much like yesterday, Shelly's hair and makeup were done. Her makeup was painted on as if she might be going to the club. Her long lashes were obviously fake and she had on so much red lipstick that it kept getting stuck on her teeth. Tobi sat next to her. She was covered in tattoos all the way down her arms and her husband's name was branded across her chest. Unlike Shelly's short bleached-blond hair, Tobi's hair was long and dark. She flipped it over her shoulders and twirled it constantly. Her hair and makeup were done the same way as

Shelly's and she wore a low-cut tank top even though it was freezing. Denise was the quiet one among them. Her hair and makeup were done too, but not nearly as dramatic and her boobs weren't spilling out of her shirt like Shelly's and Tobi's. The three of them seemed to be competing for some kind of prize, but I couldn't imagine what the competition was for. I watched them as they dipped their Lorna Doone cookies in milk. I couldn't eat cookies or drink milk. My stomach still felt too weak to eat.

"You don't have to sit there if you're not going to eat," Shelly said as if I was doing something wrong. A minute ago we were laughing and having fun playing cards, but now she looked at me like she couldn't stand me and I had no idea what I'd done to offend her.

I got up and went back to the couch. Rose still wasn't back yet. Matt was the only other one who wasn't eating. I hadn't seen him eat yet, but unlike Rose, nobody cared that he didn't. He stared out the window like a statue. His face was a blank slate. Did he ever speak? Is that what was going to happen to me if I stayed here? Was I eventually going to join him by the window? The thought of being him seemed less scary than ending up like Rick and Darin. They were tortured and on edge every moment of the day, but Matt was completely unaffected by his surroundings. Maybe he'd permanently left his body. Was his mind empty too?

"Did you miss me?" Rose plopped down next to me.

"Yes."

I felt more comfortable when she was around. It was a new feeling, because the only female friend I'd ever had was Emily.

"Sorry you had to eat with those three," she whispered, gesturing over to the table where Shelly and her crew were still eating cookies. "They're crazy." She laughed. "You know what I mean. We're all crazy. Just different versions. Pick your poison."

"Shelly's odd. She makes me so uncomfortable," I whispered back. "I don't trust her at all. I don't know why Tobi and Denise like her so much. They never leave her side."

"Totally. I don't either. She's all in your business if you let her. She got here first and didn't talk to anyone for the longest time. All she did was wail and threaten to kill herself. She was so dramatic all the time. She'd throw herself all over the place, sobbing hysterically and screaming she was going to cut herself until staff came running. Then Tobi got here and she totally mellowed out. They've been best friends ever since. I think Denise only hangs out with them because she wants friends, but I can tell Shelly embarrasses her sometimes." She leaned even closer. "I think Shelly and Tobi are *together* together. I caught them kissing. And they're both married."

Polly's voice interrupted, "Rose, stop."

What did it matter that Rose was talking about them?

"I'm not doing it," Rose whined.

Doing what?

"I've been watching you do it since you sat down. You know you're not allowed."

I looked over my shoulder at Polly and back at Rose. She folded her hands on her lap and frowned.

"Fine," Rose said.

We sat in silence for a few minutes, except for Rose's occasional exaggerated sighs.

"I'm not allowed to move around after I eat. They think I'm exercising by moving my legs or something. Another one of my rules," she said. Her hands were folded on her legs. Every few seconds, one of her legs would spasm and then stop. She looked like she was in pain and it hurt her not to move.

"Do you ever get to exercise?"

"Nope. Never." Her eyes welled with big tears.

I wanted to give her permission to jump up and run around the room. Exercise couldn't be that bad for her. I'd let her do laps every once in a while so she could get it out of her system. I patted her on the back, feeling her sharp and pointed bones underneath.

"So, how are you doing?" she asked.

"I'm go—" I stopped myself from finishing the lie. "I don't know ..."

It was the first honest thing I'd said about how I felt since I'd woken up in the hospital. It felt good because I hated lying. I couldn't stand it. It was one of the things I said I'd never do after watching Mother lie more than she ever told the truth. I preferred to say nothing instead of saying something untrue.

"Yeah. I feel you. It's hard to be here. At least you're not puking anymore. I'd be on more restrictions if I did."

"Oh, so you don't puke?" I thought everybody with an eating disorder puked.

"Nope. But maybe I'll have to start," she said. "Did you hear that, Polly? I said I'm going to start puking."

I stared in awe at Rose's ability to make jokes all the time. She'd adjusted so well to being here and I couldn't imagine how she did it. Did she feel like I felt when it was her first time? Did the doctors put her through the same mental tests they were putting me through? Did she pass hers? Had I passed mine this morning? Was I ever going to get a clue what the right answers were?

Mark, the group leader from yesterday, appeared and on cue everyone stood to crowd around him. We made our way down the hallway in the same manner as the day before. We took our seats and I was more prepared for the bizarre ritual about to repeat itself. It began shortly after we were settled, with everyone's eyes on Mark as if he was some type of god to be revered, although I was unsure what he'd done to gain that type of status.

"Let's start with introductions."

He recited the same script. Everyone went around the room taking turns. Everyone said their name followed by a list of mental illnesses and then recounted how many days they'd been in the hospital. When my turn arrived, I followed the same script exactly like I did before. I expected to be left alone like yesterday. Instead, the focus remained on me.

"So, you tried to kill yourself, huh?" Shelly was peering at me from across the room with an even angrier look than she'd had earlier and I couldn't figure out how I'd unknowingly angered her again. "Does that mean you're depressed?"

I shook my head.

"Are you a drunk?"

I shook my head again.

"What's your deal, then?" Her eyes narrowed to slits and her lips pressed together to form a silent challenge.

I shrugged my shoulders. "I guess I don't know what you mean."

Shelly threw her arms up in the air and turned to look at Denise, who nodded in agreement. "This bitch drives me crazy."

Mark interjected, "Shelly, I need you to watch your language." He nodded at her as if to give her permission to continue and I couldn't imagine why he'd be aligned with her.

"Do you even know where you are?" she asked.

I nodded. "Yes, I do."

I hoped my answer would be good enough to get her to focus her attention on somebody else besides me.

"You're in a nut ward. And not just some pansy-ass 'oh, poor me, I took too many pills because my boyfriend broke up with me' kind. We're talking about being a step away from the state hospital. That's where you are. And like I said earlier, you don't end up here by accident."

There were different types of psych wards? Who knew these kinds of things, anyway? And why did she care so much? I wanted to ask her, but I didn't want to make her any angrier. Anger scared me. It didn't matter who was angry—I didn't like it.

Rose piped up, "Leave her alone."

"Leave her alone," Shelly mimicked her, the same way a five-year-old might. Her friends on either side of her burst into giggles. We'd all been playing cards a few minutes ago, but now Shelly was looking at me like she wanted to claw my eyes out.

"Look, she really doesn't have any idea why she's here or

what's going on," Rose said.

Was that true? Should I be insulted?

Shelly's face relaxed and became curious instead. "Like she's psychotic? Out of it, you mean? She really doesn't look like one of the psychos."

Mark interrupted a second time, "I'm going to have to ask you to watch your language again."

Was she swearing?

"Kinda," Rose replied, turning to look at me apologetically.

"Oh." Shelly relaxed in her chair, as if she was satisfied now.

Part of me thought I should be offended because Rose referred to me as a psycho, which is never a good name to be called no matter where you were, but for some reason I wasn't. I was simply glad the moment was over and the attention had shifted away from me.

12

Dr. Larson met me in the hallway on the way out of group.

"How was group?"

"It was fine," I said.

I'd been left alone after Shelly's initial obsession with me. The focus had moved to Tobi. She'd filled most of the hour crying and talking about how her husband was verbally abusive to her and her frustration with not being able to leave him even though he treated her badly. She blamed her inability to leave him on being beat up by her stepfather when she was a little girl. Her stepfather had beaten her with a wooden paddle since she was three and started raping her when she was nine. He'd gotten her pregnant when she was fourteen, and her mother had forced her to have an abortion. She'd married her husband when she was seventeen so she could leave home. I was amazed she could talk about her experiences so openly with people she barely knew.

"Great," he responded as if this made him happy. "The team is waiting for you."

My stomach lurched forward and for a second, I was sure I was going to throw up again. I swallowed it back down. Dr. Larson walked down the hallway and I followed. It was not an invitation or even a request, because even without being told, I knew nothing was optional in this place. I'd only been here for one day, but I'd already learned I was expected to follow the leader at all times and do as I was told. My heart beat faster and faster. By the time we reached the door, I was dizzy and lightheaded as if I'd sprinted there from fifty yards away.

The team was assembled in the same way as the previous day. They looked like they were seated in the same places, but I couldn't be sure. I didn't remember any of their names. I took the seat at the head of the table once again, and much like yesterday, all eyes were on me. I had to pay attention. Stay focused.

Dr. Larson didn't waste any time getting started. "We know you had a rather rough morning. We're all wondering how you're doing with the information we processed in our individual session this morning."

There was a long, drawn-out pause.

"And how are you doing?" he prompted.

"Oh, I um ... I'm sorry. I didn't realize it was a question. I guess, um ... I'm doing all right?"

"Really?" The woman to my right spoke up, raising her eyebrows.

I snuck a peek at her name tag: Karen. Karen Heimer, Ph.D. Her hair was in the same tight ponytail it'd been in yesterday.

"I guess so. I felt better after a nap."

What was I supposed to be saying?

"Maybe you could take some time and tell all of us about your session with Dr. Larson," Dr. Heimer said.

This time, I knew she was asking me a question without asking me a question and I was supposed to respond.

Think, Elizabeth. Think.

"We talked about Emily," I said.

There. That was good.

There was another long, drawn-out pause. Some of them exchanged glances, others scribbled in their notebooks, and the rest continued to stare holes into my face. The clock on the wall ticked. Their pens scratched their papers.

Dr. Heimer broke the silence. "Tell me more about it."

I cleared my throat. "I think Dr. Larson was checking to see if I was crazy or not. I think he was seeing if I knew what reality was."

Dr. Heimer glanced at Dr. Larson and then back at me. "And how did he do that?"

I looked away from her peering eyes for a moment and stared at the black marble table in front of me. "He told me Emily has been dead for two years."

My head was rolling and becoming unattached. I willed it to stay.

"Why do you think he would tell you that?" she asked.

I didn't like her questions or her. I wanted her to leave me alone. Why wouldn't she let someone else talk? I forced myself to look at her and to speak.

"Like I said, I think he wanted to see if I was crazy."

"Saying Emily has been dead for two years would be a test to see if you were crazy?"

I was doing good. It would be over soon.

"If he could convince me of something as ridiculous as Emily being dead for two years, then it would mean I didn't know what was going on or how to tell the difference between reality and fantasy. Basically, he gave me a test to see if I'm psychotic like some of the other people here."

I was proud of myself. It was a great answer. Nobody could argue with it.

"Elizabeth, I want you to listen to me carefully." Dr. Heimer was speaking slowly now, enunciating every syllable perfectly as if I had difficulty hearing. "Dr. Larson was not trying to test or trick you in any way. Dr. Larson was telling the truth. Emily has been dead for two years."

I hated her. I wanted to lunge across the table, grab her pen, and stab her with it.

"Do you understand what I'm saying? Emily died two years ago," she said, not breaking her gaze.

"Stop it!" I screamed, jumping up from my chair. "You're doing it too. You're all in on it. You're horrible people. What kind of monsters are you? How can you mess with someone's head? Why are you doing this to me?"

"We aren't trying to hurt you," someone said. "We're trying to help you. No one is lying or trying to trick you. Your sister has been dead for a long time."

"Shut up!" I lunged at Dr. Heimer. I couldn't help it. I wanted to make her be quiet.

I screamed wildly in her face. I saw the spit flying from my mouth and my fists shaking as I reached for her throat like I was going to choke her. The room around sprang to life. I watched as the doctors in the room rushed around us and tried to grab me. I was screaming at them too. Clawing at them, as if I was a wild animal just released from captivity. One of them hit a button on the wall and three big men rushed into the room. They pulled me away from Dr. Heimer and I flailed my arms and legs as they pinned my arms back. My screaming was becoming incomprehensible. Only sounds. They were carrying me to my room. I looked down at them as they stuck a needle in my arm and then relaxed as blackness enveloped me. The screaming stopped.

My eyes snapped open.

I have to get out of here.

I tried to sit up, but jerked back towards the bed. I strained against myself. I could move, but couldn't go anywhere. I looked to my right and then to my left. Each arm was being held down by a belt tied around my wrists and attached to the bed rail. I couldn't see down to the end of my legs, but I was sure they were tied up in the same way because I couldn't move them either. I was chained to my bed. I moaned.

Polly was by my bedside instantly, peering down at me.

"How are you feeling?" she asked.

I refused to try to answer her question.

"They put you in restraints in case you were still fighting when you came to," she said. "I can take these off of you, but they will be put right back on if you can't behave."

I'd never been in any kind of trouble before. Never. I'd always followed the rules and done what I was told, but I nodded to assure her I'd be good. She released my arms first and I sat up while she undid the belts tied around my ankles.

"You missed dinner, but I saved your plate. You want it?"

I shook my head.

"You probably only have a few minutes before your visitors get here, so we can just wait here and—"

"No visitors. I don't want to see anyone."

"Are you sure? You should feel fortunate to have people that want to come see you—"

"No visitors."

I had no desire to see the Rooths or Thomas. The only thing more horrible than seeing them right now would be meeting with the team again. I didn't want to see or talk to anyone.

"All right, then. Have it your way. We'll go have a seat in the family room with everyone else." She smiled down at me as if we were friends.

Shelly and her gang were in their usual position playing cards. They paused to stare at me as I walked into the room and exchanged glances with each other. I scanned the room for Rose and she looked up at me like she'd been waiting for me. I took a seat next to her on the couch.

She smiled at me when I made eye contact. "You're one of us now."

There wasn't any maliciousness or mockery in her smile. It was completely welcoming. I didn't understand anything that had happened with the doctors today, but I did understand one thing—Rose was right. I was one of them. I didn't know when I'd become one of them or if I'd always been one, but I was now. I'd been initiated into whatever strange society this was.

Rose didn't ask me why I freaked out. She started prattling on about celebrities and makeup. I was thankful I didn't have to see the Rooths or Thomas because I was too exhausted to handle one more emotional confrontation. I was more tired than I'd ever been. I felt as if I could sleep for days. My thinking was muddled. I nodded off on the couch listening to Rose talk and trudged to my bed when we were allowed to go to our rooms.

Morning came too soon. I wanted to lie in bed in a state of emptiness and nothingness. And then I remembered—it was day three.

My seventy-two hours were almost up, and this entire ordeal was going to be over soon. I'd made it. Rose had been right when she'd said these would be the longest three days of my life. I felt as if I'd been in the psych ward for weeks instead of days. It was like being engaged in psychological warfare, but it was finally about to end. Soon I wouldn't have to think about any of their questions or torturous mind tricks again.

I was excited to get out of bed now and was one of the first to arrive in the family room. It was empty except for Matt and Arlene. Arlene was sitting in front of the TV, even though it wasn't turned on. I grabbed my coffee from the breakfast tray and decided to take a seat near Matt since he wouldn't bother me. Dr. Larson summoned me before I had a chance to finish my coffee. We took our usual positions in his office.

"How are you feeling this morning?"

I was sick of everyone asking me how I was feeling. Did things have to happen the same way day after day in here?

"Tired."

"I suppose you are." He folded his hands on his desk. "Is there anything you'd like to talk about?"

I didn't want to talk or answer any more of his questions. I didn't know how I felt and didn't care to find out. I wanted him and everyone else to stop looking at me and messing with my mind. I only wanted out.

"I'm wondering if there are any papers I need to sign before I leave. Do I have to do anything with my insurance company?"

Dr. Larson cocked his head to the side and eyed me quizzically. "I'm sorry, I don't know what you're talking about."

"Today is my third day. I've been here seventy-two hours."

"I still don't understand."

"I thought I was going to be leaving today."

"What gave you that idea?"

The look on Dr. Larson's face filled me with dread.

"I heard people who try to commit suicide are only here for seventy-two hours." My heart sank as I watched his expression change.

Dr. Larson shook his head. "Each case is different and your case is very unusual. We have a lot of work to do before you're ready to leave."

The thought of having to go through another day like yesterday made me want to cry and filled me with anxiety.

"I think I'm ready to leave. What if I don't want to stay?"

"Nobody has explained this to you?" he asked.

A horrible sense of impending doom enveloped me. The room got even smaller. I shook my head. My voice had left.

"When you were in the hospital, your therapist, Lisa, worked closely with Dalila and Bob as your advocate. She helped Dalila complete the necessary steps to take over as your power of attorney. This means Dalila's responsible for all of your medical decisions and your care. Lisa advised her to retain a 5150 and Dalila followed her suggestion." He looked at me expectantly, as if I was somehow supposed to know what he was talking about. I was sure Rose knew what he was talking about, but I didn't have a clue.

"I don't understand."

"A 5150 is issued in order to confine a person to a psychiatric facility when they're a threat to either themselves or others. This allows a person to be hospitalized against their will. In many situations, it's only for seventy-two hours, but in certain cases, it can be extended for up to fourteen days. In your case, we felt you needed an extension."

"I have eleven more days here?"

"It's not quite so simple. If we feel you're ready to leave after that time period, then we'll discharge you. But, if we still feel you need to be kept safe then we can continue to hold you."

I wasn't leaving. I was trapped here. Ice water shot through my veins.

"I'm sure it feels overwhelming. You went through a lot yesterday. But we are all here to help you. How can I help you today?"

I shrugged my shoulders. We sat in silence for a few moments. It was unnerving.

"We're going to have to start talking about Emily. I think a good place for us to start would be to begin with easy things. Maybe not easy, but at least easier." He paused. "You did a significant amount of work with Lisa in therapy before, right?"

I nodded.

"How about if you tell me about what your therapy experience was like working with Lisa?"

"What do you want to know?"

"Anything you feel comfortable sharing."

I launched into talking about Lisa. It was the only time it'd been easy to talk to Dr. Larson. I told him how I was scared of her at first, but how that it wasn't unusual because back then, I was scared of anyone who wasn't Emily.

Lisa was different from everyone else who tried to help us. People who met us felt sorry for us and looked at us with pity, but Lisa never looked at us that way. Even Dalila and Bob did it, even though it wasn't intentional. Our individual sessions were the one place where I felt like a regular kid, and I never got to feel like a regular kid, especially not in the beginning. It was a welcome break not to be treated as so special and fragile.

Our sessions with Lisa followed the same structure every time. The first part consisted of cramming the Rooths, Emily, Lisa, and me into a room so small that it felt as if we were sitting on top of each other. I didn't like the family session time because Emily and I were expected to sit still and listen while the Rooths and Lisa talked about things I never understood. They spent the first few minutes talking before we began our activity. Even though there were lots of toys in the room, we could only play with the toys when it was a part of an activity we were all doing together. We went over and over charts, rules, and consequences. But afterward, Emily and I each had our special time with Lisa where we got to be alone in the room with her. In those early days, it was the only time I tolerated being away from Emily.

During my special alone time with Lisa, I didn't have to sit still or be quiet. I could play with whatever toys I chose and got to play how I wanted. Lisa played beside me and let me make up the rules. While we played, she talked to me about things or asked me questions, but she never made me speak if I didn't want to. She was content to sit in silence while we brushed the doll's hair or changed the stuffed animals' clothes.

I had a favorite doll that I fell in love with during our first session because of its beautiful mane of blond hair. I named her Annabelle and rarely made it through a session without picking up the brush and pulling it through Annabelle's hair from scalp to end. There was something soothing and calming about it for me. Whenever I started to get upset about something we were talking about, Lisa would notice my anxiety and hand me Annabelle and her brush. It never took long before I relaxed.

We stopped meeting with Lisa for sessions when we were eleven, but she never disappeared from our lives. She became more like a close family friend who occasionally came for dinner and was always at any special event we had at school.

In a few short years, when Emily spiraled into her depression, we started meeting with her again, but this time, the attention was focused on Emily rather than the two of us and we no longer had family sessions. Although Lisa always made time to check in with me for a few minutes to see how I was doing, the therapy she did happened with Emily. In the beginning, I was in the room with them, but eventually, once Emily felt comfortable enough, I'd sit in the waiting room doing my homework or reading a book while they met. I never asked what they talked about and Emily never told me. She seemed embarrassed to be meeting with Lisa so I never pushed her. It didn't matter to me what they talked about with each other, only that Emily was in better spirits when their sessions were over.

It was easy to talk to Dr. Larson about therapy with Lisa. The words flowed freely from my mouth and I didn't feel like I was under constant scrutiny to say the right thing. Maybe it was because I was talking about the past and the past didn't seem nearly as questionable or as frightening as what was going on right now.

"It sounds like you felt safe when you were in her office," he said after I finished telling him a story about how we used to play "Feelings Candyland" when we were kids and how we'd continued to play it even when we were teenagers. It was like regular Candyland, except each color represented a feeling, and when you landed on a particular color, you had to give an example of when you experienced the emotion.

I shrugged.

"Do you think it would be possible that therapy with me could represent the same kind of safety you experienced with Lisa?" he asked.

"Probably," I said.

There was no way he believed I was telling the truth. Therapy with Lisa was different from whatever kind of therapy we'd been doing. I'd felt comfortable with Lisa because she was the only person who hadn't looked at me like there was something wrong with me, which was not the case here. There was no mistaking that Dr. Larson thought something was wrong with me. My favorite part about therapy sessions with Lisa when I was a kid was being able to play. I was willing to play Feelings Candyland with Dr. Larson, but I was pretty sure it wasn't what he had in mind. But most importantly, I liked that she allowed me to be silent and never pushed me any further than I wanted to go. Dr. Larson didn't just push me, he shoved me right over the edge, and Lisa would never think of acting that way towards me.

"Good." He clasped his hands on the desk. "That makes me feel happy. I think a lot of progress could be made if you would allow yourself to open up in here."

He seemed pleased. Maybe he did believe me.

"I understand yesterday was a very intense day for you. I'm completely willing to talk about it if you'd like to do so, but I'm also open to letting you take some time to let it all sink in before we process it further. What do you think?"

What was I supposed to think? Yesterday he'd told me Emily had been dead for two years even though I'd been with her every day. The suggestion that she'd been dead when she was alive was unbelievable. What I didn't understand was why all of the doctors were lying to me. Why were they trying to get me to believe something that wasn't true? Dr. Heimer said they weren't testing me, but what else could they be doing? The only other possibility was that they were telling the truth, but that was unimaginable. There had to be another motive for them to lie to about Emily.

"I'm not feeling like talking about Emily."

"I can respect that. Anything you'd like to talk about? Any questions?"

I shook my head.

"I'm always here to answer any of your questions."

I was glad our session had ended. Unfortunately, tomorrow I would be back in the same chair, following the same routine. Maybe tomorrow I would have some questions for him, but not today. Today it was over and I couldn't get out of the room fast enough.

13

"I'm not leaving. I'm here for at least eleven more days."

"No way, really? I thought for sure they'd let you out in seventy-two hours. You seem perfectly fine to me." Rose reached over and gave me a quick squeeze. "Don't be mad, but I'm glad you're still here. I like having you around."

I couldn't bring myself to say the same thing even though I liked Rose. I couldn't handle more days. All the life had been sucked out of me. My brain felt like it would explode at any minute and spray pieces of me all over the linoleum floor. The day crawled. It was worse than any shift I'd had at my job. Our morning group was filled with Shelly's drama.

"I want to drink so bad," she said, skipping her long list of disorders.

"Why do you think you want to drink?" Mark asked. "What's the trigger?"

"There doesn't have to be a trigger. Maybe I just want to drink. Have you ever thought of that? This shit is stressful."

"Maybe you could learn a healthier way to deal with your stress." Mark looked around the room. "Does anyone have any ideas for Shelly about how she might be able to deal with her stress in a way that doesn't involve drinking?"

Shelly didn't wait for anyone to respond. "It's not like I can drink anyway even if I wanted to. I'm in the fuckin nut ward."

"Remember, we don't like to use that language."

"We don't use that language." She mocked him in the same way she mocked anyone who upset her.

"I think it's time to move on to someone else. I'm not willing to fight with you or talk to you when you're being disrespectful, Shelly. We've talked about this before. Tobi, let's continue checking in with you."

Tobi began but was interrupted by Shelly's loud sobbing.

"I'm so sorry. I don't know why I'm acting this way," she wailed, getting louder and louder as she went. "Nobody understands me. Nobody. For once, just once, I want someone to know what it's like to be me. Why doesn't anyone get it?"

Tobi reached out to her and tried to hug her.

"Don't touch me!" Shelly slapped her hand away.

Shelly's anger turned a switch on in the room, setting everyone in motion. Arlene started rocking rhythmically and pulling her hair. Rick and Darin became animated, as if someone had plugged them in. Tobi started sobbing as loudly as Shelly. Denise looked back and forth at each of them, trying to decide who she should comfort first and clearly afraid to make the wrong choice.

"Shut up. Shut up. Shut up." Doris joined the chorus.

Besides Matt, who didn't seem to notice the noise, Rose and I sat in silence. I watched as Mark worked frantically to keep things under control. I was the newest member and wondered if I'd have a role in the group after I'd been here a few more days. Would I respond to their agitation in the same way they responded to each other? How long would it be before I joined their ranks? What would happen to me in eleven more days?

I turned to Rose, who was watching them in the same way I was, but not participating. How had she managed to stay so normal through all of this? She'd been here the longest, so shouldn't she be the craziest? I was curious to know more of her story.

Mark ended group early once he'd managed to get everyone calmed down without having to call in the bouncers. I didn't know how he did it, but he'd methodically worked his way around the circle, talking in a hurried voice to each person while managing to sound like he wasn't hurried. It had worked.

I started asking Rose questions as soon as we got to our spot. I was surprised at how easily she talked to me about her stuff. Everyone here shared intimate details about their lives as if it wasn't a big deal.

"The only friends I ever had as a kid were imaginary ones," she said after she'd explained that she was an only child and had grown up without any other kids around.

"I'm a twin."

"No way, are you serious? That's so cool. Are you guys identical or fraternal?"

"We're identical."

"You guys must be super close. I'm so jealous."

"We are—were ..."

I didn't know how to talk about Emily.

"Is she going to come visit tonight with your family? Can I meet her?"

I shook my head. Rose's face fell.

"It's not because I don't want you to meet her. She's ... she's ... dead." My words got quieter and quieter as I spoke. *Dead* came out as a whisper.

Rose's eyes got huge. "Oh my God. When? How? My God, I feel so bad for you."

How was I supposed to answer her questions? The only thing I knew for sure was that Emily was dead. It was the one piece of information everyone agreed on.

"It's really complicated," I said.

My brain was still reeling from yesterday. I was trying to think logically about what Dr. Larson and the team had said, but my thinking was muddled like I had a brain full of cotton. I wanted to remember something. Anything that would help me comprehend what was happening, but it was like digging through quicksand. Each time I felt like a small hole might be opening up in my memory, it was quickly swallowed up by a feeling of panic.

"Were you guys close?"

"Extremely. She was my everything."

"I'd probably want to die too if I lost my twin."

"I do. Nothing feels right without her." A huge lump rose in my throat.

She moved closer to me on the couch. "I'm so sorry."

Her words were simple and matter of fact, but no one had acknowledged my loss and it touched me. Her words made their way into my center and for the first time in my life, tears started to fall down my cheeks in front of someone other than Emily. I wiped them away.

Rose put her arm around me. "It's okay to cry."

It was as if her words released a bag of rocks I'd been carrying, and I began to sob in a way I'd never sobbed before. Rose didn't say anything, just moved to hold me, and I fell into her embrace, sobbing against her collarbone. My guttural cries were from somewhere deep inside me. I didn't notice Shelly, Tobi, and Denise had come up behind us until I heard Tobi's voice.

"What's wrong with her?" she asked.

"Just leave us alone, please," Rose said in a soft voice. "Please ... Please."

I didn't know if they'd gone away or if they still were there, but I didn't care. Rose held me until my anguished cries became silent weeping and kept on holding me until the grief had gone beyond tears and sounds to find its way to my center, where it would never leave. I lay limp in her arms like a lifeless doll.

I'd never let anyone comfort me or see me cry besides Emily. Not even Thomas. I'd started swallowing my tears as a little girl when I figured out that the only way Mother knew she hurt me was if I cried and I was determined that no matter what Mother did to me, she would never know she'd hurt me. By the time I was five, I'd quit crying whenever she beat us. I never shed a tear or showed any emotion.

It was the same way with the special friends. Emily cried silently throughout their games, but I refused. I would watch what they did to me without making a sound or moving a facial muscle, and when it was over I put my clothes back on, took Emily's hand, and walked out of the room. Sometimes the pain was too great and I had to cry to release it, but I only did it in front of Emily or by myself. There'd been times where I'd been close to crying in front of someone else, but I'd always been able to pull my emotions back inside. Until today. Today was different. Something had shifted.

My intimacy with Rose compelled her to tell me more of her story. She spent the rest of the day sharing details about herself she'd never told anyone before, not even any of her previous therapists. She told me she never had anything to do with her dad. He'd left when she was only six months old to be with an eighteen-year-old girl who he'd been having an affair with during her mother's pregnancy.

"My mom said she was some itsy-bitsy little thing who was as dumb as a box of rocks and only interested in him for his money. But she was young and beautiful, which I guess is the only thing he cared about."

She'd never seen or talked to him since.

"Did your mom ever talk about him?" I asked.

"Nope. It was like he never existed. She called him my sperm donor whenever she talked to other people about him, and I think people believed she'd conceived me by in vitro fertilization all on her own."

She'd never gotten a Christmas gift or a birthday card from her dad. At least she knew who her dad was. I had no idea who my real dad was. Mother never talked about him. She didn't refer to him by any name, negative or otherwise.

Before we lived with the Rooths, Emily and I didn't know

what a dad was. We weren't aware you could have more than one parent. The Rooths had obtained our birth certificates during the adoption process. The line reserved for the father to sign acknowledging paternity was filled in as "unknown." When the Rooths' lawyers questioned Mother about our father, they were met with evasiveness every time. She told them she didn't know who our father was and didn't care to find out.

"Did she have boyfriends?" I asked, remembering the steady stream of men in Mother's life.

"Nope. I mean, I'm sure she had men she was sleeping with, but she never brought anyone home and she was definitely not in a serious relationship with anyone. Ever. She cared too much about herself and her job."

"What'd she do?"

"She was a lawyer." Rose rolled her eyes. "The worst kind of a lawyer. She defended criminals. It didn't matter to her what crimes they'd committed as long as they kept her bank account full. I don't get why she cared so much about the money because she never used it to do anything fun. Her whole life was work, work, work. I never saw her."

"Weren't you lonely?"

"You have no idea. It was awful living alone in a huge, empty house. Not to mention that it was so clean it was like living in a museum."

She described how her mom loved to collect antiques and artwork that she kept displayed around the house and Rose wasn't allowed to touch any of it. Even her bedroom was filled with collectible dolls that she couldn't do anything with except stare at them as they lined the shelves in her bedroom.

"My mom was so mad when I didn't go to college," she said to me after we got out of group in the afternoon. Unlike yesterday, when group ended early, today's group ran late because Mark spent the first half of it trying to get someone to confess to stealing one of the nurse's cell phones. Nobody ever confessed.

"Where'd you apply?" I asked.

"I didn't apply anywhere. It was the worst thing I could've done to her. She took it so personally." She added as an afterthought, "Maybe it was personal."

Even though her mom wasn't around, she had people to take care of her. She'd had nannies that she referred to as glorified babysitters since she was two weeks old. Once she'd turned thirteen, she was on her own and able to do whatever she wanted and the only thing she wanted to do was get skinny.

She'd been starving herself since she was nine years old. It took her mother a year to notice, even though the nanny had repeatedly expressed concern. She tried to kill herself for the first time when she was eleven by hanging herself in the closet. The belt broke and she fell to the ground. Instead of dying, she got her first cast. It wasn't long until her mother started sending her away to psychiatric facilities.

"How old were you when you got locked up for the first time?"

"Twelve. It was a lot different than here. It was all other girls with eating disorders. A bunch of rich snobs and they all hated me."

"How long were you there?"

"Six months and my mom didn't visit me once." Her face looked older than I'd ever seen it.

"It's okay to cry." I gave her the same permission she'd given me earlier in the day.

"I'm done crying over my mom." She said it with an air of finality, signaling that she was done with the conversation as well. "Did you know you can play Spades with two people? Wanna play until dinnertime?"

I tried to focus on the card game, but my mind couldn't keep track of anything. I was exhausted. I didn't think it was possible to be more tired than I'd been yesterday, but I was. I couldn't keep track of Rose's conversations any longer. All of her words started to blur together.

As soon as dinner was over, I told Felicia I didn't want to have any visitors and asked if I could go to bed early. I was surprised when she said yes. As I lay in my bed, having surpassed my seventy-two-hour limit, I felt the threat of impending doom hovering around me like it had since the morning. Not being able to go home had changed everything. It had brought with it the realization that this wasn't temporary and I wasn't going to be able to get out anytime soon. It meant I was going to have to stay alive, and in a way that I'd never had to live before. The prospect of living a new way of life was more terrifying than any anticipation of my death.

14

"I noticed you refused to see your visitors again last night," Dr. Larson began the following morning.

I nodded. The morning nurse told me Bob, Dalila, and Thomas had shown up together during visiting hours the night before. I was already asleep by the time they got there.

"Can I ask why?"

It was too much of an effort to sit in my room and try to think of things to say to them. I didn't want to see the pain and rejection in Dalila's eyes. The pain and rejection had been there for as long as we'd lived in their home. Now it was coupled with the immense grief of losing Emily, which made being around her unbearable, and I was still angry that they'd had Emily's funeral without me.

"It's just too hard right now," I said.

"Bob and Dalila seem to really care about you. Dalila calls twice a day to talk about how you're doing. She checks on your progress every morning and then again at night. She seems willing to do whatever it takes to help you."

It was one of the things that made her such an amazing mother. She'd devoted her life to us. She showered us with love and affection, kissing and hugging us whenever we were within her reach. She taught us how to function in the world and cared for our health with the skill of the most experienced nurse. Our list of medical problems was endless, and since we were so uncomfortable being poked and prodded, she learned how to handle them. She refused to allow the doctors to hold us down and restrain to give us our shots, so she learned how to give them to us herself under the guidance of our pediatrician. We were so sick during our first months with them, since we had the immune systems of infants, and she spent night after sleepless night holding cool washcloths to our foreheads, rubbing our aching bones, massaging Vicks VapoRub on our chests, and singing nursery rhymes.

She didn't waste any time enrolling us in all kinds of activities because she didn't want us to miss out on any more opportunities than we already had, and she made sure we got to try everything at least once. Neither of us learned to swim despite all the classes we took, but we got good in karate and liked anything having to do with art. She hired private tutors to work with us each afternoon, and it wasn't long before we were reciting our ABCs and counting to twenty like we'd always been doing it. Taking care of us was the equivalent of two full-time jobs, but she never complained. Dalila's love overflowed and seeped out of her pores, which only made our rejection more painful.

We didn't try to reject her on purpose. We were kind to her and never spoke a mean word to her. We were grateful for everything she did for us. For the first year, we said thank you every time she gave us food to eat until she finally convinced us we didn't have to. We were polite and respectful. We grew into well-mannered girls, and much to everyone's surprise, we began to thrive in our environment, despite our horrible beginnings. But we were unable to reciprocate her love and affection in a real, genuine way. We could do everything that was expected of us, but we couldn't give her the only thing she wanted—for us to return the love that a child has for their mother. We never could do it no matter how hard we tried.

"You made Dalila cry after supper again," Emily whispered

one night as we brushed our teeth before bed.

"I know," I said.

We still weren't sure whether we'd be able to stay with the Rooths. It seemed too good to be true. We lived in constant fear of doing something wrong and being sent back to Mother.

"I didn't mean to."

I'd spilled my milk at the dinner table that night and automatically flinched when Dalila jumped up to grab a towel from the sink.

"Oh, honey," she'd cooed as she wiped up the milk spilled down the front of me. "It was an accident. You don't have to be scared if you make a mistake."

She hugged me. I stiffened my body, preparing for the blows that used to come so quickly. I saw the look of hurt in her eyes before she pulled away. It was a look that was becoming more and more familiar with each passing day.

I felt Emily's eyes on me and turned to look at her. We didn't need to speak. Her eyes told me to get up and hug Dalila. Lately, we'd been talking about how important it was to Dalila for us to hug her. The last few weeks we'd worked hard to try to remember to do it. We reminded each other about it constantly. Emily was much better at remembering than I was and she gave better hugs.

I jumped up from my chair. I went up to Dalila at the sink and put my arms around her from behind, awkwardly hugging the back of her. I was uncomfortable, but I made myself keep the position because whenever she hugged us, she held on for a really long time. I counted to twenty before I let go and returned to my seat. When I turned around, I saw her wiping tears away from her eyes. Emily must've seen it too.

I didn't know how to describe my feelings about Dalila to Dr. Larson. He probably assumed there was something Dalila had done wrong that I hadn't told him, but that wasn't the case. She'd done everything right—always had. It was simply that neither of us felt a need to connect with a mother on an intimate level. The desire might have been there if we'd gotten taken away from Mother earlier, but we'd had to squelch our desires and impulses for maternal love for so long they no longer existed.

Both of us had wanted a mother, and we'd reached out to Mother time and time again for any morsel of love and attention she might throw our way. We were happy with any scraps she might have, but the closest she ever came to affection was patting us on the head like you might do to appease a puppy you didn't want to be bothered with. I couldn't count the number of times I'd reached my arms out to her to be picked up or hugged and she'd swatted me away like a fly that had accidentally gotten into the house when the door was left open.

Sometimes when she got home after being gone for a long time, she would come in to check on us. We would sob and try to cling to her when she leaned over the crib. She'd smack us and yell at us to lie down, so we learned to stop reaching for her. If we asked for anything or tried to crawl into her arms, she would grab us by our arms and fling us back into the crib as if we weighed nothing. Eventually, we were quiet and kept our hands to ourselves when she'd appear at the door, no matter how eager or desperate we might be. I didn't know when it happened or how old we were when we gave up trying to connect with Mother. I stopped first. It took Emily a lot longer to give up.

"I know you're right about Dalila. She's a great person. I'm pretty sure there's never been a better mother, but I can't connect with her like she wants me to." I didn't want Dr. Larson to think badly of her.

"Has it always been that way?"

I nodded.

"I understand."

He did?

"When children are young, there are critical periods of development where important tasks take place. One of the biggest tasks is the attachment to a primary caregiver. As psychologists, we know this is one of the most important things to happen during the first five years of life. Sometimes when it doesn't occur, children grow up unable to form attachments with other people, or they form what we call disorganized attachment. I think in your case, because you experienced such horrific abuse, it damaged your ability to form a reciprocal attachment to a maternal figure. It's also one of the reasons your attachment to Emily was so strong. Whereas most children form their most secure attachments with one or both of their parents early on, your instinctual need for attachment was developed with Emily." He cleared his throat. "What I'm trying to tell you is that it's not your fault. Your behavior and attitude towards Dalila makes perfect sense given your childhood."

It was the first time in all of our discussions that he'd given me helpful information and didn't just confuse me. Maybe there were other things he could help me with, like explaining what the doctors thought was wrong with me.

Yesterday, Rose had told me everybody had to have a diagnosis in order to be hospitalized. She told me the list of labels everyone gave in group after they said their name was their official diagnosis. I'd always thought Rick and Darin were the most messed up because they heard voices and talked to people who weren't there, but I was beginning to think Shelly and Tobi were equally screwed up. I was starting to wonder if they might be worse than Rick and Darin because they each had three or four diagnoses behind their names and I was more scared of Shelly than anyone else on the unit. She'd get the same look in her eyes I'd seen Mother get right before she was about to beat Emily with the coat hanger or the time she made me drink bleach when I asked for water. Rick and Darin were persecuted by demons who were real to them, even if we couldn't see them, but Shelly wasn't reacting to any voice in her head. She was reacting to the evil inside her like Mother.

Rose told me there was no way I didn't have a diagnosis of my own. She even had the medical book that the doctors used to diagnose and study our disorders. All we needed to do was to find out what my diagnosis was and we could look it up.

"Does my diagnosis have something to do with attachment?" I asked.

"Your diagnosis is very complicated," Dr. Larson said.

"What is it?"

"Is your diagnosis something that's important to you?"

It was a silly question. Of course it was. Who wouldn't want to know what was wrong with them?

"Yes, it is," I said.

"Why do you think it's important?"

"If you and a team of doctors have decided there's something wrong with me—that I have some kind of mental condition, or whatever you guys call it—I'd like to know what it is."

Was it a secret? Would any doctor not tell their patient that they had cancer?

"We can go over your diagnosis." He looked secretive about it, like he didn't want to tell me. Whatever door had opened during our conversation about Dalila was closing. "We've diagnosed you with a dissociative disorder. Dissociative disorders are on a spectrum much like most mental illnesses. They range from mildly impairing to severely impairing. Your disorder is what we would classify as being severely impairing because it's negatively impacting your life on multiple levels. It's severe. You represent a unique case and something we haven't seen. Your core feature is dissociation, but you don't meet the criteria for some of the more common dissociative disorders that we see. The particular name for your disorder is a Dissociative Disorder Not Otherwise Specified."

I had no idea what he was talking about.

"What's a dissociative disorder?"

"It varies. And it all depends on which particular disorder you have. But you can have one and function in your environment.

Lots of people do. You can be a fully functioning person but have no memory of doing certain things. The person becomes fragmented from themselves in some way. They disconnect or disassociate from themselves and the environment around them."

He still wasn't making any sense. He didn't seem very sure of himself. I wasn't sure he knew what he was talking about or trying to explain.

"Maybe this will help. Have you ever lost periods of time? Has there ever been an occasion where you were awake and did something you weren't able to remember you'd done or where you were?"

I nodded my head. Maybe there was a piece of truth in his jumbled mess of words, because I did lose pieces of time and didn't know why. It started when I lived with Mother. There were times when the special friends would take me into the bedroom and I wouldn't remember anything that happened while we were there. I would be aware of going into the bedroom, but the next thing I knew I was back in the living room watching TV as if nothing had happened. But my disappearing wasn't only with the special friends. Even when we lived with the Rooths, there were times when I did things I didn't remember doing. It took me a long time to work up the nerve to tell Emily about it. I didn't talk to her about it until we were in high school.

"Can I ask you a question?" I'd started out the conversation while we were walking to the bus stop. We'd reached the point where it was no longer cool to have Dalila drop us off in the front of the school building.

"Of course," she said.

"Remember a few weeks ago when you got so mad at me for talking to Chrissy after class and we got in that huge fight?"

Emily rolled her eyes and nodded. "Of course I remember. And we're still not talking to her."

Emily struggled in math. She always had, and the more difficult it got, the harder she struggled. At the beginning of the quarter when we started algebra, they divided everyone in our grade into specialized math classes based on ability. The teachers tried to pretend it wasn't what they were doing, but we all knew it was exactly what they were doing. Emily was placed in the class with other people who struggled with math, but unlike Emily, who struggled in math but passed other subjects, the kids she was placed with failed nearly every subject. They were the ones who'd been teased since elementary school for not being smart. By the time we'd gotten to high school, they were popping pills, skipping school, and had a hardened exterior towards everything related to school. It was the first time Emily had been placed with them and she felt like a loser.

Chrissy singled her out in the hallway after the class when we'd all been given the lists. "Looks like you're going to be going to class with all the morons," she sang out while her two closest friends stood next to her smirking.

Emily glared and said nothing.

"It's too bad. I got placed in the accelerated math class. Guess we know who will be going to college and who's going to be stuck flipping burgers at McDonald's."

Everyone laughed and Emily turned bright red. That night she made me swear not to speak to Chrissy again. It was an easy promise to make. Hurting Emily was the same as hurting me. However, a few days later, Emily had found me in the hallway having a conversation with Chrissy and her friends. She'd blown up on me for breaking my promise not to talk to her. The problem was that I didn't remember talking to Chrissy. I remembered leaving the lunchroom and the next thing I knew I was in World Studies. I'd lost two periods. Rather than tell Emily I didn't remember anything about it, I told her Chrissy was trying to be nice and figure out a way to apologize to Emily for what she'd said. My deception had eaten away at me until I had to tell Emily the truth.

"The weird thing is that I still don't remember talking to

Chrissy in the hallway. I really don't. I don't have any memory of it. But that's not the first time something like that has ever happened. It happens a lot. Does it ever happen to you?"

Emily threw her arms around me and gave me a big hug. "Oh my God, I had no idea it happened to you, too. I should've said something to you about it. I always wanted to. I tried to, but I felt super weird about it. The same thing used to happen to me all the time when we were younger." I held her hand as we walked, a sense of relief washing over me. "Do you remember when Bob used to catch me stealing his lunch all the time?"

I nodded. Back in the days when Emily couldn't get enough to eat no matter how much food was around and all of the cupboards and the refrigerator were locked, she'd started stealing food. She'd gotten busted on more than one occasion with the leftover remnants of sandwiches and bags of potato chips under her bed from the lunches Dalila prepared for Bob each day. She always denied it, but nobody ever believed she didn't do it. Not even me.

"See, I knew I did it. Just like all of you knew I did it. But I swear to God, I didn't think I'd done it. I never remembered taking one of his lunches. Not one. Believe me, Bethy, I totally get it."

We shared our stories about losing time with each other, especially if one of them scared us, and it became another thing we had in common, but I'd never told anyone else. No one had asked me about it until now.

"Losing time is a big part of your diagnosis. Your psyche is disconnected and fragmented into different parts. Sometimes in dissociative states people function very differently from the way that is typical for them. When this state becomes very severe, some people develop other states of being or might even act as if they're a different person."

For a moment he had me, but he was losing me again. My psyche was fragmented?

"What makes a person have a dissociative disorder?" I asked.

"It almost always stems from severe trauma. Many people

would experience the extreme disassociation like what I'm describing from experiencing the type of horrific neglect and abuse you experienced as a child. However, you demonstrated an unbelievable amount of resiliency in managing to recover from it within a supportive and nurturing environment. When it comes to resiliency, we know that certain factors serve as protective factors that can help predict how well an individual will respond to trauma. In your case, I believe the reason you were able to demonstrate such a high level of resiliency is because Emily served as your protective factor. It explains why her death caused you to split from reality."

"I still don't get it."

I wanted to get it, though. I needed to understand what they thought was wrong with me.

"Let me try to explain this another way. Your early childhood trauma predisposed you to developing a dissociative disorder, but because of your relationship with Emily, you were able to retain a measure of stability. When she died, it was more than your frail psyche was able to handle, so instead of dealing with the reality of her death, you continued to live as if she was alive."

"She's really been dead for two years?"

"Yes. I can absolutely assure you Emily has been dead for two years."

"And this isn't a test? You're not trying to trick me?"

"On the contrary, I'm trying to help you." He paused, searching my eyes for clues. "I'm not going to lie to you. Your level of impairment is severe. I've never seen someone who was able to be so gravely disconnected from reality, but still able to maintain a relatively stable and normal life in the way that you did."

If what he said was true, then I didn't know how I'd done it either. Emily still felt real to me. She was as real to me today as she'd been two weeks ago. I wished we'd studied dissociative disorders in my Introduction to Psychology course. We hadn't covered anything like what he was describing.

"Why don't we save the rest of this for our next session? We are almost out of time," Dr. Larson said. "I'm very pleased with your progress today."

15

I couldn't wait to look up the diagnosis Dr. Larson gave me in Rose's book and see if we could make sense of it together. I wanted to do it in private but unfortunately, it wasn't possible because I was still being followed. I was the only one on the unit being followed. The team had assured me the restriction would be lifted as soon as they were convinced I was no longer a threat to myself or anyone else. It was unsettling that they still thought I was a threat, but there wasn't anything I could do about it.

We got lucky because both Polly and Felicia were off. The two of them didn't miss anything, especially not Polly. There were times when Polly looked like she wasn't paying attention, but she always knew what was going on. My substitute babysitter was the hippy-looking guy who'd been there a few nights ago. His name was James and his hippy-looking appearance wasn't solely about the way he dressed. He had the droopy bloodshot eyes to match.

Rose pulled out a big, thick gray book. It was a huge textbook. She handed it to me. The front read: *Diagnostic and Statistical Manual of Mental Disorders*. I was shocked by how massive it was. I thumbed through it quickly and discovered it had over nine hundred pages. How was it possible that there were nine hundred pages of mental disorders?

I was holding the Holy Grail in my hands. For the first time since my ordeal started, I was going to have an idea of what they thought was wrong with me. I would be privy to some of the knowledge they possessed. It gave me a small sense of control over my situation.

"Crazy, huh?" Rose giggled. "You should see your face. You look just like I felt." She grabbed the book back from me. "Let me show you what they think is wrong with me." She flipped through it easily, coming to rest on a page I was sure she'd visited hundreds of times before. She pointed to a black heading. "Here I am."

The bold black letters read:

Diagnostic criteria for 307.1 Anorexia Nervosa.

"What does the number mean?" I asked.

She shrugged. "No idea. I've asked different doctors and they all say it's for classification purposes. Whatever that means. Who knows?"

Underneath the heading were lettered lists of what I assumed were symptoms. There were four criteria and as I read through, I was surprised at how accurately the book described Rose. I did a mental checklist on the way down.

"Refusal to maintain body weight at or above a minimally normal weight for age and height."

Check.

"An intense fear of gaining weight or becoming fat, even though underweight."

Absolutely.

"Denial of the current low body weight."

Check. She really did think she was fat and even though she'd already had a heart attack, she laughed it off.

"The absence of at least three consecutive menstrual cycles."

"Do you get your period?" I asked.

She beamed proudly, "Nope. Not for almost two years. How lucky am I?"

Should've known. Another check.

"Is it dangerous?"

"Not really. They always try and make a big deal out of it, but basically I can't get pregnant, which would be great birth control if I was actually having sex." She slapped her thighs. "But c'mon, who's lining up to have sex with these big ole' things?"

"Do you really think your thighs are big?" I asked. "Your legs are the size of my arms. They might even be smaller."

She punched my arm. "Shut up. You don't see me naked. They are flabby, trust me. I can pinch an inch."

"Of skin! There's no way you have an ounce of fat on you. You have to have skin and it has to be elastic. That's all you're pulling."

"Whatever you say, Doc. Someday when you don't have to be followed around wherever you go, I'll show you what I look like naked. You'll see what I'm talking about then."

"Deal." I was excited about looking up my disorder, given the accuracy of hers. I handed the book back to her. "How do we find mine?"

"Okay, tell me again what he said you have."

I recited our conversation to her again like I'd done earlier when I came out of my session. The name of my disorder was permanently embedded in my mind. As I talked, she moved through the book with the ease of a professional.

"Here it is," she said. "I—"

I snatched the book from her. I'd been waiting for this moment all day. My eyes quickly scanned the page and landed on the bold heading:

300.15 Dissociative Disorder Not Otherwise Specified.

However, my disorder wasn't as neatly laid out in a concise list of symptoms like hers. Mine began with a small paragraph that read:

"This category is included for disorders in which the predominant feature is a dissociative symptom (i.e., disruption in the usually integrated functions of consciousness, memory, identity, or perception of the environment) that does not meet criteria for any specific dissociative disorder."

It went on to list six examples. The six examples used words I'd never heard of before. Things like "derealization" and "depersonalization." It listed "dissociative trance disorder" and the more detailed explanation used words from another language called "amok" and random letters stacked together, making a foreign word called "piblotkog."

"This doesn't make any sense. It might as well be Spanish."

"Let me see," Rose said, taking the book back from me. "Sometimes it takes time to figure it out."

She read through and crinkled her forehead as she went along. She burst out laughing suddenly and in a snooty voice recited, "Possession trance involves replacement of the customary sense of a personal identity by a new identity attributed to the influence of a spirit, power, deity, or other person. So, it sounds like you're possessed by the devil."

"Shut up." I leaned toward her to examine the text with her. "It's not just me, then, huh? This doesn't make any sense to you either?"

"Nope. Not at all. Some of the stuff in here is pretty confusing, though, so I'm not all that surprised. I was hoping you'd get an easy one."

I hoped Dr. Larson would explain it to me if I asked him, but it was unlikely. He seemed much more interested in asking questions than he was in giving answers. Even when he did give answers, they didn't answer the question asked. Like yesterday during the team meeting when I'd asked when I could stop being on a one-to-one restriction, and he'd answered that it depended without explaining what it depended on.

Rose had helped me more than Dr. Larson or any of the team doctors. For all of their education, the doctors didn't seem to have a clue about how to talk to people. They weren't like Lisa. She knew how to talk to people.

My heart sank. I'd been so excited to learn my diagnosis. I'd thought it was going to help things begin to make sense. Even if I wasn't able to put all of the pieces together, at least it would've been a place to start. I felt like crying.

What would Thomas think? He was always so logical and practical. What would he say if I told him about everything happening in here? How much did he already know? I felt the first pangs of missing him.

My reason for not seeing him during visiting hours was different than my feelings about avoiding Bob and Dalila. For the most part, I blamed myself for my situation, but there was a small piece that blamed him. If I hadn't fallen for him and been so pressured by him to meet Emily, none of this would've happened. It wasn't logical or rational, but I still felt the same way.

More than anything else, though, I was embarrassed. I was sure his image of me was shattered. I couldn't imagine what he must think of me now. He had to think I was some kind of freak. But, if anyone could look past something like this it was him. Was there a possibility he could find a way to look at me like he did before? I didn't expect him to still want to be with me, but he'd been a good friend and we could talk about anything. I missed our talks. Even if we couldn't go back to the way things were, there might be a chance we could still be friends and talk like we used to.

Over the last year, Thomas had become my support. Whenever I was excited about something, he was the person I told, or if someone made me angry at school, I couldn't wait to be able to give him the details. Even though I couldn't talk about what things were like for me at home with Emily, he had a way of making me feel like everything was going to be okay. He told me everything was going to be all right if I didn't get an A on a test or made me laugh about not making any sales at work.

As hard as it was for me to admit to myself, Thomas had slowly begun to take Emily's place as my confidante. I couldn't remember the last time I'd told her about a bad day I'd had at work or school and she'd offered me encouragement. Everything was about her and her moods. I stepped delicately around them and they dictated everything I said or did. I'd lost the Emily I knew a long time ago and I'd been mourning her disappearance for years.

It was one of the reasons it'd been so easy to fall for Thomas. I wasn't able to acknowledge it then, but the truth was that I'd been lonely. If Dr. Larson was right and I'd been creating Emily for the last two years, then why did I make her sick and give her such a miserable existence? If I imagined her because I couldn't let go of her, then why did I invent a scenario that suffocated us both and left me feeling so alone?

I wanted to talk to Thomas about it. I didn't expect him to be able to answer any of my questions, but it would be nice to get his perspective on what was happening. I told myself I was calling him because I wanted his help, but more than anything else, I just wanted to hear his voice.

16

I'd been in the psych ward for five days and hadn't made a phone call, which was unusual because everyone fought to use the phone. There were only two on the unit and there was a ten-minute limit, so somebody was always yelling at somebody else to get off the phone because their time was up. Even Darin and Rick used the phone. I couldn't imagine who they talked to, but they used it.

During the week, there were only two scheduled phone times, but it was Sunday and the phones were free on Sundays until lights out at ten. There wasn't much of a routine on Sunday because the regular doctors didn't work. They were on call if there was an emergency that the regular staff members couldn't handle. I breathed a sigh of relief to learn that the team wasn't there on Sundays either. We had something called occupational therapy instead of regular group with Mark.

A woman named Teresa, dressed in yoga pants as if she'd come right from the gym, took us into a room resembling an elementary art classroom. Everywhere you looked there were plastic boxes with miscellaneous craft materials inside. Glitter, fabric, and glue littered the two long tables lining the center of the room.

"All right, everyone," Teresa said, beginning to pull out boxes and plopping them onto the table. "Express yourselves. Really try to get in tune with your feelings and release them here."

She began digging into the boxes and pulling out crayons, colored pencils, stencils, and paintbrushes, handing them to Rick and Darin. Tobi plopped down next to Teresa. Shelly and Denise took a seat next to her.

"I'm working on my god box again," Tobi announced.

"Great idea," Teresa said. "I'll get it. Shelly, do you want yours too?"

Shelly nodded.

Teresa reached up to a shelf and pulled down two small boxes covered in construction paper and magazine clippings. Shelly and Tobi got busy. Doris wasn't with us. She'd flipped out while she was getting dressed and was still recovering from her shot. It usually took her a long time to come back to life after they'd put her out. Arlene was missing too. She'd been sick for the last two days and hadn't left her room.

"Arlene's faking being sick so she doesn't have to go to the state hospital," Shelly said at breakfast. "She knows the doctors are going to send her to the state hospital, so she's going to pretend like she has some terrible disease so they won't send her, but they'll send her. It's not going to work. It never does. The last time I was here they sent a guy with AIDS to state. If they sent him, they'll send anyone."

I didn't trust much of what Shelly said, but I was pretty sure she was right about Arlene going to the state hospital. She'd pulled so much of her hair out that she looked like she was going through chemotherapy. None of the medications the doctors forced her to take made a difference. She'd started to have accidents too, and became hysterical if any of the nurses tried to point it out or clean her up. It made the group room smell terrible.

I looked at Rose and shook my head as Denise followed suit and declared she wanted to make a god box too. Rose rolled her eyes back at me and mouthed, "Of course she does."

I had no idea what a god box was, but the mention of God

made me think about Thomas again. Rose and I took our seats, not picking up any of the art materials. Teresa didn't seem to mind that we weren't doing artwork.

"I'm going to call Thomas today," I said.

"Who's Thomas?" she asked.

"My boyfriend, I guess. At least he was. I haven't talked to him much since I got here."

"What? You have a boyfriend? I'm totally jealous. Tell me all about him. Everything. I want to know." She bounced up and down on her chair.

"There isn't much to tell, really. His name is Thomas. We've been going out for a year. We met at work."

"And then? I want the good stuff. The drama. Did he cheat on you? Is he being supportive of you being sick?"

"There really isn't drama. He's my first boyfriend who ever lasted more than a few months. He's probably the nicest guy you'll ever meet. I was super into him before the accident." The accident was how Rose and I referred to what happened before I got to the hospital.

"Was the sex good at least?"

Thomas and I never had sex. I was a twenty-year-old virgin and not because of a deep religious conviction to save myself for marriage like what kept him from doing it. I didn't like sex stuff. Never had. I wanted to like it because people were supposed to, but my body froze.

"You mean you don't think it's creepy I'm still a virgin?" Thomas asked after he'd told me about his virginity.

It was many movie nights into our relationship. It was my turn to pick and he'd pretended to suffer through another one of my romantic comedies even though I was pretty sure he secretly liked them.

"No."

It was unusual, but I didn't think it was creepy. I debated whether I should tell him my status during the car ride back to my house. I'd never told another guy I was a virgin. I always pretended I wasn't, but I took a risk with Thomas.

"I'm a virgin, too," I announced.

"You are? Really?"

He'd spent the last twenty minutes of the drive explaining his religious convictions to me before making his proclamation, but I didn't share his convictions, so my announcement was shocking.

"Can I ask why?"

"I don't like sex."

"How do you know if you've never had it?"

"I've done other things."

I'd let boys explore my body in high school. I'd let them grope and poke and prod at me. They'd grabbed my chest and squeezed and pulled till it hurt while they groaned with excitement. I'd let them play around inside me with their hands, but their insertions gave me as much enjoyment as inserting a tampon.

"And you didn't like any of it? They must not have known what they were doing." He said it with the air of confidence that assumed he did.

I'd heard it before. Every guy I dated said the same thing.

"I think I'm numb from the waist down."

I'd never felt a thing. Unlike me, Emily loved sex and couldn't get enough of it. She'd do it with strangers and I could never understand what she got out of it. She would tell me in great detail how it was supposed to feel and she'd even convinced me to try masturbating. I'd done it exactly how she instructed me, but still felt nothing. I might as well have been playing with my belly button.

Thomas belonged to the "everything but sex" club. He may not have been able to be the one who took away my virginity, but he was determined to be the one who gave me my first orgasm. I liked kissing him, though, because he was a great kisser. Guys I'd dated before rushed by kissing like it was a prerequisite to be checked off the list before they got to what they really wanted.

Thomas liked kissing as much as I did and he wasn't in a hurry to get somewhere else. I refused to take my pants off so we dry humped like teenagers and my first orgasm came as a total surprise during one of our sessions. Fully clothed. I didn't tell him it had happened for a month because I felt so silly about it. When I finally did, I was bright red because it seemed too juvenile, but he was elated. He didn't care how I'd gotten off. He was just glad to be the one to get me there. It wasn't long after and he followed suit. We had better fully clothed simulated sex than some people have real sex.

"We never had sex, but we fooled around and it was pretty good."

"What are you going to say to him when you call?" she asked. "Are you going to ask him to come today?"

I hadn't thought about asking him to come.

"Can he come today?" I asked.

"Yep. On Sundays you can have visitors anytime you like. They can even eat with you if you want them to. They have to either bring their own food or order a tray from the hospital."

I hurried to the phone as soon as occupational therapy was over. I was afraid I'd lose my nerve if I didn't do it right away. I was the first in line, and before I knew it, I was punching his number into the phone. Besides Bob and Dalila's phone number, his cell phone number was the only one I knew by heart. My heart pounded as it rang. My throat was dry and my palms were wet on the receiver. I kept wiping them off. I was about to hang up before his voicemail came on when he answered.

"Hello?" he said breathlessly.

"Hi ... it's ... it's Elizabeth."

"Oh, hey, hi." I heard the excitement in his voice. "I've been thinking about you. I'd say praying for you, but I know how mad you get when I say that." He laughed nervously. The air stretched out between us.

"How's work?" I asked.

"It's good. The same old stuff. You know. People still ask me about you. You know how they all like to gossip."

"Uh-huh."

"I don't tell them anything. Everyone thinks you went on medical leave or something. I'm sure Josh would give you your job back when you get out."

"Cool." Another long pause. "How are you?"

"I'm good. Thanks for asking." His voice was so polite. "How are you?"

"I'm good too."

More dead air. This time, it lasted longer.

"I'm so glad you called. I wanted to call or write you a letter, but Lisa said I should give you your space and that you'd get in touch with me when you're ready. I'm so glad you called. I already said that." He laughed nervously. "I hope you're not mad that I talked to Lisa. It's just that she's been so helpful."

"It doesn't bother me."

"Good. I really like talking to her. I couldn't stand talking to that Dr. Larson dude. I felt like a complete idiot every time I talked to him. I mean, would it kill him to act like a regular person?"

I laughed. It felt good to laugh.

"I'd really like to be able to visit you again. I miss you."

"Do you? I mean with all this stuff? With me being so crazy."

"I love you more than I did before."

My heart melted. He still loved me even though I was in a psych ward.

"Can I come see you? Please? Just me. I won't bring Bob or Dalila. We don't even have to talk. We can just sit together. I'd love to sit next to you."

"Yes, please come."

17

I sat next to Thomas on my bed with a stranger on guard in the doorway, more nervous than I was on our first date. I'd started crying when he walked onto the unit. I'd cried in front of Rose and now I'd cried in front of Thomas too. I was afraid to open my mouth and say anything in case I started crying again.

"You look better than the last time I saw you." He smiled.

"You do too." I smiled back. The dark circles under his eyes were gone.

We sat without touching. He stared at me while I stared at the whitewashed wall in front of me. My skin felt hot like I might have a fever.

"I'm glad you finally let me visit. I was thinking about ways to get myself locked up in here so I'd get to see you." He reached for my hand. I entwined my fingers with his like we used to do in his Honda during our lunch breaks. His hands were as sweaty as mine. I still hadn't found my voice. "Bob and Dalila seem like really nice people."

I nodded.

"Bob kind of reminds me of a skinny Santa Claus."

"He does. You're totally right."

It felt good to sit next to him. I moved closer so our thighs touched. "I'm sorry for everything. All of this. And everything before. I didn't know what was going on. I still don't. I mean—"

He put his hand up to my lips. "Shh, it's okay. Really, it is. You don't have to try to explain everything right now. I understand. I get it. I do, and I know it's going to be okay."

I wasn't sure it was ever going to be okay but it felt good to hear him say it.

"Can I bring you something? Anything?" he asked.

"A key out of here."

It was a terrible joke, but we laughed anyway to break the tension.

"Look, I'd be totally freaking out right now if I were you. I completely understand not wanting to have to worry about me and our relationship, but can I still be your friend?"

A huge lump rose in my throat. "I could really use a friend right now."

I started to cry again. I was hurting and no longer cared if anyone saw it. He took me in his arms and I clung to him like drowning people seize life preservers. He held me for a long time until the tears subsided. He didn't bother to speak because there weren't any words to fix what was happening. We stayed locked in our embrace, talking about school and work until it was time for him to leave.

He came back Monday night for visiting hours. It was nice and similar to being in his dorm room, except the shoe in the doorway was replaced with a person on a chair. I was so used to having a shadow that whoever it was seemed more like a statue than a living being. I regaled him with stories about the unit. He laughed so hard he got tears in his eyes when I told him about Doris declaring she was going to kill her mother during my first group therapy session and agreed that it was ridiculous how Shelly and her gang dressed up every day. He brought me a Subway sandwich loaded with extra cheese and jalapeños just the way I liked it. It was the first piece of nonhospital food I'd had in almost two weeks. He might as well have brought me filet mignon. I was sad when it was time for him to leave.

"I brought you something," he said, reaching for his backpack next to the bed.

"Really?"

I still remembered the first present he gave me. It was for my birthday and he'd given me Maya Angelou's *Phenomenal Woman*. This time, he pulled out a thick blue folder and handed it to me.

"I hope this doesn't make you mad. I can't imagine how you must feel, but I think if I was you, I'd feel really alone. It got me thinking and I started doing some research. I found an online support forum for people who've lost their twins. I thought it was pretty amazing. It's all people like you who've had their twin die. They talk about their experiences and tell personal stories and stuff. I thought you might like to read them, so I used up half my ink printing out a bunch of it." His face broke into his familiar wide smile. I'd missed it. "I hope you read it. It might help you not feel so alone."

I took the folder and placed it on my lap, setting my hands on top of it. "Thank you."

Rose, Tobi, Shelly, and Denise stared at him as he left. They'd missed him yesterday because Tobi and Shelly were visiting with their families. Denise had been sleeping and it was close enough to dinner that Rose was already in her private dinner session. She'd been so bummed that she didn't get to see him. He was barely out the locked door before they started squealing.

"Oh my God, he's so cute," Rose said.

"Totally," Denise said.

Shelly bounced up and down next to Tobi. "How'd it go?"

"It was nice. It went really well." I'd give Rose all the details when we were by ourselves, but I didn't trust the others. The TV was on and everyone was crowded around it. "I didn't even know that thing worked."

The rest of the group was watching an old Tom Hanks movie. Someone had even popped popcorn. I wasn't interested in the movie, but wanted to shift their attention from me because I couldn't wait to see what was inside my folder. We joined the group and I started reading while they watched the movie.

The pages were filled with people like me who'd lost a twin. There were hundreds of them. I devoured the stories as if I was a starving child who'd just been given their first meal. Their stories were heartbreaking and I related to the depths of their despair. It was like someone had crawled into my brain and typed the script. Every person talked about feeling like half of a person without their twin. They described feeling like they were the same soul in a different body and struggling to go on without their other part. Some of them couldn't move forward. Others refused to. Many of them talked about contemplating suicide. A few of them had tried. I started to cry as I read about a man who tried to kill himself after losing his brother to a heroin overdose. The comments were filled with support from fellow twins who'd turned to thoughts of suicide after losing their twin.

I was fascinated with their descriptions of the things they'd done to try to keep their twin alive. Some talked to their twin in the mirror. Others began dressing like them. A seventeen-year-old girl shared how she'd always worn her hair long and her sister had always kept her hair short, but she cut all of her hair off in the weeks following her sister's death. There were those who kept a journal or a diary where they wrote letters to their lost twin and then pretended to be the other twin writing back.

Tears streamed down my cheeks. I was no longer alone. I wasn't a freak for pretending Emily was still alive. Everyone like me had been unable to deal with the weight of losing their twin and done something to keep them alive until they were strong enough to start living without them. I still didn't know how I'd done it or how any of it worked, but I was beginning to see it was possible I had. My brain couldn't wrap itself around the enormity of the details and I didn't know if I'd ever be at a place where I could imagine living without Emily, but I was moving in the direction of acknowledging that Emily had been dead for two years. That night I fell asleep hugging the papers to my chest as if they were a teddy bear.

18

"I see you've been having visitors," Dr. Larson said on Tuesday morning as soon as our session began. He smiled.

It was the first time I'd seen him smile. It didn't fit his face.

"Not visitors. Just Thomas."

"How'd it go? Did you enjoy your time?" he asked.

I blushed and looked down. "It went good."

"I have some good news for you. During our team meeting this morning, we decided to remove you from one-on-one supervision," he said. "We no longer feel you need to be monitored so closely."

I wanted to clap. I felt better than when I won the spelling bee in fourth grade. I was so proud of myself. I had a long way to go down whatever strange road I was on, but I'd made some kind of progress in the team's eyes. I didn't know what I'd done to show them I was no longer a threat to myself, but I didn't care. It only mattered that I'd made a step forward.

"I thought we might be able to get back to the discussion we were having on Friday about your diagnosis. Did you find any helpful information about it?"

Should I tell him about Rose's book? Was it okay that she had it?

"I looked it up in a book and it didn't make much sense."

"Did you look it up in the *DSM*?" he asked.

"No, I don't think so. It was some statistical book with nine hundred pages of mental disorders."

He smiled again. It looked as out of place the second time. "That's the book. The *Diagnostic and Statistical Manual of Mental Disorders*. We call it the *DSM* for short."

"Was I not supposed to?" I asked.

"I figured you would. Most patients get better at reading it and finding their way through it than some of us. It's very normal to be curious about your diagnosis and there's no way to Google it in here." He'd smiled and now he'd tried to make a joke. It was the first time he seemed human. "Do you have any questions after reading it?"

"I didn't get it. Rose's list seemed so clear-cut and described her almost perfectly. Mine sounded like I was possessed by the devil or something."

"Dissociative disorders can be very confusing even for us. We classify disorders according to symptoms. There's a bunch of disorders that have dissociation as their common symptom. In order to have a disorder, you've got to meet a certain number of criteria. For example, let's take Rose and anorexia. I bet she met all the symptoms listed, right?"

I nodded.

"Because she has all the symptoms listed, we're able to feel confident in giving her the diagnosis of anorexia. We diagnosed you with Not Otherwise Specified. This is where it gets confusing. Basically, NOS means you have many of the symptoms of a particular disorder, but you don't have enough of the symptoms present for us to feel confident diagnosing you with the disorder. Unfortunately, your case gets even more complicated because you have symptoms that could meet the criteria for many of the dissociative disorders, but you don't meet criteria to have any one particular disorder. As we go along, we might find more information that allows us to be able to narrow down a better diagnostic picture for you, but for now, I'm comfortable with your diagnosis. Does any of that help you?"

"It does. Thanks."

Not really. It was still confusing.

"Good. I'm glad." He paused for a minute. "I'm really excited for you to begin reestablishing your relationship with Thomas. I think it's going to be really helpful for your treatment. Have you given any thought as to whether you're ready to see Bob and Dalila?"

Thomas told me they called him every day to see if he'd heard from me or if I'd allowed him to visit me. He'd avoided their calls for the last two days because he didn't want to tell them he'd seen me and he wasn't going to lie and pretend like he hadn't. I was sure they'd call again today and didn't know how much longer he could dodge their calls.

"I guess I probably should," I said. I didn't want to put the responsibility of telling them on Thomas. It wasn't fair.

"You're not going to be able to stay in the hospital forever. Part of our goal is to get you ready to be discharged, and when we discharge you, we want to make sure you have a support network in place. I think Bob and Dalila would be a great support network for you if you'd allow them the opportunity."

"I don't know if I'm ready."

"What if you called Dalila instead of seeing her? Do you think you could call her and try to talk to her at least? Or how about Bob? Would it be easier if you talked to him?"

If I had to call one of them, I would rather call Bob, but I never called him because he didn't like to talk on the phone and it always hurt Dalila if I showed a preference towards Bob.

"I could call Bob, but then I'll have to deal with Dalila being hurt because I called him instead of her."

"Dalila's an adult and she's responsible for her own feelings. Not you. If you want to call Bob instead of her, then it's perfectly acceptable for you to call Bob."

"Really?"

Dalila and Bob were a unit and I never considered having unique relationships with them. Thinking about calling Dalila made me feel heavy and depressed, but the thought of calling Bob made me feel good. It was similar to how I felt when I called Thomas.

"Yes. There's nothing wrong with it. There's nothing wrong with preferring to talk to Bob instead of Dalila. Maybe the two of you could start figuring out how you'd like your relationship to be."

We spent the rest of our session discussing what I would say to Bob when I called and what I could talk to him about that wouldn't make me feel uncomfortable, but I wasn't all that interested or focused. I was too excited to tell Rose about the twins' stories I'd read to pay attention to our session. I'd been too emotional to explain things to her last night, but this morning I couldn't wait to fill her in on what I'd found out.

"You okay?" she asked as soon as I sat down next to her once my session with Dr. Larson had ended.

"I'm okay."

"Well, that's great. Really great," Rose said. She turned away from me.

I looked towards her and noticed her lower lip was quivering.

"What's wrong?"

She shook her head. "It's really stupid. I'm being dumb. Just ignore me."

"Did your weigh-in go bad?" I asked. She was always in a terrible mood after her weigh-ins.

She laughed and shook her head again. "I told you. I'm just being dumb, but I thought you were like me."

Like her? Like her how? I raised my eyebrows. "I don't get it."

"I don't have any friends."

She never used the phone and didn't get any visitors. I'd been here for a week and no one had come to visit her. Now it was my turn to laugh.

"You think I have friends? I've had one friend my whole life and that's it. You're the first girlfriend I've had who wasn't Emily."

"I told you I was being stupid. But even the nutjobs get phone calls." She motioned to the rest of the group scattered in their respective positions around the room, hanging out. "And you had your boyfriend here. A real boyfriend. I've never had one."

"You act like I've had so many of them. Seriously, he is my first real boyfriend. Ever. And I mean ever. I told you before that I'm still a virgin. Clearly, I'm not experienced when it comes to guys."

"Did you guys mess around while he was here?" She was back to her old self that quickly.

I rolled my eyes at her. "Sure, we did. We got naked while staff watched."

"I could never take my clothes off in front of a guy. Never. Can you imagine what they'd say?" She shuddered.

"Yes, believe me, they'd just be happy your clothes were off. And besides, I'm sure you'd look amazing."

"I'd look fat is what I'd look."

I rolled my eyes again. "Come on, get up."

"Why?"

"Just get up. I've got to show you something."

I grabbed her hand and pulled her off the couch.

"Where are we going?" she whispered.

"Follow me." I turned to look at Felicia and called out to her. "We're going to the bathroom. We'll be back in five minutes."

Felicia nodded.

"What? You're off restriction?"

"Yep. As of this morning, I'm free to move about without a shadow." I continued to pull her along down the hallway to the women's bathroom. "And we're celebrating my freedom."

I pushed open the bathroom door on the right side of the nurses' station. Rose looked at me, bewildered, but she followed me anyway. I shut the door behind us and checked underneath all of the stalls to make sure there weren't any shoes.

"Take your clothes off," I said.

Rose burst out laughing. "What are you talking about?"

"I'm talking about you taking your clothes off." I giggled. "Now take them off. You're always saying you're going to show me what you look like naked. I want to see it."

"Really? Are you serious?"

"Sure am. How many times have you said I haven't seen you naked? Well, now it's time for me to see you."

"You'll see." She pulled off her shirt and tossed it at me with a big grin on her face.

I stared in horror. She wasn't wearing a bra, but she didn't need to because she didn't have any breasts. There were only nipples. Her chest looked like a twelve-year-old boy's chest. I could see every one of her ribs, and her stomach was concave. It went in so deeply, it looked like I could lay my head down in it if I wanted to.

"You're the skinniest person I've ever seen."

She lit up. "Really?"

"Yes." I didn't know people could get that skinny.

She took off her pants and stripped down to her underwear. Her stick-thin legs bowed out as if they might snap. I didn't know how they held up her body. How did she walk without breaking?

"What do you think?" she asked with her hands on her hips. They jutted out like dinosaur bones.

"I think you need to gain some weight."

"Ugh, so that's what this is about." She reached down to find her shirt, scowling.

"No, stop." I grabbed her shirt back from her. "You keep saying you're fat over and over again, so I want you to show me where there's fat."

"That's easy." She lifted up her arm and pointed underneath her forearm. "See this flab? It jiggles."

There was nothing there.

She grabbed some of the skin on her stomach and pulled it out. "And this? This is what I've gained since I've been here."

She was only pulling on skin. There was nothing there either.

She pinched her thighs, but came up empty-handed, so instead she slapped them. "Look how they flap when I hit them. So gross."

The skin on her thighs hadn't moved. It was stretched so tightly the bones threatened to poke through.

"Now do you get it?" Tears welled in her eyes as she stared at herself in the mirror.

I put my arm around her. "No, Rose, hon, I don't get it. You don't have any fat on your body. There's nothing there. I'm looking right at you and there's nothing there."

She shook her head, disbelieving. "You're only trying to be nice. I'm staring in the mirror and it's there. I see it."

I looked into the mirror at her emaciated body with her oversized head attached to her bony neck. She didn't see what I saw. The fat on her body was real to her even though it didn't exist. She was staring in the mirror and seeing things that weren't there.

My heart started to pound in my head and my stomach rose into my mouth. I stared at her in the mirror as she pinched and poked at fat only she could see. Her brain had tricked her. Hypnotically, I began to undo my jeans and dropped them to the floor slowly as she continued to prattle on, listing each area of fat she found. I locked eyes with my own eyes in the mirror, afraid to look down at my body.

Just do it. Look. Just look.

I felt dizzy and all the air left my body. I gripped onto the sink in front of me, forcing myself to breathe, and then I looked down at my legs. They were mutilated. Jagged red cuts sliced through the skin, creating butchered deformations.

These are my legs.

I squeezed my eyes shut, counted to ten slowly, and then reopened them. I forced myself to look again, hoping I'd been wrong. The angry red scars were still there, screaming at me. Tangled wounds wrapped their way up and down from hip to calf, some of them chaotic, as if they'd been released in a fury, others methodical and clean as if they'd been done with deliberation.

Adrenaline shot through my veins as if a gun had been fired. I scrambled for my jeans as fast as I could, pulled them up, fumbling to do the zipper and button as if I were a two-year-old. And then I ran. I sprinted as fast as I could out of the bathroom and away from the mirror.

19

I lay in bed staring at the ceiling tiles and not sleeping. I saw my legs every time I closed my eyes.

My legs. My wounds. My scars. My body.

How could I do that to myself? How could I hack my legs and not remember doing it? My brain had tricked me in the same way Rose's brain tricked her. What was wrong with me?

A few hours ago, I'd experienced my first glimmers of hope, but it'd been destroyed in the bathroom. It was one thing to pretend and make-believe Emily was alive, but it was insane to butcher and brutalize myself without having any recollection of doing it. I was terrified. If I'd done something so awful to myself and had no recollection of it, what else had I done? Were there other things I didn't remember? Fear shot through my body over and over again.

Talking to Dr. Larson wasn't an option. If he knew what I'd done to myself, I was never going to get out of the hospital. There was no way he wouldn't tell the team and they'd probably send me to the state hospital. I could tell Thomas, but we'd barely scratched the surface in our discussions about what had happened before the hospital. He'd listen like he always did, but he wouldn't have any clue how to help me. Somewhere around three o'clock, it dawned on me that I could talk to Lisa. She knew my history, understood me, and I trusted her. Bob had told me she wanted to visit when I was ready, and I was more than ready now. Thoughts of Lisa calmed my brain enough for me to fall asleep.

I didn't wait for Dr. Larson to ask me how I was feeling during our session the following morning. "I want to work with my old therapist," I said before he had time to get out his notebook.

"Your therapist? Do you mean Lisa?"

It seemed like a good idea in the middle of the night and was still a good decision in the morning.

"Yes. Her. I want to see her."

"I'm sorry, but it's hospital policy that you work with the psychologists provided for the patients on staff." He looked insulted.

"Why?"

"The team works hard to provide you with consistent care. It's really important that the care you receive is consistent among caregivers."

It sounded like more psychobabble to me, which was exactly why I wanted to see Lisa. She talked like a regular human being. I wasn't giving up on being able to see her.

"And why would Lisa be inconsistent?" I'd never argued with him before and he was taken aback.

"She's not part of the treatment team," he said. "She doesn't have access to your charts or any of your treatment plans that we've created while you've been here. You can see her as your outpatient therapist when you leave if you'd like. I'd be more than happy to arrange it for you. I think it'd be a great idea. We can talk more about arranging it once we're closer to your discharge. We still have quite a lot of work to do until we get to that point."

"I want to see her now."

"Can you tell me why?"

"I think I would be more comfortable talking to her."

"I'm sorry, but it's hospital policy." He shrugged. "Maybe we could talk more about why you would feel more comfortable talking with her than me or one of the other therapists here."

He wouldn't understand even if I explained it to him. He looked at me like I was a cell in a Petri dish.

"Can she visit me? She doesn't have to do therapy with me since it would violate hospital policy, but can she come during visiting hours?"

He frowned. "I guess she could, but I wouldn't recommend it. It might be confusing for you, but I can't control who comes to visit you. You would have to add her to your list of visitors."

Our session was rushed and hurried. I wasn't paying attention to anything he wanted to talk about because I was focused on counting the minutes until it would be over. Our session couldn't end fast enough and when it finally did, I leaped up from my chair and raced to the nurses' station. I called out to the closest nurse and told her I needed my visitor log. I scribbled Lisa's name on the line. Then I scurried off to wait for the phone. I was there forty-five minutes ahead of schedule and first in line. I looked up her number in the yellow pages while I waited.

I tapped my feet together as it rang.

"Can I speak with Lisa?" I asked when the receptionist picked up.

"I'm sorry. She's unavailable right now, can I take a message?"

"It's an emergency," I said. "I really need to talk to her."

"I'm sorry. She's in session, and I can't interrupt her session."

"Please? It really is an emergency. Please? I've got to talk to her. I'm not going to be able to call back."

"Listen, I understand it's an emergency. She gets lots of emergencies. I can take down your information and have her call you."

I could tell by her tone she was getting irritated.

"Okay, can you write all of this down?"

"Go ahead," she said.

"All right. Tell her Elizabeth Rooth called and that I'm in Galston United Hospital and I'm in the psych ward. I really want her to visit me. Tonight, if at all possible. And I don't know the number here. Damn. I have no idea what the number is."

"I'm sure she has the number. What time are visiting hours?"

"Six until seven. Can you please get her this message? Will you tell her it's super important?"

"I will. Anything else?"

"No."

"Okay. Have a great day."

Click.

I didn't have any choice except to hang up the phone and wait. I wandered back to the family room and settled in to wait out the day.

"What's up with you today?" Rose asked.

I shrugged. "Nothing."

"You've been acting funny all day." She stuck out her lip. "Are you mad at me or something? Did I do something wrong? You still haven't told me why you went running out of the bathroom last night. Was I that hideous?"

"Not everything is about you, all right?" I snapped.

"Fine," she huffed, grabbing one of her magazines. "I don't want to talk to you either."

I'd hurt her feelings, but I didn't have the strength to try to make her feel better. Not today. Panic threatened to overtake me. I kept seeing my legs and each time, a flood of terror washed over me, making me feel as if I was going to throw up.

It was the longest day at the hospital I'd had, even longer than my first day. Each minute dragged. I told myself not to look at the clock, which only made me look at it more. Every time I was sure a significant amount of time had passed, I'd look up to discover it'd only been a few minutes. It was excruciating. I wished there was a fast-forward button I could press to take me to visiting hours. I was as scared of Lisa coming as I was of her not coming.

I was acutely aware of my surroundings all day. The lights were too bright and the voices of everyone around me were too loud. I could hear the nurses talking to each other at the nurses' station and most days their voices didn't even register. Shelly's exaggerated laugh was so shrill I wanted to cover my ears to drown it out. I heard my heartbeat in my head.

By the time visiting hours arrived, I was exhausted from feeling as if I was at a starting line waiting to begin a race all day. I couldn't eat my dinner. I was glad I didn't eat because when six o'clock arrived I was in the bathroom dry-heaving clumps of yellow-and-green slime into the toilet. I ran into Lisa at the nurses' station on my way out of the bathroom.

"Hi, Elizabeth."

"You came." My body was buzzing.

She threw her arms around me and squeezed me. "I'm so glad you called."

"I'm glad you came."

The only person I would've been happier to see was Emily.

"Should we go to your room to talk?" she asked, linking her arm with mine.

I nodded and we walked to my room in silence. She closed the door behind us and the room felt so much smaller with it closed. I never got to shut my door even at night. She must've been given special privileges since she was a therapist. I was glad we got to be alone and uninterrupted.

I settled onto the bed and she grabbed the desk chair for her seat. She smiled at me. Unlike Dr. Larson, she didn't start out by asking how I was feeling. She reached into her bag and pulled out Annabelle. I gasped. She handed her to me.

"I thought you might be able to use her."

I was sobbing before all of the words were out of her mouth. I grabbed Annabelle from her and clutched her against my chest. We sat for a few minutes while I cried. When I was finished, Lisa handed me the familiar white comb and I started brushing her hair in the same way I'd done when I was a little girl. My breathing slowly relaxed now like it did then.

Unlike my sessions with Dr. Larson, I got to take the lead. "I have some questions for you."

"Okay. I'd love to answer your questions," she said.

"I don't know how to explain this, but I'm going to try. Emily was always the cutter. I never cut, ever. She's cut since we were kids, but not me—only her. I couldn't. I tried. More than once, just because I wanted her to see how it felt. But I—I ... could never do it—at least, I thought I could never do it." I felt like I might throw up again. The taste of bile was in the back of my throat. "I'm rambling. I know I am ... I'm trying to tell you this—ask you this, or something. I really am. It's just so weird, and it's hard. I don't know ... It's crazy, or I'm crazy. I mean, I think I really am crazy, and I don't know what's going on. I thought if I talked to you—if I talked to you, I don't know ... I just thought ... I just thought, you know, talking to you—"

Lisa got up from her position on the chair and moved to sit next to me on the bed. She put her arm around my shoulder. "Elizabeth, take a deep breath."

I tried to take a deep breath, but it felt like I would choke on the air. "I don't know what's happening." I took another deep breath. This one went past my throat and filled my lungs. I let it out slowly.

"Okay. Emily was a cutter. You remember that, right? The first time she got caught?"

Lisa nodded. I sighed, happy she remembered.

I'd kept my promise never to tell anyone about how Emily hurt herself. From the start, she'd kept her cutting private and in the beginning, she didn't do it often, so it was easy to keep hidden and secret. Her favorite spot was her thighs because nobody besides me saw her legs since I was the only one who saw her naked. Neither of us liked anyone to see us naked and once we'd learned how to bathe ourselves, Dalila and Bob had respected our privacy and allowed us to shower by ourselves.

Initially, her cutting wasn't very deep and stayed on the surface, never drawing a lot of blood. I never knew when she was going to do it, but she always showed me her wounds. She had an odd measure of pride about being able to do it. She was giddy each time she presented her scrapes and scratches to me. Months would pass at a time and she wouldn't do it. I'd hope she was done for good, but it was only a matter of time before she presented me with another new trophy.

Emily had always been emotional. Unlike me, anything could make her cry. Sometimes nothing was going on and she'd begin to weep. Any expression of anger was sure to elicit a meltdown. The upside to her emotional lability was that she also had the ability to experience extreme happiness as well. She had an infectious laugh that made everyone around her happy too. She was so alive she was on fire when she was feeling good and bounced with energy. Her emotional bottoms were manageable because they were fleeting. But something happened when we turned thirteen.

Her sadness and negative emotions no longer passed quickly. She plummeted into periods of deep despair and anguish where I couldn't reach her. She cried uncontrollably, which she'd always done, but unlike before, she became inconsolable. The happiness and light she'd used to emit so brightly were extinguished.

Her cutting became almost daily. She carried a purple velvet pouch in her backpack that held a razor blade and a shard of glass. She had it with her at all times. She'd sneak into the bathroom like a heroin addict during lunch or study hall and silently slice into her skin. Her cuts grew deeper, to the point where it was difficult to stop the bleeding. I became her nurse. I watched YouTube videos to learn how to clean and bandage her damage and quickly became skilled at creating butterfly bandages and tight wraps to contain the bleeding as best I could.

I'd never forget the day Dalila found her in the bathtub. I was in the kitchen making a peanut butter and jelly sandwich, my favorite after-school snack. Emily had been locked in the bathroom for the last hour. I never disturbed her when she was in there. I knew what she was doing, but I hated seeing it. My job was to be there when it was over.

Dalila's scream was shrill as it rang out and reverberated throughout the house. I dropped the plate on the floor and the shattered porcelain echoed as I took the stairs two at a time. I sprinted into the bathroom to find Dalila standing in the middle of the bathroom, frozen in terror as she stared at Emily's bloody naked body in the tub. Emily clutched a long butcher knife from the kitchen wood block in her hand. Her legs lay spread wide open, one on each side of the tub, with trails of blood pouring from the middle of them as if she was in the middle of a gruesome miscarriage. She'd scrawled her name in blood across her chest.

I shoved Dalila out of the way and ran toward her. She stared upward at the ceiling with a look of pure bliss in her eyes as if she'd been catapulted to another world. I shook her, trying to snap her out of her dreamy reverie.

Her head flopped to the side to look at me, eyes rolling slowly as if she was on drugs, and whispered, "Bethy. Hi. I love you so much."

"I love you, too, Em," I said. "Let's get you cleaned up."

Dalila hadn't moved from her spot on the tiled floor. She stood as still as a statue in shock as I began to run the bathwater and erased "Emily" from her chest while her legs continued to bleed. When I got to "i," Emily's eyes closed. Dalila sprung to life.

"Oh my God. Dear Jesus. We have to call someone." She fled from the bathroom.

Dalila shook with silent sobs the entire ride to the hospital. She was too upset to provide Emily's information in the emergency room so I had to do it for her. It was Emily's first set of stitches. She'd gotten twenty on her right inner thigh and forty-two on her left inner thigh. The doctors said it was lucky we'd found her when we did because she'd already lost a lot of blood. Emily swore she wasn't trying to kill herself and she'd only wanted to feel good. She said doing so much damage to herself had scared her enough to stop cutting. She promised never to do it again. Emily had to sign a "no-harm" contract in order to not be admitted to the psychiatric hospital and Dalila assured the doctors she would get her psychiatric help.

We'd stopped seeing Lisa for therapy sessions a few years before, but after Emily's incident, we started going back to see her. Emily refused to meet with Lisa unless I went with her, so I accompanied her to all of her sessions. Dalila kept Emily out of school for two weeks and took off work to watch her. She drove us back and forth to Lisa's office every other day.

"Emily kept cutting even though we told everyone she'd stopped. It didn't take long until she started cutting again. She switched to cutting on her stomach instead of her legs for a while just in case anyone asked to see her legs, but nobody ever did. I'm not sure why Dalila never asked to see her legs or check her body to see if she was doing it. I think she preferred to think she was better. I'm not sure she ever got over that day. She never looked at Emily in the same way again. From then on, Emily made sure to always hide her body. It's why she never wore shorts or went swimming. She was never afraid of the water."

"You always did protect her secrets, huh?" Lisa asked.

I nodded. "Cutting was Emily's thing. Never mine. That's why it makes this so weird. Yesterday, I went to the bathroom with Rose. She's a friend that I've made since I've been here. She's anorexic like those super skinny chicks you see on talk shows and *Dateline*. She's convinced she's fat and no matter what anyone else says to her, she still believes it. I thought if I made her look at herself in the mirror she would see she really isn't fat."

It had seemed like such a good idea yesterday.

"She took her clothes off with me standing next to her and she's even skinnier than I thought. She's completely emaciated. I asked her to show me where she saw the fat, and she kept looking in the mirror and pointing at fat all over her body. The entire time I kept wondering how it was possible she could look into the mirror and see something that wasn't there. She was literally looking in the mirror and seeing something that wasn't there. But then, but then ... I just knew. I don't even know how I knew. It just hit me. You can see things that aren't there ..."

Lisa waited for a few minutes for me to go on, but I couldn't.

"Did you see something that really wasn't there?"

I shook my head. Tears dropped onto my favorite jeans. I hadn't realized I was crying.

Lisa took my hand and held it. Finally, I found my voice again. I had to tell someone.

"My legs have cuts on them. Everywhere. Just like hers. Just like Emily's."

My brain felt fuzzy, like I was halfway between awake and sleep. Lisa squeezed my hand. She squeezed a second time, harder this time. I felt less muddled.

"Why do you think you have cuts on your legs?" she asked.

I shrugged my shoulders and shook my head back and forth. I looked at her. "Please, help me, Lisa. Something's seriously wrong with me. I'm really messed up. I don't know what's going on anymore. I'm so lost and scared."

Lisa took me into her arms in the same way Dalila had done hundreds of times, but instead of rejecting her like I rejected Dalila, I let myself sink into her support. I didn't have a choice because I was afraid if I didn't then I would fall off the bed. Annabelle was sandwiched between us.

"Let's talk about this together and see if we can figure it out. Do you want to do that?" She waited for my nod before continuing. "Are you sure?"

I nodded again.

"I know the doctors have explained to you that Emily has been dead for two years, but has anyone told you what happened to her?"

I shook my head.

"Do you want to know what happened to Emily?" she asked.

"Yes."

Maybe if I knew what happened to her I could figure out what had happened to me.

"It was a week after the two of you graduated from high school. One of your friends had a party and you went to it together. On the way home from the party, you got into a car accident. It was really bad." She paused, letting her words sink in and giving me time to process them before going on. "Emily was thrown from the car. Unfortunately, she didn't make it, but you did. You were devastated. You didn't speak for three days. Not one word."

"God, that's horrible. She was thrown from the car?"

Lisa nodded. "Do you remember anything about it?"

I closed my eyes and willed the memories to come. There was nothing.

Lisa let go of my hand and patted my leg. "Losing Emily was more than you could handle. There's probably nobody who will understand what the loss must've been like for you. Sometimes when people experience significant trauma, their brains will disconnect to protect them from the loss. After the accident, your brain unplugged itself for a while because it had to shut down."

I'd experienced the same thing she was describing two weeks ago when I'd woken up in the hospital and thought I'd lost Emily. My entire system shut down. It was only beginning to turn back on.

"The thing that was so surprising to everyone around you was how fast you went from being catatonic to walking around and talking like everything was fine within a few weeks of the funeral. You'd been wracked with grief and then bam—you were totally fine. The oddest part was how determined you were to move out of Bob and Dalila's. Bob tried to talk you out of it, but you were convinced it was what you had to do. Dalila was still reeling from losing Emily and so immersed in her own loss she wasn't able to be there for you. If she was, she might've been able to get you to change your mind. Shortly after you moved out, Bob called me and told me he'd just spoken to you on the phone and you were talking about Emily like she was still alive. He was baffled and had no clue what to do."

I caught a glimpse of myself packing boxes in Emily's old bedroom at Bob and Dalila's. I remembered how I'd packed all of her clothes and thoughtfully chosen which of her crime books to take and which to leave behind because there were too many to take them all to our new apartment. If Emily had been alive, she would've packed her own things. She never would've let me pick her books because she was so particular about them and would've wanted to be the one to choose which ones should go and which ones should stay.

Lisa reached out to stroke my head. "People's brains are powerful. Extremely powerful. You'd be amazed at what they can do. This is just my opinion and I could be wrong, but what I've seen with the clients I work with who've experienced traumatic losses is that our brains don't let our bodies die from grief even if we want to and it feels like we might. Eventually, our brains force us to start functioning again. Emily being dead was more than your brain could process, and for you to function at all, you had to act as if Emily was still alive. You believed she was still alive. And for you, she really was. Your brain continued to create Emily. But in reality, you've been both Emily and Elizabeth for two years."

I digested her words slowly. I kept swallowing, trying to get my tongue unstuck from the top of my mouth.

It's why she's here. You have to ask her.

"I put the marks on my legs, didn't I?"

She nodded, confirming what I'd become aware of last night. Much like Rose looked into the mirror and saw fat that didn't exist, I'd been looking into the mirror for two years and seeing smooth, unblemished skin that didn't exist. In reality, Rose didn't have an ounce of fat on her body and I had mutilated legs that looked as if I'd been sliced with glass after being thrown through a window. Rose wasn't able to see her reality, but I'd seen mine. And I was terrified.

20

I couldn't stay in my room alone after Lisa left, as much as I wanted to. Even though staff dangled the privilege of gaining time alone in your room, no one was allowed to have it. I was exhausted but stood in line waiting for Shelly to get off the phone because I'd promised to call Thomas. Unlike everyone else, who whispered and talked in hushed tones whenever they were on the phone, Shelly made sure everyone heard her conversations.

"C'mon, baby. You know you still think I'm hot," she giggled. "You know you want it. I'm going to. Yep ... Oh, baby ... not here ... I can't. Not here ... yes, I'm horny!"

She kept looking over at me, making sure I was hearing her conversation. It was impossible not to, even the nurses looked uncomfortable. Thankfully, I'd caught her during her last few minutes of her scheduled time and before long I was punching in Thomas's number. He answered on the second ring.

"Hey!"

"Hi."

"How was your day?" he asked.

"It was really long and hard."

"What's up? Your voice sounds sad. Are you okay?"

"Not really."

"Do you want to talk about it? Tell me about it? You don't have to if you don't want to, though. No pressure."

I didn't know how to explain things. I wanted to talk to him in person, but he had classes tonight and tomorrow night so I wouldn't see him until Thursday. He couldn't afford to miss any more classes since he'd missed a week of class while I was in intensive care and was still trying to catch up on all of his homework. I didn't have a choice except to try to explain things to him now. I felt rushed and hurried to do it since I only had ten minutes before I had to give up the phone to the next person in line.

"Last night something really weird happened to me when I was in the bathroom with Rose. I'm not sure how to explain it. I don't even understand it myself, but I'm working on it. I'm trying to figure out what's wrong with me."

How was I supposed to tell him I wasn't the person he thought I was? I'd been lying to him since I'd known him, but unlike most liars, I didn't know I wasn't telling the truth. Was it considered lying if you weren't aware you were doing it?

"I'm crazy. You need to know that."

I didn't want to hurt him any more than I already had.

"You're not crazy."

"Yes, I am. You have no idea. Emily really has been dead for two years and I've been doing more than pretending she was alive. I've been doing what she did." My voice cracked. "I chopped up my legs. If you don't believe me, you should look at my legs. I'll show them to you on Thursday. You'll know why you've never seen me naked then."

He was silent. All I could hear was the occasional sound of him breathing.

"I have seen you naked," he mumbled.

"What'd you say?" I asked.

He cleared his throat, "I said I've seen you naked."

"Huh? When? What are you talking about?"

"You really don't remember, do you?"

"No, I don't. What are you talking about?"

"I knew you didn't really remember having sex. You always

said you didn't, but I thought maybe you felt bad about it so you pretended like it never happened. And well, honestly, I felt guilty too, so it was easier to forget about it and play along with you. But I always kinda had a feeling you didn't have any idea we'd done it."

I had no memory of it. How could I not remember having sex?

"I'm not a virgin," I said out loud. I couldn't believe we'd had sex.

"You still kinda are. I mean, we tried ... but, uh, it didn't really, um ... work."

How did sex not work?

"When did we do it? Or try to do it. Whatever. When did it happen?"

"It was the first time you stayed overnight."

"I stayed overnight?"

I never stayed overnight anywhere. Not ever. I'd always been too scared to leave Emily home alone because of what she might do while I was away.

"You don't remember sneaking into the dorm?"

"No."

He described how we'd decided to spend the night together while his roommate went home to be with his family over the long Presidents' Day weekend. There were plenty of other guys who snuck their girlfriends in to stay the night, so there was already a well-practiced plan for getting girls into the dorm. All of the guys took turns being the decoys in front of the cameras at the front door by jumping around after footballs and smashing up against the wall to block the view. It worked for us too and I'd walked in undetected. We got carried away in the moment and had sex. I made him tell me the details of the story a second time and I still couldn't remember any of it.

"I've got to tell Lisa."

"When did you talk to her?" he asked.

"After I saw my legs last night, I was so freaked out, I could barely sleep. I knew I needed to talk to somebody, but you've met

Dr. Larson and he's impossible to talk to. Plus, he doesn't know my history or Emily's. There's something comforting about talking to somebody who knew her. I called her office earlier today and she came to see me tonight. She brought me an old doll I used to hold when we did therapy as kids." Lisa had given me Annabelle to keep during my hospital stay. She'd even left her brush. I would've still been hanging on to her, but I didn't want Shelly and Tobi to tease me. "I told her about my legs."

"Can I ask you a question?"

"Sure."

My heart began to thump.

"Your legs. You never looked at your legs?"

I could hear the disbelief in his voice and didn't blame him. I wouldn't believe it if someone told me the same thing. It seemed impossible. I didn't know how it was possible, but it was true. I'd been going to the bathroom all day to look at my legs to make sure I hadn't made a mistake. I'd confirmed my self-deception over ten times.

"Of course I looked at my legs. I looked at them all the time. I just never saw the marks and I don't remember putting them there either. That's why I'm crazy. It's why I called Lisa. I had to talk to her about it."

"What'd she say?" he asked.

"She told me Emily and I got into a car accident after our high school graduation and that's how she died. She thinks her death put my brain over the edge, so I kept on pretending she was alive."

"That makes sense. It must feel good to feel like you can start moving on now."

It didn't feel like I was moving on. I felt more lost and confused than I'd ever been. I shrugged my shoulders. "Maybe."

"My turn. My turn. My turn."

Doris was in front me.

"My turn. My turn."

"Look, I have to go. My time's up," I said.

I did my best to stay out of Doris's way. She flipped out at least a few times every day. Her eruptions almost always ended in something getting thrown or somebody getting hit. So far, I'd been lucky enough to stay out of the way of her rages. Tobi hadn't been so lucky. She'd taken a dining tray to the left eye yesterday during lunch, and today she was walking around with a black eye.

"Okay. Can I still come on Thursday? I can't come tomorrow, but—"

"Of course you can still come."

I was amazed he still wanted to see me.

Doris was muttering louder and she was tracing an angry trail back and forth in front of me. I had to get off the phone fast.

"All right. Bye."

I nodded at Doris, but she wasn't aware I was there. She moved past me and grabbed the receiver from the wall. I walked into the family room and took a seat next to Rose. She didn't bother to look up when I sat down.

"Hey," I said.

She ignored me.

"Rose? Can I talk to you?"

"Oh, now you wanna talk."

"C'mon, I know I totally freaked out after last night. It's been weird for me all day long. I'm sorry. Will you let me explain? Can I tell you why?"

She rolled her eyes, but let me explain everything I'd experienced in the last twenty-four hours. I did better explaining things to her than I'd done with Thomas. It was easier to tell her because she understood mental illness so well. I tried my best to articulate how I'd become aware of the marks on my legs last night while we were in the bathroom without hurting her feelings, and that the only explanation was that I'd put them there myself. By the end of it, she'd scooted her way down next to me and was almost sitting on top of me.

"Wow. That's wild. So, Emily really has been dead? For like

two years? And you totally thought she was alive?"

I nodded. "I still can't wrap my head around it. Any of it. All I keep thinking over and over again is that nobody's been trying to trick me or mess with my mind. Emily's been dead for two years. Two whole years. None of what I went through with her even happened."

"I remember reading a book about something like this when I was in high school. I can't remember what it was called. Anyway, it doesn't matter. The girl in the book wasn't a twin, but she had a daughter who died. I don't know how she died. I think it was drowning or something. Whatever. It doesn't matter how she died. But she was kinda like you. She still saw her daughter all the time and talked to her every day. She thought her daughter was alive."

She kept describing the book and explaining different scenes, but I quit paying attention. I was too busy searching my mind for any kind of image or memory of Emily dying besides the night I thought she died. There was nothing. My mind always returned to the night in the apartment when I found her in the bathroom. I could remember it so vividly. How could it seem so real and not be?

I had so many questions. How did I fight with someone who wasn't there? How did I come up with the idea to pretend she was alive? Was it a choice? Did I wake up one day after the funeral and decide to do it? Did I think about it beforehand?

"What do you think? Does it help?" Rose interrupted my thoughts.

"Sure," I replied, even though I had no idea what she was talking about.

"Did I tell you my mom is coming in for a meeting tomorrow with the team?" she asked.

"No. Really? For what?"

"No idea. Dr. Heimer told me about it in our session. I wanted to tell you earlier today, but you've been ignoring me all day, remember?" She stuck out her lower lip in an exaggerated pout.

I giggled. "Sorry, but you've got to understand, right? I mean, wouldn't you be out of it for a while if you figured out you'd been the one butchering your legs and didn't remember doing it?"

She laughed. "I guess. You've got a point. I'll forgive you this one time. Just don't let it happen again."

21

I expected to have a hard time sleeping again, but much to my surprise, I got the best rest I'd gotten since they'd taken me off my sleeping pills. Up until two days ago, I'd been taking two pills a day since I'd gotten to the hospital. A white one in the morning and a pink one at night. But even without my sleeping pill, I fell asleep as soon as they turned off the lights and put on the hallway dimmers.

"I'm really curious to hear how your meeting with Lisa went last night," Dr. Larson began while we walked down the hallway that grew more familiar each day. I couldn't believe it, but I was beginning to like the structured routine of doing the same things in the exact same way every day. I was starting to feel comfortable in an environment where nothing ever changed.

"She told me Emily has been dead for two years," I said as soon as he shut the door behind us.

"How do you feel about that?"

I was used to his favorite question and wasn't surprised when it was the first thing out of his mouth. "I'm trying hard to remember the real night she died."

"I want to be clear—are you telling me you believe Emily's been dead for two years and didn't die a few weeks ago?"

I nodded. "I just—"

Dr. Larson interrupted, "Do you realize this is the first time you've acknowledged Emily's death happened two years ago? This is very significant progress." He looked pleased, like he might want to give me a high five. "I think it would be helpful if you said it out loud again and not by saying someone else told it to you. You've said that before, but I want you to acknowledge Emily's been dead for two years. It's important for you to make it your own truth."

I swallowed hard. Swallowed again.

"Emily has been dead for two years."

Since the moment I'd looked at my legs in the bathroom and seen the wounds, I knew what they were telling me wasn't an elaborate scheme to test my insanity. If I could cut my flesh without having any recollection of it, then I could make-believe my sister was still alive even though she was dead.

"What does it feel like?"

I shrugged.

"Elizabeth, I want you to work hard at getting in touch with the loss. Part of the reason you created Emily was because you couldn't deal with the grief of losing her. It's important for you to experience the grief so you can begin to heal. You've got to let her go in a meaningful way. Part of that process means allowing yourself to feel the feelings you've been burying. It's the only way you'll be able to move past this and you want to move past this, don't you?" He peered at me over the table.

I felt guilty, but I did. Spending time with Thomas again reminded me why I'd taken the risk of starting to separate myself from Emily in the first place. It felt good to be close to someone who was capable of reciprocating it. I couldn't remember the last time my relationship with Emily had been reciprocal. It'd been a lot longer than two years. I'd lost her when we were teenagers. She'd given in to her pain and I'd never been able to get her back. Not fully. I'd been surviving on pieces of her, and brief moments of who she used to be, for a long time. In the days before the hospital, I'd begun to believe I was capable of separating myself from her and beginning to live my own life. I wanted to feel that way again and not feel guilty for it.

My motivation was based on more than my feelings for Thomas and wanting to get back what we had. Rose was my first real friend who wasn't Emily and I liked our friendship. It gave me hope that other people besides Emily might like me and want to be close to me even if they knew how messed up I was. Rose and I had so much fun laughing and joking around. It felt good not to be serious all the time. The weight of carrying Emily around with me was heavy and overshadowed everything I did. It always had. What if I could live without the weight? What if Lisa and Dalila had been right all along about letting her go and moving on?

I didn't have to do it alone. Other twins had done what I was trying to do. They'd gone through what I was going through and somehow made it to the other side. They'd learned how to be half-alive. If they could do it, was there a chance I could do it too?

"I want to get well."

It felt good to say it. I was finally letting go and allowing the recovery process to happen.

"Getting well is going to be one of the hardest things you've ever had to do. One of the most important things we need to do is to get at the root of your dissociation. Dissociation stems from trauma and we need to go back to where it started. The reason you were able to disconnect from Emily's death and create an alternate reality is because of your ability to separate yourself from pain. I believe the practice of disengaging yourself from hurt to protect yourself was already in place before you lost Emily. Most likely, it began in your childhood. We've got to go backward and find those places where you disconnected in order for you to move forward."

He was losing me again like he always did.

"I don't understand."

"People dissociate to protect themselves. You learned how to disconnect from reality when you were a child because of the things you went through. You're going to continue to dissociate unless we go back into your childhood and walk through the trauma you experienced. We have to reconnect the connection to reality that was severed a long time ago."

"Do we have to do this?"

He nodded. "It's important. We can start small. Were you sexually abused as a little girl?"

That wasn't starting small. Not at all. I didn't need to talk about what had happened to me when I lived with Mother. It had nothing to do with what was going on now. I shook my head.

"It's time to start talking about what happened to you when you were a little girl. You're safe now."

I wanted to go back to talking about Emily. I'd do any other work he wanted me to—just not this. Anything but this. I froze, my mind paralyzed.

"When kids experience trauma, they often describe leaving their bodies. They talk about being outside themselves and watching themselves do things, but without any emotional attachment. Has that ever happened to you?"

How did he know?

I flashed back to the ceiling tiles in Mother's bedroom, where I would hide and watch as the special friends played their games with my body. Each ceiling tile was filled with tiny holes and I would pick one to focus on and send my brain into it. Sometimes I watched as they poked and prodded into my body, putting their evil inside of me, splitting me in two. Other times I disappeared into nothingness for a while.

"Yes. I know what that's like." I didn't recognize the sound of my voice.

Dr. Larson spoke slowly, enunciating every syllable. "Tell me about it. Try to remember where you were and what happened. What it felt like. You're safe now. It's okay to talk about it."

"I ... um—I ... it was ..."

I remembered the searing pain ripping through my whole body, so hot, it felt as if I was on fire, like my entire insides were being burned. I saw Emily's face filled with terror and her small body shaking violently as she watched me from the corner of Mother's bedroom, knowing she would be next if the monster didn't get his fill from me.

Oh my God. I can't do this. I said I never would. I don't want to remember. Please don't make me. Please.

Dr. Larson rose and pulled his chair next to me on my side of the desk. He was on my side. He was too close. I didn't like it. I couldn't breathe. What was he doing?

"You're safe now. Nobody is going to hurt you. This is an important part of the process. Give your brain permission to remember."

I can't do this. I won't.

It felt like someone shoved my head underwater.

I can't breathe. There's not enough air.

I saw myself as a little girl lying on the bed, the monsters hovering over me. The black stones where their eyes should've been. My thoughts raced so fast I couldn't discern them.

"They hurt me. Bad men. Really bad men," I whispered as if the special friends were in the room with us and might hear. I started coughing and choking. There was something in my throat. I gagged but nothing came up. I heaved again and this time when I opened my mouth, gut-wrenching wails pierced the air. Loud animal screams from someplace deep within my core.

I can't stop screaming. Please, make it stop.

It went on and on. Dr. Larson moved to stand beside me and placed his hand gently on my knee. He didn't hug or embrace me like Lisa would. He simply stood on guard as I came apart. And I was shattering. My entire body hurt. My insides were on fire. The sobs ripped through me again and again. Tears stung my eyes as the images of Emily and me huddled together in our room after the monsters had gone played in my mind. The pain devoured me. My body shook as if I was having a seizure. Snot dripped on my knees as I began to hiccup. I kept hiccupping and my body kept shaking until the sobs finally ceased. I was empty. I felt like a woman whose baby had been ripped from her womb. I pushed Dr. Larson's hand off of my knee.

"Can I go back to my room?" I asked, refusing to look at him, ashamed at my explosion.

"I'm not sure it would be a good idea."

"Please, just let me go. Please."

He motioned for the door. I shuffled out the door and down the hallway. I moved in slow motion on the way to my room. I fell onto the hospital paper sheets and curled up on my side, hugging my knees to my chest.

Just like Emily.

I sat up and looked around, expecting to see her. I'd laid in the same position I'd found her in so many times over the last two years, but it wasn't her. It was always me.

"This is how I lay when I'm Emily," I said out loud.

It was comforting and familiar. I saw myself in our apartment, lying exactly as I was now—alone. I saw the image clearly. My eyelids were heavy and I didn't fight their descent. I closed them to the darkness. It was like being covered in a warm blanket.

I was startled awake by Rose shaking my shoulder. "Are you okay? Are you sick? Get up before you get into trouble."

I sat up, rubbing my eyes. "I'm sleepy. How long have I been asleep?"

She pulled me up. "I don't know. An hour. Maybe two. You were gone when I got back from my breakfast and then I noticed Dr. Larson was meeting with Darin, but you weren't anywhere to be found. Now, c'mon, get up or you're going to get in trouble. They still don't know you're in here."

I groaned and stood. I wanted to crawl back into my bed but instead followed her into the family room. I curled into a ball on the end of our couch. She sat next to me and put her arms around me. Shelly and her crew stared at us from their spots at the table. Shelly whispered in Tobi's ear and before long, Tobi walked over to the couch. I hid my head in Rose's chest.

"What's going on? Is she okay?" Tobi asked.

I didn't have to look up to know she was feigning exaggerated concern or that Shelly was straining her ears trying to hear the conversation.

"Get out of here. Leave her alone," Rose said.

"Look, we just want to be here for her."

"I said get out of here. I meant it. Go bother someone else."

I heard her footsteps walking away. Rose rubbed my head and smoothed my hair back and forth like I used to do to Emily. It made me start to cry again.

"What's going on?" she asked. "Did something happen? Do you want to talk about it? You don't have to if you don't want to."

"My session with Dr. Larson was really intense. He made me talk about my childhood."

Rose rolled her eyes. "They love to talk about your childhood. I swear to God, I've talked my childhood to death. The shrink I see outside of the hospital is obsessed with getting me to talk about the time I was raped when I was nine, but really I'm so over it. I've—"

I sat up and looked at her. "You were raped?"

"I've never met a girl in here who wasn't."

"Are you serious?"

"You've heard how everyone talks in group. It's always like that. People don't end up here unless they've been through some really tough stuff. Was today the first time you've ever talked about your childhood?"

"Yes, but I didn't actually talk. I just completely freaked out in his office as soon as he started asking me questions about it."

She reached out to pull me close to her again. "It gets easier the more you talk about it. I swear it does. But I know what you mean. The first time is super intense and then once it's out there, you can't take it back, you know?"

I started to cry again. My secret was out. This time, my sobs were soft and quiet. There was no violence with them, only an overwhelming sadness.

"Shh ... shh ... it's going to be okay. You're going to be okay."

The way Rose soothed me reminded me of how I'd comforted Emily in the last two years, but the moment I thought about Emily I wanted to scream at myself to stop pretending. I was never comforting her. I was only comforting myself. I was both the wounded and the savior.

Rose didn't ask any more questions. She just kept holding me.

"I'm sorry," I mumbled.

"Sorry? What are you sorry for?"

"Being such a mess."

"Pshht, we've all been there."

I lifted my head. Shelly and Tobi were still staring at me, whispering back and forth to each other. Their concerned looks were gone and replaced with their snotty adolescent looks, as if I'd insulted them. Rose noticed them at the same time I did and shot them an icy stare. They didn't pretend to be bothered by it. They never did.

"Do you want to hear some good news? Something not so depressing?" Rose asked.

"Sure."

"You're never going to believe this. I'm totally freaking out right now," she said. "I get to go home." Her smile stretched across her entire face. Her eyes sparkled with new life.

"Are you serious?"

"Remember the meeting I told you about yesterday? That was what it was about. My mom showed up this morning and of course, she was totally annoyed because I'm sure she had to miss a court date or something, but whatever, I don't care. Dr. Heimer was there and so was Mark. They went into this long explanation about how the team doesn't think I'm ready to go home yet, but my insurance won't cover my stay here any longer." She was still grinning. "The team wants to send me to an extended care treatment facility for eating disorders, but my mom would have to pay for it and it's like one of those super fancy treatment centers so it's really expensive. And guess what? My mom won't pay for it. She said she's done paying for me to go to treatment centers that never make me better."

"What are you going to do?" I asked.

"Oh, it gets better. I get to live in my own apartment. My mom doesn't want me to come back home. She hates having to worry about me, so she's paying for me to get an apartment. I get to live on my own. I'm so excited."

I couldn't help but remember all of our conversations when she shared how she hated her mom being gone all the time because she had to be alone, and she didn't like being alone. She always said she couldn't stand it. I guess living alone was better than living here.

"It's probably not going to be for a couple more days. There's all this paperwork that needs to be done and my mom has to find me an apartment, but I'm going to start packing. You want to help? It might get your mind off things."

I nodded. I was afraid if I started talking, I'd start crying again. What would I do when she left? Would I ever see her again?

"Hey, Polly," Rose called out to the nurses' station. "Can you come with us to my room? Pretty, please?"

Polly followed us to Rose's room and went back to reading her book outside the door. I'd never been in her room before, and an elaborate collage covered an entire wall. It must've taken her hours to complete. It was plastered with pictures of stick-thin supermodels intermingled with dark and depressed poetry. I plopped on her bed and watched as she attacked the collage, tearing everything off, rolling the paper into balls, and tossing them into the garbage.

"I'm not taking any of these. I don't want to remember anything about this place." She ripped more off the wall. "I mean, of course I'll remember you. I'll still talk to you. I'll call you on the phone. It's not like I don't know the best time to get a hold of you. You can fill me in on all the daily drama."

I smiled back, suddenly feeling awkward. "I'm going to miss you. Do you have any idea when you're going to get out?"

"I don't know. Hopefully, in a few days."

I wanted to be excited for her, but couldn't bring myself to do it. I wanted her to stay with me.

"I have an idea." Rose leaped onto the bed next to me and grabbed my shoulders. "You should totally live with me. We can be roommates. Oh my God, it'll be so much fun!"

"Really?"

I hadn't given a thought to what I would do when I got out. There was no way I was going back to Emily's and my apartment. I couldn't live with the reminders of our life staring me in the face every day. The thought of it gave me the same underwater feeling I'd had in Dr. Larson's office earlier. If I was truly going to start over, I wanted a fresh start. Maybe living with Rose was what I needed.

I started helping her tear down the collage while she chattered about how we would decorate our apartment, the colors we would use in the bathroom, and furniture ideas for the living room. She wanted to paint the bathroom yellow and her bedroom blue. She carried on about all the movies we'd see together and the restaurants we'd eat at like she was ready to start eating dinner again. It sounded so normal and I liked the way it sounded.

22

Lisa came to visit during visiting hours like she'd promised the night before. I spent the first part of our time filling her in on the breakdown I'd had in Dr. Larson's office.

"I'm sure it felt horrible, but I agree with Dr. Larson. He's right about your ability to disassociate and going back in your history to where it started. It's the only way to do it if you want to get better. As painful as it is, you're going to have to start talking about your childhood and working through it."

I'd never talked about the special friends. Not ever. Not even with Emily. It wasn't as if there'd been a time when we agreed not to talk about it, but we didn't need to. What had happened to us was unspeakable.

"It's too awful." My voice sounded weird again, like it did in Dr. Larson's office.

She took my hand in hers and gave it a gentle squeeze. "Why don't you give it a try with me?"

"Mother wasn't the only one who hurt us. She only started letting us out of the bedroom so other people could do things to us."

"You mean the special friends?"

"Oh my God, you know? How do you know?"

"Emily told me."

When did Emily tell her? She never said anything about it. Why didn't she tell me that she'd told her?

"Wow." I didn't know what else to say.

"We always knew you girls had been sexually abused. It was included in the medical report, but we never knew who did it. Bob and Dalila were convinced it was your mother, but I always suspected other people were involved. They didn't think it mattered who'd done it and I respected their wishes. I never pushed."

"When did Emily tell you?"

"Remember when the two of you came to see me after Emily got caught cutting?"

I nodded.

"Those weren't the last sessions I had with Emily. Emily started coming back to meet with me during your junior year. I saw her in therapy for the next few years. We were working together right up until she died." Her eyes filled with tears.

I couldn't help but feel betrayed. Why wouldn't Emily tell me she was going to see Lisa? Why would she keep that a secret? Anger shot through me.

"You look upset," she said.

"I am." I didn't want to be, but I was. Emily had told the one secret we shared while I'd always kept all of hers.

"She was embarrassed to be in therapy again. She thought it made her weak. That's why she didn't tell you." Her voice was thick with emotion. "Elizabeth, do you know how hard it was for her to struggle while you did so well? She talked about it all the time in our sessions. She wanted to have your strength. She hated who she was and the things she did. She was ashamed of her cutting and mortified by her behavior with boys."

For years, she'd gotten into trouble for the things she did with males. In elementary school, she got caught playing doctor on the playground with boys from our class and by middle school, she'd progressed to performing sexual acts on them. She lost her virginity when she was thirteen to a seventeen-year-old guy she met on the Internet. He took her to Chick-fil-A, then to the backseat of his car, and after they'd done it, she never saw him again. She was constantly in trouble with girls at school for sleeping with their boyfriends. Bob and Dalila caught her on more than one occasion posting naked pictures of herself online and in chat rooms with older men. She'd spent half our adolescence grounded from the Internet and her phone.

She didn't keep any of the things she did with guys a secret from me. She was proud and talked about it all the time. She swore she liked it and her level of excitement rose the more risqué the conquest. I believed her. I thought I was the one with the problem. Not her. I thought there was something wrong with me for not wanting anyone to touch me.

And then, she suddenly stopped. She quit dating and stopped talking about hooking up with guys. I asked her about it a few times and she laughed it off. She said she was thinking about becoming a lesbian. I'd figured it was another effect of her depression, like she'd given up another thing she enjoyed in the same way she'd quit painting.

"I remember when she stopped. It was the summer of our junior year. She used to be boy-crazy and then all of sudden she didn't have any interest."

"Emily was never boy-crazy, even though that's what it looked like from the outside. What she didn't understand was that she was reacting to the sexual abuse in her childhood. One of the things I explained to her is how sexual abuse affects sexuality. When girls are sexually abused, they tend to behave in two ways— they either become extremely promiscuous, or they end up avoiding all forms of sexual behavior and become unresponsive to sex. I spent a significant amount of time with Emily explaining this relationship to her. She found it comforting that her sexual behavior was common given what she'd been through."

I couldn't help but recognize that I was the other extreme Lisa was talking about. I swallowed the lump in my throat.

"We spent months doing a form of therapy called trauma-focused cognitive behavioral therapy. It's a type of therapy that helps people work through sexual abuse and trauma. She found it helpful and she was able to stop her self-destructive behavior with men." Her eyes filled with tears again. "Even though our work helped her stop acting out with men, I couldn't stop her from hurting herself. It didn't matter what kind of therapy we did or what techniques I used. Cutting herself was something she wouldn't give up no matter what. I've never felt so powerless."

She let the tears spill down her cheeks. I understood her powerlessness and she might be the only person who understood mine. This time, I took a hold of her hand. We sat in silence for a few moments, but unlike the silence of Dr. Larson, it was a comfortable silence.

"Emily was a tortured soul, but you don't have to be. I've always stressed the importance of seeing the two of you as individuals and separate people."

She must've said it thousands of times to the Rooths over the years and probably as many times to me during our private sessions.

"Even though it might not feel like it, the two of you are not the same person. Remember when you came to see me the week before you tried to kill yourself and how you told me that you loved Thomas? It was clear you needed permission to love someone else besides Emily. Dalila used to call me all the time to talk to me about how you believed and acted like Emily was still alive, but she hadn't called me in months. I figured you'd finally come to terms with Emily's death and weren't still living like she was alive. When I saw you that day, you seemed like you were doing well. Better than I'd ever seen you. You'd fallen in love and needed permission to let go of Emily." She paused, looking deep into me. "I'm giving you that same permission again. It's okay to let go of the hold she has on your life and create a new life for yourself without her."

It wasn't that easy to let go. I still had questions that wouldn't go away.

"What I don't understand is why the last night happened. Ultimately, I was killing myself and there wasn't any reason to kill myself. If I created the story about Emily, wouldn't I just have to rewrite the script? Or stop pretending she was alive? Why'd I have to die?"

I'd existed as two people in order to keep Emily alive and it was surprisingly logical, especially since all the other twins I'd read about did similar things. Maybe not to the extreme I had, but all of them had made efforts to keep their twin with them and not face their loss. I didn't want to deal with Emily's death, so I pretended it hadn't happened and then I created a make-believe Emily and pretended to be her whenever I needed to. It wasn't the part of the story I had a problem with anymore, as bizarre as it was. Killing myself was the one crucial piece of the puzzle that didn't fit in the explanation.

"I think you were finally ready to let Emily go," Lisa said.

She still wasn't answering the most important question.

"But then why did I try to kill myself?"

I could tell she'd never thought about this part of the scenario. The explanation about creating an imaginary Emily so I didn't have to let go of her was understandable. Needing to let go of the delusion of her existence once I'd fallen in love with Thomas also fit perfectly with the explanation. All of it did, right up until the point of trying to kill myself. Why was I the one person who saw a problem with this part of the puzzle?

I'd asked the same question I was asking Lisa at the team meeting earlier in the morning and no one could answer it then either. They'd stared at me until finally someone spoke up.

"That's a very good question. It's one we are hoping you're able to answer once you begin feeling more comfortable," one of the female psychologists said. All of the others had nodded their heads in agreement in their typical fashion.

Lisa's response was similar to hers. "I guess you're the only one who knows why you did it. It may take a while for you to be able to remember why, but unfortunately, there's also a chance you might not remember. You may never know what happened or why you did it. Some people never recover memories from traumatic events. There may come a point in your recovery where you have to just accept you'll never know. You might have to learn to get comfortable with not knowing."

"So, I'm just supposed to forget all about it?"

"Is it important for you to know why you did it? Do you think knowing why helps you to get better?"

"Wouldn't you want to know why you tried to kill yourself?" I asked.

"Yeah, I'm pretty sure I would. Do you want to know what I think happened?" She didn't wait for me to respond. "I think you were acting as Emily when you tried to take your life. You'd acted as Emily for so long that the line between where you ended and she began was completely blurred. It was almost nonexistent. And Emily very much wanted to die. Even when she was alive. My guess is you tried to kill yourself while you were acting as Emily, even though you didn't want to die. You weren't trying to kill yourself, but you were unable to step back over the line into Elizabeth again in time to stop it. Does that make sense?"

I shrugged. "A little. I guess it could've happened like that. How did somebody find us? I mean me?"

"You took pills and slit your wrists."

I looked down at my arms and saw the scabs and stapled stitches working their way up my arm like a ladder. For some reason, seeing my wounded arms for the first time wasn't nearly as startling as it was when I saw my legs. I didn't react to them. It was as if I half-expected the damage to be there. Now I knew why Shelly and Tobi acted the way they always did towards me—their eye rolling and knowing looks with each other. They saw my arms.

They always had. They thought I was lying to them or playing games. And Rose. My sweet Rose. She'd always seen my injuries too, but knew enough not to say anything. Not to push me until I was ready to talk. It made me like her even more.

"You were in the tub when you did it and you became unconscious before you turned off the water. You'd called Dalila earlier in the night and something in your conversation scared her. She came over to check on you and heard the running water, but she couldn't get you to open the door or answer the phone. She talked the apartment manager into letting her into the apartment. They are the ones who found you." She paused before going on, "Unconscious and not breathing."

I had a fleeting glimpse of the white porcelain tub in our apartment splattered in blood. An arm hanging over the side of it. Words written in blood on the tiled wall that I couldn't make out before the image was gone.

"A few more minutes and ..."

"I wouldn't be here." I finished the sentence for her.

Poor Dalila. It must've been so awful for her. I was sure finding me had reminded her of the time she found Emily in the tub. We sat in silence again, each of us in our private thoughts.

Lisa broke the silence. "Do you think it would be helpful for you to see Emily's grave?"

My stomach flipped at the suggestion. "I haven't ever thought about it."

"Dr. Larson thinks it would be a good idea for you to see Emily's grave," she said.

She went on to explain how she'd talked to Dr. Larson twice since our visit yesterday. She assured me they'd only talked about my progress and how he believed seeing Emily's grave might help me in my recovery process. The thought of seeing Emily's grave made me catch my breath and felt like someone had put a clamp on my chest. I'd gotten used to saying Emily was dead. It rolled off my tongue easier and easier each time I said it. It was amazing how quickly it'd happened, but something about physically going to see her grave made it too real. It would make it a reality I'd never be able to take back. It would be more saying good-bye. More letting go.

"I'm not sure I want to. Do you think I should?"

"I think it would be a good idea. It might help you heal and bring closure." Her eyes were serious. I'd never seen her look so serious. "There's a possibility seeing her grave could help you to remember her death and fill in some of the gaps in your memory. Or it might not, but it could bring you more acceptance of her death and the motivation to continue moving on."

Moving on. Thomas had said the same thing last night.

"How would it work?" I hadn't seen anyone leave the hospital yet. I didn't know it was something you could do.

Dr. Larson had given Lisa permission to take me. He'd already written the order and gotten permission from the team for me to go. All Lisa had to do was tell him when. She was excited about it. She rambled on about how good it would be for me and all of the ways it would help my growth. She'd even got permission to attend the team meeting after we went to the grave so she could be there when we processed the experience. Apparently, Dr. Larson and the others had changed their views on allowing a therapist who wasn't affiliated with the hospital to be part of the treatment team. I still wasn't convinced it was a good idea for me to go to the grave, even if both of them thought it was.

"When would we go?" I asked.

Although the conversation had started out with her asking me if I thought it would be a good idea, it was beginning to feel like I didn't have a choice if Dr. Larson and the team were involved. Would they think I wasn't making progress if I didn't go? Would they send me to the state hospital if I refused?

"We could go as early as tomorrow morning."

"Tomorrow morning?" My mouth dropped.

I hadn't expected her to say tomorrow. Not at all. I thought she'd say a few days or a week, but tomorrow morning? I wasn't ready for that. I needed more time to prepare myself.

"I think you should take advantage of being here. This is the best facility in the entire state. There's no way to know how you'll react to seeing Emily's grave, and doing it while you're here gives you a safety net to work through your emotional response. Your days here are numbered and we want to be able to help you as much as we can before that time gets here. This is a very safe environment for you."

I hated to admit it, but she was right. I felt safe and sheltered. My world had shrunk to the four walls of the family room, but the walls contained me. I found it oddly comforting to be surrounded by people who had serious mental problems because I didn't feel so screwed up. I'd gotten used to how everyone shared horrific events from their past. I'd never known people who'd experienced trauma like I had and it relieved me. I'd grown to like living in such a small world. I liked doing the same things every day in the same way.

I took a leap into the unknown in hopes that she was right.

"I'll go to Emily's grave."

If she thought it was going to help me, she was probably right. Seeing Emily's grave might propel me to begin taking the necessary steps to rebuilding a new life for myself outside of the hospital, as scary as the prospect seemed. A life that existed without any version of Emily. Make-believe or otherwise. I started crying even though I didn't want to.

"Is it always going to feel this way? I hate crying and falling apart all the time."

"I wish I could give you a date for when it'll be over, but I can't. I can tell you from experience, though, that it will get easier. I grieved the loss of my childhood for years and there are still times when I have to allow myself to cry over it, but it's no longer as overwhelming and as all-encompassing as it used to be, like I'm sure it feels for you right now."

"I feel like it's going to swallow me up."

"I understand."

I knew she did because she'd spent the first five years of her life eating out of garbage cans. She'd had a big brother who took care of her while they lived on the streets in the same way I took care of Emily. She handed me a handful of Kleenex from the box on my desk. I wiped my eyes and blew my nose while she explained how she would set everything up for the morning and that I didn't have to worry about anything except trying to get some rest.

I couldn't fall asleep that night. I lay awake feeling as if I'd drunk two pots of strong coffee before going to bed. My mind was on a frenzied search. Every time I closed my eyes, I relived pieces of Emily's and my life. I saw glimpses, like stilled shots of Emily and me in our apartment. Ones where I was sitting at the table doing my homework and she was in the kitchen, laughing and joking as she cooked us dinner. She loved the weekends. They always made her smile.

I replayed scenes over and over again. Us going to the movies. Us going shopping like we used to do when she wasn't depressed, digging through piles of clothing at Goodwill looking for the perfect find. Her nudging me to get up when the alarm clock was going off after the third time I'd hit snooze while I pulled the pillows over my head.

I rewound our childhood, remembering the stories we told each other. Stories of princesses with knights who protected them and kept them safe from evil. Imagining candy that grew on trees and whipped cream popsicles. I remembered how happy we were when we got to live with the Rooths. Our first Christmas with presents. Getting to go to school together. Learning how to ride our first bikes—the ones with the pink streamers and the baskets in front with big purple flowers.

But I didn't only remember the good times. Memories of all her struggles and pain flooded through overshadowing the times she was happy. All the blood she shed. The journal filled with bloody writings I'd found hidden in her closet when we were sixteen. The pink flesh of her wounds. All of the hours I spent holding her while she sobbed, promising her it would be okay while she argued with me that it was never going to be. Her begging me to let her die as I fought to force her to throw up the pills she'd taken, sticking my finger down her throat since she couldn't bring herself to do it.

Lisa had called Emily a tortured soul and she was right. No matter how much I loved her, she still hated herself. She'd never recovered from what Mother had done to us, and Mother's special friends had done more than violate her body. They'd violated her insides in ways I'd never let them get to mine. There was a lot wrong with Emily that was never wrong with me. She'd been saying she wanted to die since we were nine and trying to kill herself since we were thirteen. Maybe it was time to give her what she'd always wanted.

I tossed and turned. There wasn't any spot where I felt comfortable. I kept telling myself not to look at the clock, which only made me look at the clock more. At four, I gave up on the idea of sleep.

I threw my covers off and stood. I peeked out my door. The hallway was empty and dark, except for the small glowing lights along the floor. The nurses' station was still illuminated with light. There was only one nurse behind the desk and she was busy working on the computer. I opened my door a bit more and slid my body through. I tiptoed down the hallway and stopped three doors down. I looked back over my shoulder to make sure the nurse was still occupied and breathed a sigh of relief that she was.

I crept through Rose's doorway. She was sprawled out across her bed as if she'd been wrestling in her sleep. I walked towards her bed.

"Rose," I whispered. Waited. "Rose."

I jiggled her shoulder. She startled and turned to look at me.

She rubbed her eyes.

"Elizabeth?" she asked.

I was flooded with embarrassment. I felt like a little kid creeping into their parents' bedroom at night after having a bad dream.

"I'm sorry I woke you up. I couldn't sleep."

She sat up, rubbing her eyes again. She patted her bed. I took a seat.

"I'm so scared." My voice was quivering.

She grabbed my hand and squeezed it. We sat in silence, afraid to talk in case someone came in and found me in her room. I laid my head down on her lap and she stroked my hair. I fell asleep listening to the hum of the air conditioner.

23

Polly saw me in Rose's bed when she knocked on the door for the customary morning wake-up call, but she didn't say anything. I rushed back to my room, not wanting to test her leniency. In a few minutes, she was at my door.

"How are you feeling?" she asked.

It never mattered that nobody talked to her about how they were feeling. She never quit asking. I was sure she knew where I was going. Nothing was a secret in the hospital. I shrugged my shoulders. I was glad she didn't say anything about being in Rose's room.

I showered, and for the first time since I'd been at the hospital, I thought about what I was going to wear. I stared at the clothes Dalila had packed for me. I picked a pair of jeans and my favorite gray American Apparel T-shirt. I threw my hair back into a ponytail and was ready to go. I didn't bother trying to eat breakfast because my stomach was already doing gymnastics. Instead, I sat and watched everyone around me having theirs, wishing Rose could eat with us.

"I can't believe you get to go out on a pass today," Shelly said. "I'm so jealous."

"Me too," Denise said.

She always agreed with her. Shelly could say Denise had

orange eyes and even though her eyes were green, she'd nod her head in eager agreement.

"Where are you going?"

"To see my sister."

"You have a sister? I didn't know that." Shelly moved from her chair and plopped down in the chair next to me. "Older or younger?"

"Older." I didn't add by three minutes. I didn't tell her because it would only elicit more questions from her.

Tobi joined in the interrogation. "What are you guys going to do? How come you're getting together? Is it some kind of family emergency? It usually has to be some kind of emergency for them to let you out."

"It's not an emergency. Just a visit."

I hated when I got cornered by them without Rose. She was so much better at shutting them down and getting them to mind their own business. How was I going to get away from their questions when she was gone?

"Where are you guys going?" Shelly asked.

"I don't know."

I had no idea where we were going. I assumed Emily was buried close, but the Rooths might have a family cemetery far away where they'd buried her.

Lisa arrived before breakfast was over and unlike me, she looked well rested. Her eyes were bright and shiny. Her face glowed and her hair was pulled back neatly from her face.

"Are you ready?" she asked.

I wasn't ready, but if I waited until I was ready I wasn't sure I'd ever go. I stood and followed her to the nurses' station. I filled out a form on a clipboard with my signature, the time I was leaving, and who I was leaving with. Lisa scribbled her name on another paper.

I followed her through the first locked door, feeling like I was somebody else. It was as if there was a ladder in my head that I'd crawled up to get out of myself and was watching my body perform from somewhere above me. I watched myself walk beside Lisa as she chattered through each twisted corridor and locked door, looking down at my faded blue jeans with the hole in the middle, wondering when my brown hair had gotten so long. We found our way to the elevator and made our way down.

We stepped outside and the blinding sun jolted me back into my body. It'd been so long since I'd been outside that the sun hurt my eyes, making me squint. The air smelled different. It was more alive, like it smelled right after it rained. Everything looked brighter and more vibrant.

"I parked across from the building. I'm cheap and didn't want to pay for parking." Lisa laughed and pointed across the road.

She drove a red Honda Accord. I slid in and was flooded with memories of all of the lunches Thomas and I took in his Honda. By the time Lisa had left last night, it was too late for our scheduled phone date. I missed hearing his voice. I couldn't help but wonder if we were ever going to be able to eat lunch in his Honda again.

I didn't ask where we were going. I stared out the window, watching the trees and houses flash by. I watched the lights flicker and turn color as we passed through them. The world still existed and had continued moving. There was a part of me that thought the world was on hold, but time hadn't stopped while I was in the hospital. Time hadn't waited for me to catch up. It had kept going and it was going to keep moving forward whether I wanted it to or not.

"Is there anywhere you want to stop before we get there? Do you want a coffee or something?"

I appreciated the gesture, but the only thing I wanted to do was to get this over with. I was afraid if we stopped the car and I got out that I would start running in the opposite direction. I would take off sprinting as fast as I could and never look back. As it was, I didn't know if I was going to be able to get out of the car once we got there.

Lisa slowed down as we passed St. John's Cathedral and put her blinker on to turn into the driveway. It was the church Dalila and Bob had taken us to every Sunday until we were sixteen, even though neither of us believed in God. At sixteen, they'd given us a choice as to whether we wanted to keep going or not. We never made another Sunday. I hadn't stepped foot in a church since then, no matter how many times Thomas had asked me to go with him.

She made a left-hand turn and followed the driveway to the back where it opened up into a large parking lot. There was a small cemetery behind it. The parking lot was empty. She pulled into a space to the side of the gate and turned the car off. Neither of us moved to get out.

"Have you been here before?" I asked.

I realized as soon as I said it that I already knew the answer. She'd mentioned being at the funeral before and I was sure she'd gone to the grave site too.

"I stood next to you during the burial. It was a beautiful service."

Dread crept up the back of my throat. "Do I have to do this?"

Lisa laid her hand on my knee. "Honestly, no. You don't have to do anything you don't want to do. We can go back to the hospital if you'd like or just sit here for a while. But, I think it would be a good idea for you to see her grave. I support whatever you decide, though. Really, it's up to you. Take all the time you need."

I stared out the window at the rows of headstones for a long time. It was hard to imagine that each stone was a marker for somebody who'd died and Emily's headstone was somewhere among them. She was out there. My legs felt like lead. The feeling of being underwater was back.

"I don't know if I can go out there. I feel sick."

"I know you're scared and how hard this must be for you. Even though your brain doesn't have a memory of being here, your body does, so I'm not surprised that you're feeling sick. Remember how yesterday we talked about how there was a possibility being here might trigger more of your memory?"

I nodded.

"I'd encourage you to focus on what's happening in your body right now and not ignore it—it might help you to get in touch with your experience. Just give yourself permission to feel whatever you feel and allow any memories to come."

I wasn't sure I wanted to. The thought of getting out of the car and seeing Emily's grave filled me with a sense of impending doom.

"I want to go back to the hospital ... I can't." I started to cry.

Lisa pulled me close and held me next to her, stroking my arm. "We don't have to do this. We can go back to the hospital. I won't force you to do anything, but I want you to know something." She pulled away from me and cupped my face in both of her hands, peering into my eyes. "You're the bravest person I've ever met. If anyone can face this, you can. I wouldn't have brought you here if I didn't think you could handle it or that it was going to help you."

"Do you really think so?"

"I do."

I opened the passenger door.

"Are you sure?" Lisa asked.

I wasn't sure, but I was going to do it. I stepped out of the car and walked to the front of it. She followed my lead and came to join me. She took my hand.

"You can do this." She squeezed my hand and started walking.

I walked alongside her robotically, as if I was in a trance. We weaved in and out of the aisles of headstones, careful not to step on any of the grave sites. There were so many. I avoided reading any of the inscriptions.

Lisa stopped, so I stopped too. She looked down and I did the same, but I couldn't bring myself to follow her gaze. Instead, I stared at my feet. New black Converse. I couldn't bring myself to look forward at the stone. I wasn't ready to raise my eyes. Lisa placed her hand on my back. My palms were sweaty and my armpits were moist. I felt hot and flushed like I was coming down with the flu. My heart was a staccato drum in my head and I was sure if someone looked at my chest they'd be able to see it pounding.

I took a deep breath and looked up slowly. There it was:
Emily Rooth (1991–2009)
Beloved Sister. Cherished Daughter.
You will be in our hearts forever.
I stared at the headstone and read the first line again:
Emily Rooth (1991–2009)
A sickening awareness flooded my body and all the air got sucked out of me. I reached down and rubbed the spot of the raised *Emily* carved on my inner thigh—the tattoo I'd put there with a razor on our fourteenth birthday. Lisa had always asked me why I carved my name into myself or wrote my name in blood whenever I cut. The answer was simple—I did it to remind me I was alive and who I was.

I'm Emily Rooth.

Panic rushed through me. Did Lisa know? Was this what she wanted me to remember? I furtively looked over at her, but she wasn't looking at me. She was staring at my headstone with tears streaming down her face, struggling with her own memories of me. There was no way she knew the truth. She was as convinced that I was Elizabeth as I'd been.

It was like I'd been living in a dream and had arrived at the spot where it was time to wake up. I was assailed with the memory of our last night. The images were unleashed from my unconscious and violently pummeled their way into my consciousness without my permission.

I was behind the wheel. Elizabeth was sitting next to me, crying. I hated it when she cried. She didn't cry very often, but when she did it was tumultuous.

"Who cares? He's just a guy. It's not like you were going to marry him or something. How many high school crushes end in marriage?" I asked.

I didn't like that Elizabeth was so hung up on her new boyfriend, Marc. She'd been spending more and more time with him and less and less time with me. Even when she was with me, I could tell she was distracted, not fully present. It wasn't the fact she had a boyfriend that upset me so much, but that she'd kept him a secret. We weren't supposed to have any secrets between us. I'd overheard her talking to him on the phone and promising him she was going to tell me about him soon, but saying she was waiting for the right time to do it because she was afraid of how I'd react. It bothered me that she thought I was so fragile that I couldn't handle her having a boyfriend.

I'd started eavesdropping on their conversations more and more. I couldn't stand the voice she used when she talked to him. It was fake. So phony. I'd never heard her giggle and laugh the way she did when she talked to him. It wasn't long and she'd started ending their calls by responding, "I love you too."

Maybe she loved him, but there was no way he loved her. You couldn't love someone if you didn't know them and there was no way he knew Elizabeth. Nobody besides me knew her. If she started thinking someone else understood her, then she might not need me as much and there was no way I was going to let that happen.

I'd set out to prove to her that Marc didn't know her like she thought he did. My plan had been simple. I'd pretend to be her and kiss him. If he was in love with her then he should've been able to tell he was kissing me and not her. I was only trying to show her that he didn't know her. If he couldn't tell the difference between the two of us, then he wasn't right for her and Elizabeth shouldn't be with someone who wasn't right for her.

I'd gone to the party dressed in one of her outfits and

straightened my hair intentionally because she always wore hers that way. She couldn't stand how frizzy our hair got when we left it curly, but it never bothered me. But it wasn't as if I'd gone to great lengths to pretend to be her. That wasn't the point. The point was that what we looked like on the outside shouldn't matter. If you loved someone, then you knew their insides.

I'd followed her to the party. She'd lied and told me she was going to the library to study, but I'd been reading their email exchanges all week, so I knew she was meeting him at the party. I'd waited until she'd gone to the bathroom and then I approached him.

"Hey, honey," I'd said, wrapping my arm around him.

He'd turned to look at me. "That was quick."

"Come here." I'd smiled, pointing to the open bedroom door next to the bathroom.

He'd raised his eyebrows. "Are you serious?"

I'd motioned seductively for him to follow and he'd eagerly followed me into the bedroom. "I've wanted to do this for so long." I'd pulled his face close to me.

He'd pulled back before I kissed him. "What changed your mind?"

"I don't wanna talk." I'd grabbed him and started kissing him passionately. He'd stuck his tongue back in my mouth hungrily. It was only a matter of seconds before he was moaning and his hands were up the back of my shirt.

And then Elizabeth had walked in. Just like I'd wanted her to. Her face had gone white and she'd looked as if she was going to throw up on the floor. Marc had pulled himself away from me and looked back and forth between the two of us. He had no idea who was who or which one of us he was supposed to be talking to. Elizabeth hadn't said anything. She'd just turned on her heels and stormed out the door. I'd followed her outside, but she'd refused to get in my car and taken off walking down the road. I'd trailed beside her with the window down.

"Please, Bethy, get in the car, please," I'd begged over and over again as she stomped down the road. "I can explain. Just let me explain."

I'd pleaded with her for five minutes before she finally got in the car. When she slid into the passenger seat, she began sobbing hysterically and I didn't know what to do. I hadn't expected her to react so strongly.

"It's not just a crush!" she screamed at me from the passenger seat. "I love him!"

She'd never screamed at me before.

"He doesn't love you!" I yelled back. "He kissed me. He kissed me and had no idea it wasn't you!"

"What was he supposed to do?" Elizabeth asked. "You came to the party dressed exactly like me, and we've never dressed alike. Not once. You looked totally like me. You even straightened your hair and you never straighten your hair. You knew exactly what you were doing! Don't try to pretend like you didn't. How could you? How could you do that to me?" Elizabeth hadn't ever raised her voice at me and now she was screaming. I didn't know how to stop it or make it better. She was the one who knew how to make things right.

"He should've known! That was the entire point!"

"How could you? How could you do that?" She was crying so hard she was on the verge of hyperventilating.

"Bethy, don't be upset. I was just looking out for you. I really was. You've got to know that. I knew he wouldn't be able to tell the difference between us because he doesn't really know you or love you. I had to show you."

Her shoulders continued to shake with sobs.

"Don't you see? I did it for us. He was going to come between us. He already had." I was desperate to calm her down. She'd never been so angry with me. "Please, I'm sorry. You've got to understand. Don't you see? I was only thinking about you and trying to protect you. He was going to hurt you. They always do."

"I really liked him. I mean, I really did." Elizabeth turned her head away from me.

"Please, look at me. Don't be mad. Please!"

I was crying now too. I couldn't take her being mad at me. I didn't know how to handle it. I was becoming unhinged. Elizabeth kept her head turned towards the window, refusing to look at me. I reached over to touch her shoulder. She jerked it away.

"Leave me alone, Emily. I just want you to leave me alone!"

"C'mon, don't be like that. You can't stay mad at me. Please, look at me, Elizabeth." I grabbed her again. She shoved me off and moved further away. I reached for her another time.

And then it happened. It all took place so quickly. The bright, glaring lights in my face, blinding me. The loud horn screaming at me. The screeching. The squealing. The deafening crunch followed by the darkness.

I opened my eyes slowly. It was hard to breathe. The airbag smashed my face. My head hurt. My seat belt was ripping into me, cutting me in half. I turned to look. She was gone.

"Elizabeth! Elizabeth!"

The windshield was shattered. Pummeled through savagely. I pushed open my door. The headlights were blaring in my eyes. The horn still roared in my ears. A semitruck lay on its side next to us. There was smoke. Lots of smoke everywhere. It burned my eyes. Hurt my head.

"Elizabeth!"

I ran down the road in the darkness, screaming and searching wildly. My lungs hurt and the throbbing pain in my legs was excruciating, but I didn't care. Nothing mattered. Nothing except finding her. I spotted a body on the side of the road. Crumpled. Twisted. Grotesquely contorted. I ran to it.

I knelt down. Her face was splattered with blood. Her clothes ripped to shreds. Her arms and legs were twisted at odd angles as if they'd been snapped in half. Her stomach was gashed open and pieces of her insides lay around us, sprinkling the side of the road.

Her eyes were wide open. So wide. And dark, filled with terror. I brought my face down to her face. Nothing. I knew before I touched her that she was dead. I placed my hand on her neck, then her wrist, and finally her chest. Nothing. Elizabeth was dead and I'd killed her. My life was over.

I laid my head on her chest, sobbing. Primal sounds were released from a place inside me that I didn't know existed. Her blood pooled around my head. People were running, screaming, calling out to each other. Red lights blinked. Sirens howled. And the smoke. There was so much smoke.

Big black boots at my face. A strong arm shook me. Shook me again. "Miss, what's your name? What's your name?"

I couldn't move. I couldn't breathe. I couldn't live.

"What's your name? Do you know your name?" he asked me again, shining a flashlight into my eyes.

I lifted my head off her chest slowly and nodded at the police officer.

"I do. My name is Elizabeth. Elizabeth Rooth."

Epilogue

It had been three weeks since I'd been to my own grave. For a brief moment on the ride back to the hospital, I'd considered telling Lisa who I really was, but I pushed the idea aside in favor of keeping it a secret. If I told her, she and the doctors would make me go back to being Emily and I didn't want to be Emily anymore. I'd never wanted to be me and had spent my life hating myself.

Mother had been right about the two of us. She'd always said Elizabeth was the strong one and I was the weak one, that she was smart and I was dumb, and I should try to be more like her. Even after we were rescued from Mother and went to live with the Rooths, everyone still compared me to my sister. They measured my progress against hers and I never measured up. Nobody ever came right out and said it as cruelly as Mother had, but it was always there, hidden beneath the surface. Bob and Dalila were too kind to say it to me, but I saw it in their eyes the first time my elementary teacher called to tell them I'd been caught playing doctor with two boys on the playground during recess. Then, there were other times when I heard the two of them talking about how messed up I was when they didn't know I was listening. Like when I got home from the hospital after Dalila found me in the bathtub and I'd overheard her crying to Bob, "I just don't understand. Why can't she be more like Elizabeth?"

I would've given anything to be more like Elizabeth. I'd spent just as much time wishing I could be her as I had hating myself.

Everyone always raved about how alike we were as if we were the same person and how we lived in our own world, but the latter part of the story was the only part that was true. We lived in our own world because she was the only person who understood me, but we couldn't have been more different.

She was born with a steel guard around her heart that protected her from evil. I, on the other hand, wasn't born with any form of protective shield. I didn't have any boundaries to contain me and keep me safe from others. She had her armor and I had nothing, which meant my body and soul were never my own and anyone could reach in and invade me. There wasn't a single part of me that had gone unmarked.

I grew up watching Elizabeth with awe, wondering how she could be so invincible. It started with Mother and the special friends but continued after we'd been taken away and our life unfolded with the Rooths. She was solid and strong, full of so much grit and fortitude. Nothing penetrated her. I didn't have any idea how she did it and desperately wanted to be like her, but I never could. Not even close.

The night I killed her, I didn't intend to become her. It just happened—almost by accident. As I lay on the road on top of her body, I was devastated that I'd killed the one person I loved and who loved me more than anyone else in the world. I worshiped and needed her. I couldn't fathom a life that existed without Elizabeth, nor could I bear the responsibility of being the one who took her life. There wasn't any way I could admit she was dead, so when the police officer asked me what my name was, I told him Elizabeth.

Bits and pieces of my memory were slowly coming back. I still didn't remember anything about the days following her death. But I did remember standing next to the grave as they buried her and realizing everyone thought I was dead. They all believed I was Elizabeth and hadn't even questioned it. I was the only one who knew the truth and it dawned on me that I could go on being her.

If I didn't tell anyone what had really happened, then no one besides me would ever know. I told myself I would be giving both of us a gift—I would no longer have to be me, and becoming Elizabeth would keep her alive.

I slipped into the role of Elizabeth effortlessly. It was so simple and didn't take any effort on my part because I was already aware of every detail about her. I'd been studying her since we were little girls and knew everything about her, from the way she cocked her head slightly to the left side whenever she laughed to the way she stuck the tip of her tongue out when she focused. It was like stepping into my favorite book. It was easy to be her and I found out very quickly that I liked being her. It felt so good. So much better than it had ever felt being myself.

What I hadn't counted on was that I wouldn't go away. I'd buried myself in the ground with a headstone bearing my name, but I refused to die. I wouldn't disappear and let myself just be her. It was a constant battle between the two of us. During my first session with Dr. Larson after visiting the grave, he explained that the battle I had between selves was because I had an identity fugue that allowed me to assume a new identity while still maintaining a true identity. He described everything in the context of me being Elizabeth, because unlike Lisa, I never considered telling him who I really was. He referred to my identity fugue as my "altered state" and said it was another symptom of my dissociative disorder.

It was another instance when I had no idea what he was talking about and wished I was able to ask Lisa about it, but I couldn't. Once I was aware of the truth about who I was, I knew she was the one person I wouldn't be able to hide it from, so I had to stay away from her because I couldn't take the chance of her finding out. It made me sad and I was going to miss her a lot. But like Elizabeth always used to say—sometimes you have to make sacrifices to get what you want and giving up my relationship with Lisa was a sacrifice I was willing to make because I was committed to my freedom.

Dr. Larson was hopeful for my complete recovery. His focus during my last few weeks at the hospital had been to help me repair my identity fugue by doing what he referred to as "bringing me back into congruence" and "getting rid of my altered state." He assured me if I followed his instructions and trusted myself to the process, I would be able to begin a new life and I wouldn't have to continue living the way I'd been living. The process included grieving Emily's death and identifying the role that keeping her alive had served in my life. Dr. Larson said the goal of my treatment was to live integrated, but my goal was to live without her completely.

I was willing to do whatever it took to get rid of Emily because when I walked out of the hospital doors I wanted to be free to live my life as Elizabeth without the interference of my old self. I did everything Dr. Larson asked of me. I wrote her a good-bye letter and read it during group, talked to her in an empty chair and told her I loved her, beat on pillows and screamed about how angry I was, and finally through a guided hypnosis, visualized myself releasing her hand and letting her go. Dr. Larson promised it was possible for me to have a new beginning and I knew I could have it as long as Emily stayed buried. I just had to make sure she stayed buried this time.

By the time I was discharged from the hospital, everyone else had already been released. There was no one in our original group left, but right before my going-away party in the family room, I heard Polly telling the other nurses that Shelly was being readmitted the following day. She'd tried to kill herself by shutting herself up in the garage with the car running. I felt bad that she was coming back so soon and vowed never to come back to the hospital.

Thomas was at my going-away party with Bob and Dalila. My love for Thomas was stronger than it'd ever been. We'd stopped talking about what had happened in the past and started focusing on planning our future together. He'd begun dropping hints about marriage. Bob and Dalila were as proud of me as they'd been at my high school graduation. Bob brought flowers and Dalila gave me a beautiful book full of inspirational quotes. The nurses brought in a cake with *Congratulations* scrawled across it in pink frosting. No one was more proud of me than I was of myself.

I'd been out of the hospital for five days now and I sat in my new bedroom in the apartment I shared with Rose. She'd gotten out two weeks ago and the apartment was completely furnished as if we'd been living there for months. Her mom had done an impeccable job providing us with everything we needed, including paying the rent. It meant I didn't have to work and could just focus on my schoolwork. I'd be starting my classes again next semester and was really looking forward to it.

I hadn't seen Rose eat anything except lettuce and she'd already dropped most of the weight she'd gained while she was in the hospital. She spent her evenings locked in her room exercising. I didn't care that she didn't eat and had to complete two hundred sit-ups and leg lifts before going to bed because not eating and exercising made her happy. I wanted her to be happy. She deserved it.

Since she was occupied in her room at night, I was left alone to do as I pleased. So far, I'd been spending my nights reading the book I'd picked up at Target on my first day out or talking to Thomas on the phone. We never ran out of things to say to each other. But tonight was going to be different. Earlier in the day, I'd suddenly found myself back at Target in the health and beauty aisle even though I didn't know how I'd gotten there. I didn't have any memory of taking the bus or walking into the store, but there I was running my fingers along the fresh packages of razors.

I watched myself as I unwrapped the film and pulled out a shiny new razor blade from the container. My heart beat faster and my body started buzzing as I marveled at the way the light caught the blade, making it glimmer. I checked to make sure the bedroom door was locked before I went any further. It was, but I pulled my desk chair over and leaned it up against the doorknob as an extra precaution.

I brought the cold metal to my skin and pressed slightly, then a bit harder, just so I could feel the sting. I felt the familiar bite and hot energy shot through me. I had to have more. I pushed deeper and felt the ecstatic release as it broke through my flesh, revealing the pearly white of my insides before the first red droplets began to form their red trail. Once I saw the blood, I had to go further and bleed the evil out of me. I dragged the razor across my skin and felt the undeniable pleasure of my soul being set free. I could breathe again. As I closed my eyes and felt the familiar rush, I promised myself I'd be careful. I wouldn't go too deep. This would be the last time—just one last time.

ABOUT THE AUTHOR

Dr. Lucinda Berry is a clinical psychologist and leading researcher in childhood trauma. She uses her experience to weave psychological thrillers that blur the lines between fiction and nonfiction. She is the author of PHANTOM LIMB and MISSING PIECES. She lives in Los Angeles with her husband and son. You can find her on Facebook or https://about.me/Lucindaberry.

Read on for a thrilling excerpt of her next novel, BOY DISRUPTED, coming soon.

1

Noah being charged as a sex offender sucker punched our entire suburban community. Child molesters were adults—dirty, old men who lured children into their cars with promises of candy and treats. They weren't A-honor roll students who ran varsity track and went to mass every Sunday. I still cringe inside every time I say it, but our nightmare is finally about to be over.

Noah is getting out of The Harsh Foundation in three weeks. I've counted every day he's been gone. I pulled two of his boxes out of the garage before my husband, Lucas, got home, hoping their presence would force him to talk about Noah's homecoming. I put them in a neat stack next to the couch, but when he walked into the living room, he skirted around them as if they weren't there just like he dodges anything related to Noah.

After he tucked our youngest, Katie, into bed, he planted himself in front of the TV with the remote control in one hand and his phone in the other, shifting his attention back and forth between the two screens. I stare at him from the kitchen, trying to muster up the strength to approach him.

He isn't classically handsome but he's always been attractive to me. The dimples in both cheeks make him look playful despite his khaki pants and buttoned-up shirt. He's six feet tall with a leanness that passed as athletic years ago, but decades working in an office have taken a toll on his body. His muscles have begun to sag and the bulge hanging over his belt grows more and more pronounced each year. I take a deep breath before heading into the living room to join him.

I plop down on the couch next to him and do my best to appear relaxed. I cross and uncross my legs, rearrange the magazines on the coffee table, and wipe away imaginary crumbs as I work up the nerve to bring up the subject he continually avoids.

"Do you think we could talk?" I ask.

He stares at the screen in his hand without looking up. "Sure."

"About Noah."

His body stiffens the same way it does each time I mention his name.

"What's there to talk about?" he asks.

There's no way he doesn't know Noah is getting out soon no matter how hard he tries to remain oblivious to what's happening with his case.

"Come on, Lucas. Don't be difficult."

"I'm not being difficult. What's there to talk about?"

"Maybe the fact that your son is getting out of treatment in three weeks, and we haven't discussed what we're going to do about it?"

"You already know how I feel about it."

"But that was a year ago. We haven't talked about it since."

I ignored him when he said he didn't want Noah to come home after treatment. It was only two months since he'd been locked up and his discharge date was so far into the future it was the least of my concerns. I was worried about how Noah was going to survive being locked up with criminals and sexual deviants, anxious about how well he'd be supervised around them, how he'd sleep in a strange place, and if they were feeding him food he liked. Wondering what we'd do when he got out was the farthest thing from my mind.

"I still feel the same way," he says, his eyes glued to his phone. I want to slap it out of his hand.

"Are you serious?" I try to keep my voice calm.

He lets out a deep sigh. "I don't want to get into it with you again. Please, don't start this."

"Start this? I'm not trying to *start* anything. We have to prepare and figure out what we're going to do. This is happening, whether you want it to be or not. I've given you time to pretend like he doesn't exist, but you're not going to be able to do that anymore. Not when he's here. You're going to have to see him and God forbid, you might even have to talk to him."

When Noah first got locked up, I forced him to come with me on the weekend visits and family sessions because the treatment staff stressed the critical role families played in the child's rehabilitation process. Lucas is an affectionate man, but he could barely bring himself to touch Noah during our visits. He shook his hand with the formality of meeting a business acquaintance for the first time. He rarely looked at him, his eyes sliding over him before looking away, unable to hide his contempt and disgust. He only spoke when spoken to during the family sessions and sat mute whenever we met with Noah alone.

I breathed a sigh of relief the first time he pretended to be sick so he wouldn't have to go. Even though all the experts told us how important family support was for Noah's recovery, I didn't think a father who looked at him like he was a pariah qualified. It was better I went alone. The next weekend rolled around, and he said he needed to stay home with Katie to work on her science project, and I happily agreed. He didn't bother to make up an excuse the next week, and I pretended not to notice. We didn't speak about it again. I went alone each Sunday, and he never asked how Noah was when I got back. It wasn't long before his silence extended to all things concerning Noah.

I try not to be angry about Lucas's attitude toward him. His response is better than some fathers. He didn't react like Jamar Pickney's father who shot his son in the head when he learned he'd been sexually abusing his sister or the father in Detroit who slit his son's throat for taking naked pictures of his sister and selling them online.

There are only two fathers who attend the groups at Marsh. Most of the kids didn't have fathers in their lives before their offenses and the ones that did either disappeared or disengaged after their sons were convicted. The other mothers I've met assure me men process their emotions about it differently. They were confident Lucas just needed space to deal with things in his own way and would come around eventually, so I'd given him his time, but his period of avoidance is over.

"Okay. Let's talk about where he's going to live," he says. He turns off the TV and lays his phone on the coffee table.

"He's seventeen, where else is he supposed to live?" I can't keep the emotion out of my voice no matter how hard I try.

"I was thinking we could help him become an emancipated minor. I already looked into the process. It's pretty easy, especially if the parents are on board with it. All you have to do is fill out an application saying that all parties agree to the emancipation. Then, you go before a judge to put his official stamp of approval on it and after that, it's done. He's free to live on his own." Unlike me, his voice is devoid of all emotion.

"Really? How's he supposed to live on his own? What kind of a job is he going to get when he doesn't even have a high school diploma? And did you forget he'll be a registered sex offender? He's not even going to be able to use the Internet."

"He'll have to figure it out."

How is he going to do that without any help? How can Lucas consider sending him into the world alone when he doesn't have any of the basic skills he needs to survive? He's still a kid.

He takes my hand in his. "I know you love him and how hard this must be for you."

I jerk my hand away. My body shakes. "I love him? What about you? You act like he's some stranger. Like he's not even your son. He's still your son, Lucas."

"He stopped being my son when he raped those girls." His lips are set in a straight line.

"He didn't rape them, don't say that," I snap.

There's a difference between rape and what he did. He touched the girls, but he didn't rape them. Rape is different, and I cling to anything that separates Noah from being a monster. He made a mistake. That's all. One mistake. We all make mistakes in adolescence.

"Calm down."

I don't want to calm down. I want him to care about his son the way I do—the way he used to. It's as if nothing from before matters and he's erased the memories he used to hold so dear. How can he forget the way he cried when Noah was born or sat up with him all night in the shower when he had croup? He squealed like a child when he took his first steps and taught him to ride his bike without training wheels when he was only four-years-old. How could he push aside the way his heart swelled with joy the first time he called him daddy and every other milestone along the way? He'd coached his baseball team every summer since t-ball and never missed a swimming competition even during tax season when he was the busiest. He used to have an entire wall in his office devoted to his artwork, tracing the lineage of his childhood from his scribbled drawings when he was a toddler to the self-portrait he'd created in junior high art class. Now, those images are gone, torn down, and all that remains is a blank wall with leftover pieces of tape, hinting at the story the wall used to tell.

Lucas can't see past what he's done, but I can. He is our son and we can't just wash our hands of him. Society is going to throw him away, but we can't.

"How can you make him live somewhere else? It's so cruel."

"I'm protecting my family." His jaw is set. The same angular line as Noah.

"He's your family and if you'd gone to any of the family meetings you'd know how important it is for us to be there for him. All the statistics say family support is one of the biggest factors in his recovery. It's the thing that's the most important. We have to help him, offer him encouragement. It's what—"

"I can't have him under our roof. I won't put Katie in danger."

Anxiety curls in my stomach at the mention of her—our Peanut. She's never gotten out of the twenty-fifth percentile on the growth charts. She's dainty and delicate with a small face and piercing blue eyes that constantly study and take in the world around her. Unlike most babies of the family, she hides from the limelight, painfully shy, and never likes to be the center of attention.

I roll my eyes, shaking my head. "He'd never hurt Katie. Never."

"She's the same age as those girls."

"Yes, but he's better now," I say it with conviction, hoping my words have the power to make it true. "I'm meeting with the treatment team on Tuesday to come up with a safety plan. You should come with me."

"If he's better now, then why do we need a safety plan?" He raises his eyebrows.

He doesn't understand. Part of a safety plan is keeping him out of situations where he might look guilty even if he's innocent.

"We can put locks on her doors just like we did before. We could even put a lock on his door too. Maybe one that locks from the outside and we can make sure they're never alone together."

He scoots down the couch and puts his arm around my shoulders. "Listen to yourself. Do you hear what you're saying? Locks on doors? Constant supervision? And putting a lock on the outside of his door? So, we'd basically be locking him in his room every night and letting him out in the morning like a prisoner? What kind of a life is that for him? For any of us?"

I bite my cheek to keep from crying. I hate this. Every part of it. It never gets easier.

We sit in silence, staring at the blank TV screen lost in thought about what life used to be like for us and the family we'd been, all the dreams we had for our kids and each other. The vortex of depression threatens to pull me inside, but I'm not going back. I've spiraled there before and crawled my way out. I'm not doing it again.

"I can't let him live on his own. He's still just a kid." The tears I've been holding back spill down my cheeks.

"You could live with him."

I jerk my head up. "What are you talking about?"

"The two of you could get a place together. It could be somewhere nearby so you'd still be able to see Katie whenever you wanted to." He takes a deep breath.

"Are you kidding me?" I jump up, throwing his arm off me, and pace the living room.

We can't separate our family. We've been apart long enough. I've waited eighteen months for this day to come. He knows how excited I am for Noah to come home and all of us to be together again. How can he be so insensitive?

"I know it sounds crazy, but it's not all that crazy if you stop to think about it. The other night I watched a documentary about a family who had a daughter with schizophrenia who was psychotic and violent. She had a younger brother and started attacking him whenever she went into one of her fits. They couldn't live together anymore because they were afraid of how she'd hurt him, so they moved into two different apartments in the same complex. One where the girl stayed and one where the boy stayed. The parents went back and forth between them. They still spent time together as a family, but it kept the boy safe."

I can't believe we're talking about keeping Katie safe from Noah. He adored her from the moment we told him he was going to be a big brother. He was ten when she was born and insisted on learning how to do everything to care for her. He changed her diapers like a pro and fed her bottles like he'd been doing it his entire life. We were so grateful for the extra set of hands during those early months because unlike Noah, Katie was a difficult baby who didn't like to go to sleep without a fight and never slept for more than a few hours.

He spent hours lying next to her, reading her books, and dangling toys over her head. She was mesmerized by him, and he quickly became her favorite person. Her eyes searched for him whenever she heard his voice and toddled after him from room to room after she learned to walk. Her first word was "No-nah" and sometimes she still refers to him by it.

Unlike Lucas, Katie begs to go with me every week to see him, but staff only allows siblings to visit on pre-arranged monthly outings. She created a calendar with her visiting days circled in pink hearts and tacked it on the bulletin board in her room. Each week she creates care packages for me to take, filled with letters she's written and pictures she's drawn for him. When she's able to visit, she throws herself at him with a huge hug and cries all the way home when we leave. She's going to be as devastated as I am if he doesn't come home to live with us. How will we explain it?

She doesn't know what he's done. Not in words. At least we tell ourselves that. She knows he made bad decisions and hurt kids because his brain wasn't working right at the time. We told her he had to go away so he could work with doctors to fix his brain and help him make better choices in the future. What will we tell her now?

How can I function away from her? Noah's absence sucked the life energy out of me, but she breathed new life into me. She was the reason I got out of bed in the morning when all I wanted to do was pull the covers over my head and stay there. Her schedule organized my life and kept me grounded when everything was spiraling out of control. I was determined to keep her sheltered from all the tragedy as best I could and protect her innocence for as long as possible, so I put on a brave face for her and worked hard to keep up with her routines and maintain the order in her life.

What will I do without fixing her peanut butter and jelly

sandwiches for lunch or making sure her leotard is clean for ballet? How will I go to sleep without the angel kisses I place on her forehead each night? What will she do when her nightmares startle her awake, and I'm not there to lay with her and rub her back until she falls back to sleep?

Noah will suffer from her absence too. She's the one person who can still make him smile and bring life to his eyes no matter how badly he feels. It won't be lost on him that we don't trust him enough to live in the house with his sister. What kind of a message does that send for his recovery?

But in the last eighteen months, I've learned I'm much stronger than I thought. I've been blessed with an easy life and never would've thought I was capable of going through what I've been through and not being devastated beyond repair. There aren't any parenting books about what to do when your son is a sex offender, and I've figured it out on my own. It's like stumbling through a dark hallway alone, feeling your way through, and hoping for a glimmer of light to reveal your next step. It's too much to hope for a light at the end of the tunnel. I gave up on that long ago, but if I look hard enough, there is always light on my next step. Is Lucas right? Is this the next step for our family?

I let out the breath I hadn't realized I was holding.

"Okay," I say. "How would it work?"

Printed in Great Britain
by Amazon